No Molasses
in Rhum

J Duval

Published in North America and Europe by RIZE. Visit Running Wild Press
at www.runningwildpress.com/rize Educators, librarians, book clubs (as well
as the eternally curious), go to www.runningwildpress.com/rize.

ISBN (pbk) 978-1-955062-07-7
ISBN (ebook) 978-1-955062-13-8

To Brunia and Yves—in distinct ways—
you forced me to see art in everything.

PROLOGUE

February 5, 1994

"Passport." The clerk held out his hand.

Ti Zoot removed the document from his shirt pocket and handed it over.

The clerk raised the book and studied the photo against his subject. The long scar that ran from behind Ti Zoot's ear to his neck kept the man's interest. The clerk's eyes shifted between the image and Ti Zoot. The photo could have been taken that very morning, but the clerk took his time as if there was a discrepancy and the image hadn't matched at all.

"Wesner Phillipe?"

Ti Zoot nodded.

"Where do you live?"

"Brooklyn," he answered.

Ti Zoot couldn't take his eyes off the man as he logged his notes. In particular, he couldn't help notice how deft the man was at using his pen despite his meaty paws. After what seemed like an eternity, he finally directed Ti Zoot to another exit lane.

At the baggage claim area, Ti Zoot rummaged through his pockets, skimming past keys and several items in the charcoal suit, until he found his pager. He'd powered the device after the plane landed, but the screen remained blank. It was taking forever for his suitcase to hit the conveyor, so he checked a half-dozen times for one particular message that never came through.

"Son of a bitch," he blurted when his search for coins produced pennies. He was about to leave the conveyor for a pay phone when he spotted the large brown suitcase. He maneuvered around dozens of people and pulled the mostly empty suitcase off the belt. It was mandatory for him to travel to Haiti with a massive suitcase. He was accustomed to bringing friends and relatives all sorts of provision, but it always came back two-thirds empty. A case of rhum here, some artwork there, but the suitcase never landed at JFK as crammed as it had left.

At the pay phone, he dialed Ernse's pager then punched in codes 0-5-2 and 8-8-3, hurry and beep me, respectively.

Minutes later, he exited the terminal and lugged his suitcase onto the curb where the cold air slapped the sweaty forehead he'd sported at Port-Au-Prince International hours before.

Ernse was his ride home, and Ti Zoot had left his coat in the car when he'd been dropped off at the airport the week prior. Ti Zoot looked around, but all he saw was a sea of yellow cabs. Ernse was nowhere in sight, and he wasn't returning pages. Maybe he was stuck on the rampway's traffic? Ti Zoot watched so many cars approach and exit the ramp that he started counting them. "Can't count on this fool for anything!"

He checked the pager then shoved it in his pocket. The force ripped the pocket seam, and he dropped the device onto the concrete. "Shit!" He grunted as he picked up the device then sprinted to an approaching cab.

Close to an hour later, rain flurries woke him up and he realized the driver had reached Ernse and Nancy's block.. He looked at the pager and noticed a crack on the corner. The screen's dim yellow light came on and a page came through;it was Fiona so he disregarded the message.

Thecab came to a full stop, he sat in the back seat and squinted down the far end of the block. He thought his car was still parked in the same spot he left it. Stepping out of the cab, he could see it was indeed his car. After paying the driver, he rolled his suitcase over to his vehicle and shook his head in disbelief.

There's no way Ernse forgot to move the car. Maybe he was lucky enough to find the same parking spot twice.

However, the pair of neon orange envelops on the windshield wiped away hisguess . Thetwo drenched parking tickets were barely legible because of damage from the rain.

"Who is it?"

That was Nancy.

"Me...Ti Zoot."

Had it been Ernse, Ti Zoot would've cursed him through the intercom and until he'd made it up to the fourth floor.

Upstairs, he banged on the door until Nancy answered.

"You're wet," she remarked. "And where's your coat? It must be freezing out there."

"Where is he?" He looked in the direction of the living room. "Where is he?"

"I don't know." Her voice couldn't mask her worry. "He hasn't been home in days."

"Days?" He stared at her, confused. "I told him not to go anywhere!"

"I know, but he only listens to his inner voice. I'm tired of it. He comes and goes as he pleases." Her exasperation was unmistakable.

"I haven't been able to get through to him, Nancy. He never moved my car. I got two parking tickets because of that!"

"I'm sorry." She walked into the living room and sat on the couch.

"If he just called and told me, I would've moved the car myself."

"No, no. It's my fault," he replied. "I should've learned my lesson already. I can't trust or count on Ernse for anything. Where did he go? Did anyone pick him up?"

"I don't know. He said he was going out and that was it. Not so different than what he's done a hundred times before. How's your mother doing?"

"It's not good," he shrugged. "I can get a call any day now. I'll have to go back soon."

"Oh, my God. Sorry, Ti Zoot." She rose to hug him. "I was hoping things took a turn for the better."

"It's okay." He put on a strong face. "Right now, I'm a little worried about Ernse."

"How many times has he done this? I almost don't care anymore."

"That's true. But not moving the car an entire week? Even for him, that's strange. I'm going look for him."

"Thank you," sherelented.. "I couldn't bring myself to do it, and I know that's a big ask when you have your own family problems to deal with back in Haiti."

"I should've given up on him a long time ago but he's all I have. Where's Emily?"

"She's at Marie's. I'm picking her up in the morning."

"Let me get out of here. I have to change out of these wet clothes."

"Here's an umbrella," she offered.

"No, I never use them. All I ever do is lose umbrellas," He grabbed the suitcase. "I'll call you as soon as I find him."

"Thank you." She embraced him once more.

"Damn," he snapped.

"What's wrong?"

"The key. He's got my key, and I don't have a spare anymore."

"I hope he knows where they are."

Ti Zoot's eyebrows furrowed. He saw a set of keys on the rack against the kitchen wall. He studied them for a second. Since he and Ernse had similar vehicles, he thought maybe it was the wrong key. But the more he looked, it was his key. "Actually, these are mine."

"Are you sure?" she asked.

"Yes, my keys have this burn." He pointed to where someone's cigarette had melted part of the logo at a mas camp. "Was it here all week?"

"Yes, but I don't understand how I didn't realize that."

"No problem. Except for this slight burn they look identical. Thanks." He played it off, but this whole situation was really gnawing his nerves. "I'll call you."

Outside, the rain had picked up intensity, and he regretted refusing the umbrella for once. His car was down the far end of the block, but since his clothes were already wet, he gave in and continued.

On his way, events prior to his trip flashed through his mind. All of it pertained to Ernse. Not only did he fool around with a gang-banger's girl but he went as far as impregnating her. On top of that, he also beats the guy's brother silly. Ti Zoot put his best effort to make Ernse understand what his actions unearthed but wasn't sure his friend took matters seriously enough.

He warned him to stay off the streets. More accurately, he threatened him.

If I come back and I even hear you went to the corner store because the baby was crying for milk, I'll kill you myself!

Too much was going on in the neighborhood, and Ernse was its current focus. Nancy witnessed the conversation between them, but they encoded their discussions so she wasn't privy to the mechanics involved.

Near the corner, a smoke-tinted SUV pulled up and double-parked next his car, blocking him in. He lugged the suitcase faster in an effort to signal the driver he was about to leave the parking spot, but the rear window of the SUV came down and a head popped out. Even in the rain, he could make out the face. He had seen this guy many times. He was associated with the crew Ernse had static with.

Ti Zoot stopped in his tracks and considered his limited options. He could dash down the street in the other direction to force anyone inside the SUV to chase him on foot since the street was one-way and hard to navigate in reverse with any speed. The other choice was to run into the basement corridor of the closest building. He was familiar with that basement and knew he'd be able to lose them and escape through an alley that led to another street.

"Ay, primo!" The guy called from the window. "Where's your friend? I don't see him no more."

Ti Zoot remained silent and released his grip on the suitcase's handle.

"We'll see him around!" The guy yelled before the vehicle sped off.

He had to settle this for Ernse before it was too late. The guy in the SUV pushed the tempo. Things were about to get real, and time wasn't on his side.

He thought about the exchange and tried to figure what other angles they would have coming. The guy's question bothered him. He also wondered about Erne's whereabouts. He remained preoccupied with his thoughts while he took a peek in the backseat. His coat was still there. He had tossed it in the back knowing he was returning to cold weather.

He grabbed the suitcase again and was about to place it in the trunk but heard something that stopped him for a second. The rain made it hard to figure out what and where the sound emanated from.

Sure enough, he heard it again. It was distinct.

He pushed the key-fob, and the trunk popped open. Just as he was about to place the suitcase inside, a heavy-duty garbage bag blocked him. Confused, hepulled the trunk down but did not shut it.

He recognized the sound. It was similar to the buzz his own pager made when he placed it on his nightstand. He raised his head, but all he could see was the haze the streetlight formed between heavy raindrops. His heart sank weakening his legs in turn. Helifted his head again,this time, so slow he focused on the sound the raindrops made bouncing off the trunk. It was a sound he hated from the time he was a child spending summers with his grandmother in the mountains. During storms the rain would pound her steel roof without mercy forcing him to cover his ears in hopes of suppressing the sound.

He tugged the bag, and the pungent smell of blood escaped. He tore through the plastic and fell upon a lacerated, bloody torso. Pockets of blood had already dried onto the trunk's lining.

He hadn't seen a face yet. He would have to remove that end of the bag to confirm, but he already knew who it was the moment he opened the trunk.

It was Ernse

CHAPTER 1

April 12, 1996

Sunlight poked through a handful of blinds, hitting Ti Zoot in the face and still he hadn't moved. His eyes never blinked. Instead, his stare remained solely on the ceiling.

On the other side of the bed, Fiona woke, her sleep interrupted by the same light. She turned over and saw a familiar sight: Ti Zoot had failed to sleep another night. She had stopped counting when the number reached a hundred.

"Sleep." She caressed his cheek. "Sleep for once, please."

She took a moment to stare at his ebony skin, studying the crevices on his hard face. She rose from the bed, stretched herself, and chose underwear from a dresser drawer. From a glance in the mirror, she saw a tear form in the corner of his eye. It traveled slow, but finally came down his face.

She had never seen him cry. This worried her. Just as many other things worried her. Like the time she found blood on his pants when he came home one night. There was another incident someone keyed a giant 'ur next' on the hood of his car. He never led onto what was going on. Instead, nothing, don't worry about anything was all she ever got as an explanation.

She couldn't shake the feeling his cry signaled he was in the crosshairs of danger.

***

It was 7:08 pm, and Marie's car service was three minutes behind schedule. She'd been working late hours the entire quarter. Things were going in the right direction for her career wise, but it was happening at such a rapid pace, she rarely had moments to absorb it. Involved in structured finance in the mortgage backed securities group, she was recently bumped from analyst to associate. So she kicked her efforts into overdrive to prove management made the right call in promoting her. The hours were taxing, but that's just the way things had to be, plus she moved out of her mother's apartment and had to pay her own way. Rent was not cheap.

"Where's this stupid car?" She said looking down the far end of 6th Avenue when her pager vibrated through her cherished Bvlgari bag

The screen read, "1-2-3."

"It's not me you miss, Rudy." She tossed the pager back into the vast cavern of her purse.

"Are you Ms. Alexandre?" asked a voice over her shoulder.

She hadn't noticed the sleek black sedan pull up to the curb.

"Yes." She ignored the way the man butchered her last name. "Where have you been? I've been standing here forever." She slipped into the back seat.

"Sorry, it's the traffic," he explained through a thick accent.

"Yeah, yeah it's always the traffic. Brooklyn please. Take the Prospect Expressway and I'll direct you from there."

Again, the pager went wild alternating between a series of beeps and buzzes. This time it was Nancy.

"Can I use the phone?" she asked the driver.

"Is $1.50 a minute."

"I know the rate. Don't worry, my company pays for it."

He handed over the blocky Motorola.

"Hello, what are you cooking now?"

"Couz, are you on your way?" Nancy's voice was cheerful.

"It's late Nance. I'm just getting off from work. I'm tired."

"Come now, couz."

"No. I'm already in the back seat of a cab going home."

"Is no cab," the driver interrupted, "is car service."

"Uh, I'm on the phone," she said in his direction.

"You okay Nancy wondered.

"I'm fine, couz. But no, I'm not coming over tonight."

"Come on, couz. Fritay!"

"Aww, come on. Don't do that to me. I shouldn't be eating that stuff, especially this late."

"Come on, couz, we haven't been spending time together," Nancy pushed. "Ti Zoot is here. Just the other day, you were saying how you haven't seen him in forever."

"That crazy old fool is there? I'm not coming!"

"Whatever, couz. Just stop by and take some food home."

"Hmm. Okay. I'll be there in, like, a half hour."

"Great! Couz, one more thing, think you can babysit Emily tonight? I'll pick her up early tomorrow morning—promise."

"Urh! I'm tired as heck, but you don't have to twist my arm to spend time with my goddaughter. What do you have to take care of tonight?"

"I have a date," Nancy explained.

"That guy?"

"Yeah, him."

"Oh, didn't realize you guys were moving so fast."

"We're not. We've only hung out a few times."

"Okay," she said. "You know I've got your back."

Marie returned the phone to the driver and watched the city lights reflect off the window. She thought about how she could always count on a vibrant city most evenings, regardless how gray the day had started.

***

As soon as she set the phone down, Nancy ran into the kitchen and placed a heap of food onto Ti Zoot's plate. "Ti Zoot," she shouted. "Marie is on her way here straight from work."

"Okay, how is she doing with her new apartment?" He clicked through channels with the remote.

"I don't know. I haven't seen her much since she moved. We'll get the lowdown when she comes."

"Where's my beer and plantains?"

"Coming!" Nancy grabbed his plate and headed for the living room. "Emily, Auntie Marie is coming to pick you up. You're spending the night with her. Go brush your teeth."

Nancy was a young mom to six-year-old Emily and, at twenty-four, already a widow. She had a tight circle of family and friends, and she considered Ti Zoot both. He was about a dozen years older but struck a friendship with Nancy and her late husband Ernse. Back then, they were just some neighborhood kids showing Ti Zoot everything from the subway system to where he could buy akasan during his first few weeks in Brooklyn.

Ernse and Nancy fell for one another almost immediately and grew just as fast as 1980s New York City moved. When times were tough, Ti Zoot adopted them like a pair of younger siblings. A year after high school, Nancy got pregnant. Soon, she and Ernse were out on their own. Again, Ti Zoot was always in the mix making sure they had money and food on the table. He brought diapers by the truck load . There was never a doubt who would be Emily's godfather even though they had to beg him to attend the church ceremony.

He'd spent the day looking for a job, so the beer went down before Ti Zoot could take a bite from his meal. Knowing his habits, Nancy had another bottle on standby and handed it to him.

"Oh, by the way, Jimmy is stopping by."

"You're still trying to set those two up?" He scooped the plantain and griot.

"I'm not trying to set up anything." Nancy rushed back to her tiny kitchen. "I just invited you, Marie and Jimmy. Just a coincidence."

"Sure. Jimmy is my boy, but something is wrong with him. He's got no killer instinct with the ladies—"

"Please, Ti Zoot." She cut him off. "Unlike you, Jimmy is a gentleman. He doesn't need to bed everything in a skirt."

"Doesn't matter. He won't bite. No cookies for Jimmy."

"Mommy, teeth brushed," Emily toddled into the kitchen. "Can I put my coat on now?"

"Goodness." Nancy turned around to see if her daughter was clean as button. "You can't wait to leave mommy."

Ti Zoot joined them in the kitchen as he worked on the second beer. "Going out?"

"Uh huh."

"With?"

"Just a friend, Ti Zoot, we're catching a movie."

"So late?"

"They show movies at all times. This is New York City. Take your beer and get out of my kitchen."

He looked at her cross. She normally wasn't vague, something was different.

"Ti Zoot," Emily smiled, "I'm spending the weekend with my godmother."

He knelt and planted a kiss on the six-year-old's forehead. "That's wonderful my dear. Here," he reached into his wallet, "this is for some ice cream, okay?"

"Okay, Ti Zoot. Thank you!"

"Stop spoiling her," Nancy warned.

"She's the spitting image of you at that age," he marveled.

"I wasn't quite twelve when you met me." She swatted him with her dish rag then used it to remove a tray from the oven just as the door rang.

***

Marie dozed off before the car reached the Westside Highway. The driver had to tap her shoulder to wake her. She was so far gone, his words had failed to do so. After getting her bearings, she handed him a voucher, and let herself out.

"Miss, how do I get back to Manhattan, please?"

"This is Brooklyn not some boondocks," she was puzzled. "You must've driven through Brooklyn before?"

"Brooklyn, no, no, no."

"Mary, mother of Jesus." She sighed and directed the man back to the Prospect Expressway. She watched him make a left turn at the end of the block, after stressing twice that it was a right turn.

Her pager went off again. She rolled her eyes at Rudy's number then dropped the pager back in the Bvlgari.

***

Upstairs, Ti Zoot had opened another beer and asked for wine at the same time.

"That's Marie," Nancy announced.

"Marie?" Jimmy said, slightly antsy

"Yeah, I just buzzed her in. I'm going to go get ready since she's here now."

Jimmy tried the beer in his hand. "Where's Nancy going?"

Ti Zoot shrugged his shoulder, placed the beer down, walked to the foyer to open the door rather than answer the question.

"Ti Zoot." Marie was all business, finger pausing him before asking, "Where's Nancy?"

"Well, damn. Hello to you too," he answered. "Bathroom, I think."

Jimmy stuck his head in the foyer. He always found their interaction amusing.

Marie didn't see him. Instead, she went straight to Nancy's room to answer Rudy's page.

"Hello, I'm sorry to hear your mother's health has taken a turn for the worse." She paused to shut the door. "I adore your mother, but please don't use that as a reason to contact me! We are done Rudy." Cupping the phone between her ear and shoulder, she slid her coat off. "Accept it. You messed up a good thing. And what did I get in return? I got shitted on!"

Emily pushed the door open and hopped into the room. "Maren, I miss you!"

Marie responded with a hug and kiss. She loved when her goddaughter addressed her in creole, but she still had a bone to pick with Rudy.

"Go wait for me outside, Em." She whispered in the girl's ear. "Auntie is on a call."

"Okay." Emily skipped out of the room.

"Again, I have sympathy for your mom, but that's not going to affect anything between us. I'm sorry."

Placing the phone back on the receiver, she went over to the bathroom. "Nance, I'm here." She pounded on the door.

"Be with you soon, couz." Nancy shouted from under the shower.

Marie went into the kitchen and found some akra—a fried appetizer made of pureed coco, garlic, scallions, pepper, and herbs—sitting in a tray on the stove. She also found a bottle of white wine in the cabinet. She'd nearly filled her glass when she noticed Jimmy in the doorway.

"James, how are you? I didn't know you were in the house."

"I'm good—and yourself?" he asked, careful to downplay any enthusiasm.

"Just working hard." She turned her attention to Ti Zoot, who trailed Jimmy into the kitchen.

"Ti Zoot," she poked his arm, "I miss you mannn!"

Their relationship ran hot and cold, but that was mainly from Marie's side, she had little patience for his involvement in street affairs and resented Ernse had followed Ti Zoot's footsteps.

"Miss me?" he frowned."You're too busy for me. You moved out, got your own place, and totally forgot about me."

"I could be better." Marie picked through the akra. "What brings you guys here on a Friday night, besides food?"

"Just checking on my little sister," Ti Zoot explained.

"So, who's the new chick in your life…this week?"

"The same one you met last time," he smiled.

"That was six months ago. You must be losing it."

"He's trying to do normal things," Jimmy laughed.

Ti Zoot moved to a corner and left the conversation to Jimmy and Marie. There was more beer in the fridge, but he'd had enough and needed something with more weight. He checked the cabinet and discovered a couple of dusty bottles that Nancy rarely touched.

He grabbed the closest, a brandy, but his attention landed on a familiar bottle of rhum that he and Ernse once drank religiously. Reaching for it, he stopped. He couldn't finish the bottle without his partner. It was the same bottle he took a shot from after Ernse's repass. Nancy had urged him to take it a couple of times, but he declined saying it should remain in the cabinet. He slid the rhum to the back of the cabinet and moved a vodka bottle in front of it. The brandy would work for today.

***

Nancy dried off and wrapped herself in a pink robe and entered her bedroom. Locking the door behind her, she tossed the robe and rubbed lotion on. She was feeling good, there was an excitement that had been missing for a while.

As she lathered up, she caught her reflection in the mirror. She did a few silly poses, examined her real estate. Not bad. She smiled. Men checked her out on a constant basis, but that didn't prevent insecurities from creeping in from time to time. Tonight, was a little different. She was feeling pretty and quite sexy. She was accepting the beauty people often pointed out.

"Nance," Marie called from behind the door. "You're downplaying it, but I know a hot date when I see one."

"Just a movie." She fastened the robe as her cousin entered.

"Cute outfit." Marie noted the Indian saffron one-piece, perfectly lined on the bed. "Colors like that compliment you."

"Yeah, just a little something." She focused on the outfit. "Actually, I like that a lot."

Marie set her wine on the dresser. "Are you going to wear sexy panties?" She grabbed at the ties on Nancy's robe.

"Couz, I just stepped out of the shower, I don't have anything on!"

"Oh, please," Marie laughed. "I changed those diapers. Besides, I was in the room when you had Emily and saw your entire business in 3D."

Nancy playfully shoved her aside. "You have to stop pretending you're so much older than I am. You never changed my diapers!"

Marie laughed and sat on her cousin's padded trunk, sipping wine. She thought about everything Nancy had been through. Despite her burdens, her father murdering her mother then immediately committing suicide, Nancy bounced back from that only to experience her husband's tragic murder, she showed amazing resilience every time.

"When do I get to meet him?" Marieshifted from her thoughts. . "I've heard very little of him."

"Tall, good looking—nice teeth. Just a nice guy, so far."

"They're all nice at this point."

She knew that comment had a lot to do with Marie's last relationship. "Couz, how have you been?"

"I just spoke to Rudy," Marie said.

"He called me a few times. He must be desperate to call *me*." Nancy squeezed beside Marie on the trunk. "He says he wants you back."

"Really?"

"Yeah, his mom is not doing well."

"He's a manipulating liar!"

Nancy let her cool down before adding, "I know you're still hurt."

"I'm over it."

There was a pause until Marie looked over saw a tear coming down Nancy's face.

"Nance, what's wrong?" Marie rose addressing the tears wiping them with a tissue she grabbed on the nightstand. "Why are you crying? You're even trembling."

"I'm okay," she grabbed the tissue and massaged her sniffles. "It's just you gave him so much, you gave Rudy your all and he did knocks up someone you know. I feel so bad for you."

"You feel bad for me?" Marie blotted more of her tears. "With all you've been through in your life? Don't worry about me darling. I'm fine. I'll be okay, I promise."

"I know you will. Women in our family are built strong like that."

"Exactly," Marie cosigned. "And that little girl in the other room gets it too and built just like us."

"True."

"I much prefer to have gone through that ordeal instead of you, Nance."

Nancy shut her eyes, welcoming another hug.

***

Three young men huddled around a mailbox on a street corner. Steve, lanky and bright eyed, perched himself atop the receptacle as he spoke. Eddie aka E-Flow listened as Fredo engaged in an animated back and forth with Steve.

"I'm telling you, duke was very disrespectful. I don't care who he is."

17

"Shut the hell up Fredo," Steve yelled. "Enough with the drama."

"What the fuck is he talking about?" Fredo turned a beady-eye to Eddie before addressing Steve again. "You wasn't there man! How the hell you gonna say I'm on some drama shit? Slow your roll, man."

"Look, either way, I don't need beef on my block. Homie is always in the neighborhood," Steve pointed out.

"All I'm saying, I better not run into duke again, or shit is on." Fredo spat hard and watched the blob fly past the curb.

"Well we know the rules have changed," Eddie tried to reason. "We have to run everything by Max."

"Man, kill that noise," Fredo took a step back. "Ain't no one coming here making rules and all this type of bullshit up."

"I'm just saying, that's the way Pap laid everything out," Eddie pointed out.

"E, don't entertain this bullshit with Fredo. He damn well knows that's what Pap wanted. I visited Pap in the joint twice and he broke it all down. Fredo knows this. I'm not trying to do a bid for any of his stupidity and bullshit beef. Lay low. That's the name of the game."

Fredo looked at Steve dumbfounded. "I don't lay down for no motherfucker man. You keep that bitch attitude to yourself."

"I said lay low. No one said lay down," Steve responded before turning to Eddie. "You see all this bullcrap? That's why I don't put up with him too long."

"Yeah aight," Fredo nodded. "Shit needs to be loose just like when Pap ran it for years. I'm not down with rules."

"You were a just one of Pap's gofers," Steve said, punctuating it by pounding the mailbox.

Just then a car pulled alongside the trio. It was Max.

Steve was all too happy to end his conversation with Fredo and leapt off the mailbox to greet Max with a pound.

Max towered over his associates. That height along with his broad shoulders, gave him the look and stance of a basketball power-forward. He had goodheat; ladies wanted to be with him, guys wanted to be like him. There was an edge to him balanced by unbelievable poise.

"Max, we got beef." Fredo crammed the words into a single breath.

"We got nothing," Steve interrupted.

"Yo, shut the hell up," Fredo hollered. "Max this dude rolled up on us—"

"Eddie told me about it earlier." Max cut him short. "We don't need to address this like beef. Let's just let homeboy know we roll mob deep. If he tries to save face, we lay him out. If I bark, I don't have to bite."

"It's not that simple, Max," Steve explained. "I think you're still kind of new to the game out here. This isn't like Miami, man. Dude is an O.G. and respected. I don't think he's just going to lay down after a threat."

"You hear this bitch?" Fredo was furious. "Yo, I got a burner with duke's name on it, whoever he is—"

Max placed a firm hand on Fredo's chest backing him down. "Steve, hear me straight, I hope you didn't mean any disrespect by what you just said. I've done what I do from Baltimore to Virginia, right down to Miami. I'm up here now. This isn't new to me. Now, I just told Fredo how we're going to handle this. Whoever this dude is, if he has issue with that, he's going travel down the wrong road. I can't make that any clearer. You got that?"

"Got it," Steve replied. "I'm just saying, we don't need the heat."

Max remained firm. He didn't respond but gave Steve a glare. From behind, Steve could also feel Fredo's stare, which raised the hairs on his neck.

"All good, Max." Steve offered a hand. "I'm with you all the way."

"Good man, good." Max welcomed the handshake.

"Things dried up after Pap." Fredo pipped in feeling left out of the truce. "You came in and put us back on the map."

"Beautiful," Max said. "Let's just keep things like we're doing, simple under everybody's radar, including people in the block."

"Okay," Fredo nodded but added, "That's different from Pap."

Max didn't appreciate the comparison but let it slide.

"Anything going down tonight?" Eddie asked, breaking the tension.

"Whatever it is…I'm out." Max walked back to the car. "I'll stop by tomorrow night."

He sat in the car for a minute and listened to the trio. As usual, Fredo's screechy voice overpowered everyone else's, beating his chest in Steve's direction. Even after Max started the car, he could still hear Fredo's banter and act

"…what Max said is exactly right, we stand hard. You motherfuckas gonna learn they don't call me The Pounder for nothing."

***

"Love it." Marie perked up when Nancy stepped into the living room in her outfit. "But everything looks great on you. You were always curvy in the right places."

"Look who's talking," Nancy said with a hint of discomfort, taking compliments was never her thing.

"Okay. So, what time is this date picking you up? Can't wait to inspect him," Marie joked.

"You make him sound like furniture," Jimmy pointed out his brandy to Nancy who declined with a nod.

"That's about right," Marie joked. "Well, I need to see if this guy can score at least a three in my five-star rating."

"No thanks." Nancy emptied the brandy into Jimmy's glass. "But my criteria is a little different."

"You know I won't steer you wrong. I'm checking homie out."

"Nuh-uh couz, that's not happening—you guys will be leaving soon and so will I—we're meeting elsewhere."

"Elsewhere?" Marie mimicked.

"That's what I said," Nancy couldn't hold her smile.

Off to the side, Ti Zoot was silent, downing his drink. He grabbed the brandy from Jimmy, only to find an empty bottle. As always Ernse had a space in his mind. He would always remain there. The time span between Ernse's murder and present day, sometimes felt like it just took place, but other instances it started to feel like a memory that started to slip away. To counter that, he found himself reliving the sequences they took over his dreams. It was two years, but was that enough for Nancy to start anew? Was she mentally and emotionally in a good space?

He needed a refill, so he went back to the cabinet. When he opened it, he blinked at the sight of the rhum in the front part of the cabinet again. But it wasn't—he had only imagined the image upon pulling on the door.

He shook his head against the image and reached for the vodka used to block the rhum. Two fingers worth went into the glass, and he downed it like a shot. But when he placed the glass down, it missed the edge of the counter and shattered on the floor.

"You okay?" Nancy appeared in the doorway careful to steer clear of the mess on the tiles.

Ti Zoot remained mesmerized by the shard glass.

"Careful. I'll clean this up." She reached for the broom.

"No!" He sway against the alcohol but held on tight to the counter. "I'm cleaning this up!"

"It's okay, Ti Zoot," she said.

"I said, no! I'll clean this up alone, by myself!" He snatched the broom from her hand, as Marie and Jimmy watched the odd exchange in the background.

"Okay," Nancy relented. "There's some vinegar in that bottom cabinet. You can use it to clean up."

Marie made eye contact with her and nodded in the direction of the living room, suggesting they leave the scene. She sensed this more than broken glass. Something was wrong. Tension was in the air.

But before Nancy could exit, Ti Zoot called out, "What kind of man is he? He can't come to your door and pick you up?"

Again, Marie motioned for Nancy and Jimmy to leave. She stayed behind and leaned against the kitchen door, arms folded. She patiently watched Ti Zoot struggle with the mess.

"What was that all about?" Jimmy whispered in Nancy's ear in the living room.

"I have no idea. Is he drunk?"

"Him? Never," he insisted. "It would take more than he drank so far."

"Yeah, but something is off. Ever since he came by tonight, he's not himself."

In the kitchen, Ti Zoot did not acknowledge Marie's presence until he had to wait for her to step aside so he could sweep the entryway.

She chose her words carefully, using her softest tone, "I think she's ready to take care of herself. She's no longer the kid you fondly remember running up and down the block."

"Tiup," he snapped between sweeps.

"I understand. He's still in our hearts, still in hers."

He stopped, annoyed.

So Marie decided against pushing a one-sided conversation and retreated to the living room, joining Nancy and Jimmy, both still confused by the moment.

"Emily's bag is in the hallway. No sweets." Nancy changed the subject, hoping to ease the tension. "Turns out some little friend in school had been feeding her candy like you wouldn't believe."

"No worries," Marie assured."I can handle my goddaughter."

"Couz, mind helping me out with something?" Nancy asked. "Excuse us a sec, Jimmy."

They entered the bedroom. Nancy shut the door, "Be honest, is it too soon? Am I wrong?"

"No sweetheart," Marie answered. "It's been two years. Moving on with your life doesn't mean you love him any less. You're twenty-four, beautiful, and full of life. Go out there and continue living. Ernse would've wanted it that way."

They shared another tight hug, just like the first traumatic night Nancy came to live with Marie and her mother as a child. That night, they hugged until Nancy fell sound asleep.

The brief exchange in the kitchen with Ti Zoot shook Nancy more than it should. She'd agonized for months, coming to terms with moving on with her life. The very evening she was about to start a new chapter, she was socked in the gut by her dear friend's accusation. Marie's shoulder was all that kept her from balling on the floor as she had done many times when no one was around to see.

"He has to understand. It's every bit as hard on you as it is on him…on all of us," Marie explained. "Enjoy your evening. Let's get Emily out of here."

"Hold on…one more hug."

"You got it baby, couz. Love you, Nance."

Ti Zoot finished with the floor, grabbed his jacket, and kissed Emily good night.

"Wait," Marie stopped him just as he was opening the front door. "We're all leaving together, so can one of you gentleman give Emily and I a ride to my place, please?"

"I'm driving. I'll drop you," Jimmy offered.

Marie had hoped Ti Zoot would have made the offer instead, but she wasn't going to push it.

"You all go ahead." Nancy kissed her daughter good night. "I have to tidy things up here before I leave."

"Okay. Good night, Nance." Marie blew a kiss.

"See you in the morning," Nancy said.

"No, that better be after twelve-noon. I'm not waking up early on a Saturday morning for anyone."

Nancy stood at the door and watched them wait for the elevator. It was a childhood habit. Whenever her dad was off somewhere, she made sure she saw him get on the elevator and wave goodbye.

"Be careful." Ti Zoot's words interrupted her thoughts.

"I will." Nancy's response fell on deaf ears and was replaced with a rush of embarrassment when she realized the warning was meant for Emily, who was stepping onto the elevator.

She shut the door when the group disappeared. Still in a fog, she cleared the kitchen counter then resumed her beauty preparations when the buzzer rang. She looked at the time.

Was he early?

She hit the intercom. "Yes?"

"It's Max."

"Okay, coming down."

"Great." His response was full of enthusiasm.

A sudden thought came to her. It was only a few steps from the intercom to the lobby's exit. She had a couple seconds to convey a message before he'd be back in his car and out of earshot of the crappy intercom.

"Max?"

There was a pause, but she eventually heard a faint voice. "Yes?"

"Come upstairs, please." She pressed the buzzer.

An uneasy feeling came over her. What was she going to do exactly? This wasn't planned.

If only it hadn't been so long. What if he misunderstood and was still waiting downstairs?

The hollow chime of the bell made her jump. She took a deep breath, hoping to ease her nerves.

Max greeted her with a smile and a simple 'Hi.' She forgot to return the greeting. Instead, she let him in and locked the door, glancing at his broad shoulders.

There was an awkward second where Max was unsure why she had him come up, but it didn't take long for it to register. She made the first move and kissinghim passionately. In return, he gently caressed her neck and cheek with soft kisses.

It wasn't long before they found themselves on the living room floor. She had little sense when he carried her over to the couch. Once there, she took the lead.

For a brief moment she worried about coming across too aggressive but was put to ease by his non-stop caress. And she did her own caress. His shoulders were firm and flanked by two deltoids she couldn't keep her hands from.

"Wait...w-wait...protection..." she said as his caress had slid to her thighs.

"What?" he asked in between nibbling and kissing an ear lobe.

"Protection?"

"Y-yeah...okay...yeah," he struggled for his wallet.

The harder she held on, the more aggressive his kisses became. It was a game on her part to see how desperate he was to reach the wallet. But in the middle of their kisses and foreplay—he was finally able to ease on some protection.

Again, she maintained control of the situation. Each time he tried pecking her lips with kisses, she turned away, refusing them.

It happened so fast, he did a double take—she rode along with such intensity, her climax was quick. It was unlike anything he'd ever experienced. She leapt off, falling on her side, shivering. The goose bumps spread from her breasts, and now covered the rest of her body. He reached over embracing her with a kiss, but she quickly pulled away.

"D-don't...don't touch me please...please," she panted.

25

Dumbfounded, he was just remained still until she was ready.

"I'm sorry. That's how it happens for me," she explained. "I'm so embarrassed, oh my God."

"No, don't be," his voice was gentle. "I didn't expect any of this."

"Oh my God, you'll think I'm some tramp—"

"Nancy stop. I'm not thinking anything. I was right there with you," he opened his arms offered a hug, which she happily took.

"Thanks, I hope you understand."

"I think so," he said adding a kiss. "And if I don't, make me understand."

"Think we can still catch that movie?"

"If you don't mind missing the first fifteen minutes," he smiled.

She went on to clean up in the bathroom. After she finished, she looked in the mirror and took a deep breath.

CHAPTER 2

Jimmy made a right onto Ti Zoot's block. He had already dropped Marie and Emily off. Riding shotgun, Ti Zoot hadn't uttered much since they left Nancy's, except wishing Emily a 'good night.' He looked out of the window, checked his pager once when Fiona paged him, and eventually tucked the device in the ashtray.

"Everything okay?" Jimmy asked as he pulled in front of the building. Ti Zoot barely nodded, but Jimmy knew better. In fact, things were wrong from the day he learned of Ernse's fate. Some days were better than others, but it could be tough watching him mourn even now.

"She's not ready." He murmured as he stepped out of the car. "She's just not."

Jimmy's eyes were fixated on Ti Zoot as he entered the building. As he drove away, his thoughts flashed to his first memory of Ti Zoot and Ernse back in January 1994.

He'd stopped by a popular restaurant on Clarendon Road where patrons had poured outside the joint to get a better view of a fight that had just broken out on the street. He watched from the front door where he saw a young Hispanic man in a baby blue and white rugby shirt struggle to his feet while a taller, well built young man kicked him repeatedly mostly aiming for his head. The more he struck, the more heat he drew from the growing crowd. Neither of them had on a coat.

The man on the ground's baby blue shirt was marred by blood with the drops blending into a purple hue as it layered the shirt. The taller young man with theupper hand, also sported a blue albeit a darker shade pullover hoodie also stained by that same blood. In the middle of the one-sided fight, he paused long enough to look at his messy top and pulled the hoodie strings apart, removing the hoodie from his head. Despite the cold weather, the fight warmed him up, it seemed.

The crowd's attention split once a car screeched from the north corner, barely stopping in front of the crowd who blocked a lane on the street. The driver, older than the two combatants, stepped out of the vehicle and pushed his way through the crowd toward the pullover hoodie man administering the beat down. He grabbed the youngster with one hand around his throat and the other hand on the side of his face. He then forced the hoodie young man's head backward and slammed him against the restaurant's window.

Jimmy, still inside the restaurant, watched the window respond with an enormous crack, but somehow the two pieces remained in the pane. Jimmy nudged his way out of the entrance, blending in with the crowd outside.

"It's Ti Zoot." A young lady whispered as Jimmy squeezed closer to the action.

Caught between Ti Zoot and the fragile window, the hoodie young man made no attempt to break free or fight back. His red face highlighting the single vein swelling near his temple. Ti Zoot cut him loose only to stare him down. The young man looked away—perhaps from embarrassment or even regret. Jimmy watched Ti Zoot turn around, walk back to the car, and speed off just as wildly as he sprinted onto the scene.

"Sak passé la?" a voice demanded to know.

The hoodie young man gathered himself and eased away from the cracked window. He looked around, and his gaze landed on Jimmy's face. But he ignored the spectator and simply placed the hoodie over his head once again, before parting the crowd.

"Yo, Ti Zoot was mad!" A boy bounced on his heels, stirring the crowd's hype.

"Ernse! Ernse!" A dark-haired young woman yelled after the man in the hoodie. "What happened? Why are you fighting Javier?" She threw her arms around him.

"Are you fucking crazy?" Ernse stopped in front of the man he just stomped half to death. The young woman stared at the battered man and gaped at Ernse.

"Ti Zoot is gone now." A guy wearing a Knicks bandana shouted from the crowd.

Ernse gave the man a cold stare, rejecting his inference. Again, he looked at the man on the floor; the only thing that suffered more damage than his rugby shirt was his face. A gash covered his left eye and blood ran from a partially detached ear. Ernse then shoved people left and right until he crossed the street where two cars passing in opposite directions had to honk and brake to avoid striking him.

Voices buzzed from the crowd, and Jimmy tried to absorb it all. One man wondered if they were 'dealing', noting this Javier was affiliated with a drug gang. A boy went further asking if Ernse would shoot the man later.

A middle-aged woman grabbed the young lady who tried to embrace Ernse and asked her a series of questions. "Is that your boyfriend he just beat? Are you dating both of them?"

The young lady opened her mouth twice to answer, but the words never came out.

"I wouldn't date that tall one, honey," the middle-aged woman continued. "He must have an awful temper. Look what he did to him," she pointed to the young man struggling on the floor.

The young lady again, still couldn't put words together for a response . Instead, she parted the strands of hair that blocked her vision. She looked across the street in the direction where Ernse had just scuttled off to , but he was long gone. She made her way past the crowd and left the scene altogether.

Closer to Jimmy, two women and a teenaged boy tried to help the beaten man to his feet, but he fell several times, his equilibrium was off. Finally, someone pointed to his detached ear and thought it would be prudent to call an ambulance.

The restaurant owner marched from the kitchen and demanded someone pay for his broken window. He wondered aloud what he would do with a broken window with snow on the way. The crowd laughed it off and went about their business. Jimmy walked off—leaving his order behind as the bloody scene had killed his appetite.

It wasn't long after, Jimmy and Ti Zoot became friends. But even so, he never knew the details that set everything off in front of the restaurant that day. A lot of it remained a mystery and frankly he didn't want to revisit what he saw on that cold afternoon.

***

April 13, 1996

"I'm at Claudette's. Come there instead." Marie dunked bread in her coffee. "I have no idea why I'm up so early on a Saturday...I couldn't sleep. Emily also ...so we came here."

"Okay," Nancy agreed. "Give me an hour."

Marie glanced at the clock. It was 8:56. From where she sat in the kitchen, she could see the TV's light bouncing off Emily's face as she watched cartoons in the living room. She never moved an inch unless she had to run to the bathroom between commercial breaks.

She took a bite of the coffee-soaked bread. Coffee and Haitian bread was a staple at her mom's on weekends. In the old days, Ti Zoot often kicked off the tradition by knocking on the back door at six in the morning after some party he'd attended. Marie's mother, Claudette, would let him in despite a barrage of protests and filthy words, which Ti Zoot pointed out where usually reserved for the seediest of alleys in Port-Au-Prince. After the dustup, Claudette would start the percolator and wakeup Marie, Nancy, and Ernse when he spent a night or two.

On one occasion, when Ernse and Nancy were 18 and 17, the two sat quietly at the kitchen table holding hands and ignoring their coffee and bread. When Marie joined them, she sensed a problem immediately. Later that day, Nancy disclosed the result of a pregnancy test and freaked out about how the event would impact the rest of her life. She was equally afraid of Claudette's reaction since her aunt had just started to warm-up to Ernse.

Surprisingly, Claudette took the news better than anyone anticipated by simply stating, "I can't say I didn't know you were having sex."

And during Nancy's first trimester, Claudette demanded Ernse move in and help with the pregnancy. "I'm not going to rush out in the middle of the night to take her to the hospital. You better be here and do your share." Although everything was under the guise of practicality and what was best for Nancy and the baby, it was easy to see Claudette was fond of Ernse and appreciated him.

However, that set-up didn't last long since Ernse wanted them to have their own place. Just two weeks before Nancy gave birth, he found a decent apartment and convinced Ti Zoot and Claudette to help with the lease.

This left Marie heartbroken and once again alone with her mother. Nancy had been a part of their home since age twelve and now she was gone. The house was quiet, and no one knocked on the back door at six in the morning on weekends anymore.

"Was that Nancy on the phone?" Claudette stepped into the the kitchen, interrupting Marie's thoughts.

"Yes, it was." Marie's response was flat.

"Picking Emily up?"

"Yes, soon." Marie sipped her coffee.

"Good. I'm not going to spend my Saturday babysitting." Claudette poured coffee into her mug and sat across her daughter.

"What do you have? Why are you so busy?"

"Doesn't matter. It's my one day to get things done."

Claudette fussed about everything even the things she enjoyed. She always rejected them first or followed up with complaints before she could indulge. Marie called it the Haitian Woman Syndrome.

"How is work?"

"Killing me," Marie admitted.

"You know, I'm not supposed tell you this, but Rudy stopped by last Sunday."

Marie didn't react, barely looking in Claudette's direction.

Claudette moved in. "You don't want to know what he had to say?"

"Not really, no."

Claudette added a spoon of sugar to her coffee. "His mother isn't doing well."

"Mom, I know," she sighed. "Look, Rudy and I aren't seeing each other anymore and that's it."

"His mother adored you."

"Mommie, kitè sa. Leave it alone." Marie walked to the living room. "Emily, your mom is on the way ."

"But I won't see my cartoons. We don't have cable, Auntie Marie."

Marie knelt and caressed Emily's cheek. "How about I bring you some coloring books?"

"That would be nice."

"You're growing into a little lady."

Marie peeked in the kitchen. Claudette shuffled bills around the table.

Mother and daughter had drifted so far apart. Life was great when Nancy was around because she balanced everything. Maybe Claudette took Nancy moving out harder than she let on? But there wasn't even a mile separating her apartment and Claudette's home. She was closing in on twenty-seven and Claudette was young enough to continue on with her own life.

"I'm planning on visiting his mom." Marie returned to the kitchen. "But I don't want Rudy to think this is an opportunity to start over. I'm done with that part of my life."

"No one is saying you should get back together," Claudette explained.

"But you'd love that."

"Me? After sleeping with your friend?" Claudette snapped. "I was proud you were able to walk away with your dignity intact. You showed a lot of character."

Claudette had never really spoken to Marie this much about Rudy in the four years they dated. Even when she got engaged, all her mother could muster up was a tepid congratulations. Now she sat across the table praising her decision. It was all too confusing.

"You never said much. I didn't think you cared."

Claudette inhaled. "You're my only child, how could I not care?"

"You hardly ever showed it. I'm not imagining all of this."

"Well, it's hard for me to show affection," Claudette admitted. "You've always known that."

That struck a nerve. "You had no problems showing Nancy affection or any man since we're letting this out in the open."

"Of course. That's what this bullshit is about." Claudette tossed her mug into the sink. The leftover coffee splattered onto the backsplash above the sink.

"No, this isn't bull mommy. You can't sweep this under the rug. This is how I feel and that matters."

"I sacrificed everything for you," Claudette shot back. "You little ingrate!"

"Here we go!" Marie escaped into the living room.

"Everything I've done for you, and this is what I get?"

Marie grabbed her purse, hugged and kissed Emily. "Em, your mom is going to pick you up soon."

"Where are you going, Auntie Marie?"

"I have to leave. I have something to do."

"Okay, I'll stay with Grandma."

Marie returned to the kitchen, headed to the back door, and reached for the knob, but Claudette forced it shut.

"What's your problem with me? There's always something you're harboring, but that's not my problem. I raised you all by myself! I never got a helping hand in raising you, feeding you, providing for you. Was I such a bad mother?"

"That's just it. You were a great mom…to Nancy!"

Marie ripped open the door the second Claudette removed her hand. "Why was it so hard to show me the same affection you showed her?"

"Are you serious?" Claudette shouted from the doorway. "Are you going to compare your childhood to what she's been through? Don't come to me with this mess again! Selfish little bitch!"

Claudette slammed the door so hard the window curtain above the sink fell into the pool of coffee spilled earlier.

In the driveway, Marie shook her head in disbelief. She got into her car and drove a few blocks before pulling over and lettingher tears break free.

Inside the house, Emily entered the kitchen and found Claudette with her hands planted under her chin.

"Grandma, what's wrong?"

Claudette shifted her gaze to Emily. She loved the child's big brown eyes, upstaged only by a bigger set of dimples. The sweet features favored Nancy's own, but Emily was actually a carbon copy of her biological grandmother, Veronique.

"Grandma is fine, Emo." She rose and playfully brushed Emily's hair with her fingers. "I'm just a little tired."

"Why don't you take a nap? Mommy says that always helps."

"I'm sure it helps Emo, but Grandma is another kind of tired."

***

"It's Jimmy." Fiona handed Ti Zoot the phone.

"Yeah." He growled into the line. He hated calls and directed that anger to Fiona. "Coffee!"

"I try making it, but you don't like my coffee." Fiona complained in the background.

"Breakfast? Okay," he agreed after checking the time on his watch.

Ti Zoot anticipated Jimmy would reach out to him as he left things on an odd note the night before, after they had left Nancy's place. He rarely shared his thoughts, but perhaps he could explain his behavior and rationale to Jimmy who was a good listener.

"I try to make a good breakfast. I even try to learn how to make a Haitian breakfast, Fiona ranted.

Ti Zoot placed the phone down and walked over and planted a kiss on her rosy cheek.

"Tender, but you cannot dismiss everything with that, she complained, and then went to the kitchen closet where she pulled out a brochure for sleep deprivation therapy. "I know you never look at this," she shouted in his direction. "You never listen to anything I say, Wesner."Their conversations were always one-sided. He heard everything but did not respond. Instead, he decided on a shower. As the steam rose in the bathroom, Fiona kept up her banter.

"You can't ignore everything you don't agree with. Maybe I've overstayed my welcome. Perhaps, I should draw the line. C'est le moment de parler franchement!"

Unfazed, Ti Zoot dressed himself.

"If you don't want me, please say so."

"Where's my black leather?"

"The hallway closet," she pointed. "I am attractive. I am young. I can move on."

Ti Zoot flipped the collar on his leather coat, grabbed his keys and exited the apartment.

***

"Where's Marie?" Nancy looked around.

"Mwen pa kon afè granmoun." Claudette mumbled as she swept the kitchen floor.

"You don't know grown folks' business?" Nancy should've guessed her aunt was upset. Sweeping and muttering were sure signs. She figured the best thing to do was grab the dustpan, help a little, and leave before she was forced to listen to the issue.

"Emily, are you ready?"

"Can we stay? I'm watching cartoons."

"No sweetheart, we have a lot of chores. It's a busy day," Nancy explained.

Claudette took the dustpan from her. "Chita!" She pointed to a chair.

"Okay," Nancy obliged.

Claudette scooted the dust into the trash and then sat across Nancy. "I've had enough! All these years I've raised that child by myself, and I've received nothing but aggravation and grief."

Nancy drew closer and caressed her aunt's shoulder. "What happened?"

"I gave her everything. What else did she need? School, clothes on her back, food on the table. All I get in return is disrespect, nasty comments. I've had it!"

"Auntie, what happened?"

"I'm here in my house minding my own, and she walks in here very disrespectfully and accuses me of being a whore—"

"Aunt Claudette, now I know Marie would never say that."

"Nancy, kitè sa. Leave it alone."

Nancy found herself mediating from the moment she moved in with them. Sometimes she settled disagreements about silly things like how to make the best sòs pwa, a rich black bean puree. Other times, the two would go from sharing compliments about interior design to throwing jabs that Nancy refereed without offending either side.

"Love you, Aunt Claudette." She kissed her on the temple.

Nancy hoped they'd be closer once Marie moved out, but there were no guarantees in their complicated relationship. The only constant were the ups and downs between them.

"Bye, Grandma." Emily gave the matriarch a kiss.

Claudette followed with a hug and watched mother and daughter exit her kitchen.

***

Ti Zoot looked across the dim room trying to make eye contact his waitress. Both he and Jimmy had coffee, but they still hadn't received their order of herring, eggs, and plantains.

"Yes." The waitress sidled up to their table after locking eyes with Ti Zoot.

"Tell Anul that Ti Zoot is here," he instructed. "And please, turn on the lights."

As if on cue, Anul barreled out of the kitchen with plates in hand, which he set before Ti Zoot and Jimmy.

"I wanted to be sure I was the one to serve you, Ti Zoot." Sweat dripped down his cheeks.

"What happened to the lights?" Ti Zoot asked.

"Oh, yes excuse us. We had a problem with the electricity." Anul whipped around and barked orders at his staff. "Suzie, put the lights on. Oh-oh!"

"Ignore all this theater," Ti Zoot dug into his herring, "same shit every day."

"Yeah? I've only been here once." Jimmy looked around and carefully broached his next question. "Last night, you were visibly upset when the conversation turned to Nancy's date…."

"Never." Ti Zoot replied quickly as if he anticipated the comment.

"I was confused—"

"About?"

"Well, I think without actually saying it—we were wondering why you were so indifferent when the topic was came up? I mean…I'm confused. Ernse and you were very close. Did you have feelings for Nancy too?"

Ti Zoot slapped his palm into the table. "Feelings? They were…they are like my little brother and sister."

"Sorry, I didn't mean—"

"I've known them since they were kids." Ti Zoot took a minute to breathe before going into his wallet and carefully pulling out a news article neatly enveloped by a cellophane strip. He handed it to Jimmy who was unsure what it was but unfolded it with care.

"All I meant last night was that she isn't ready."

It was a *Daily News* article dated Friday, June 1, 1984.

The paper was well preserved for the years it had spent in Ti Zoot's wallet. Jimmy's eyes landed at the bottom of the article where he recognized a familiar name, Claudette. He looked a third of the way up and saw two photos side by side, a man and woman. Both people were attractive, but the man didn't look happy, which was a sharp contrast to the woman's warm smile.

Brooklyn Man Commits Uxoricide Then Kills Himself

A Brooklyn man shot and killed his wife then turned the gun on himself as their 12-year-old daughter slept in their apartment. Neighbors heard the shots and called 911. Upon arrival, officers from the 77th Precinct found the couple lying on opposite ends of the room.

Marc Bourdeau, 39, kept to himself and drove a cab during the day. His wife, Veronique, 36, a nurse at Coney Island Hospital, was more approachable, according to long-time neighbor Katia Jacquet.

"They arrived from Haiti, very down to earth, good people and two years later they had a little girl," Jacquet told reporters. "Veronique loved that child. They both did."

Sources say the hardworking couple's focus was first and foremost their daughter. Homicide and forensic experts were able to determine murder and suicide with relative ease based on the placement of the weapon and the male victim's self-inflicted head wound.

"When I heard the shots, I knew it was the Bourdeaus," Michael Lubin explained. "They were quiet sometimes, but mostly you could hear him arguing with the wife. It was always like that."

Once he entered the scene, Officer Vic Mona located the troubled couple's twelve-year-old daughter in a corner, seemingly in shock from finding the bodies. Mrs. Bourdeau was found stationary on the couch with two gunshots to her skull.

Mona's partner, Officer J.T. Bannon, examined Mr. Bourdeau and the weapon. "We are still in the nascent stages, but we're able to determine there was no foul play and that Mr. Bourdeau committed the murder prior to taking his own life." Bannon noted to the reporters on the scene.

Jimmy was stunned.

"She's not ready," Ti Zoot repeated.

He took the article, folded the cellophane, and inserted the item back into his wallet.

"Add that to what happened to her husband?" Ti Zoot pondered aloud. "No way."

"I never knew that's how Nancy's parents died," Jimmy rubbed his eyes, the details he just learned in the article was almost too much process.

The waitress came with a tray and set both their orders in front of them. Ti Zoot examined his plate as if he was expecting some abnormality, only to attack his herring and eggs with verve.

"I'll never forget the day I first saw you and Ernse," Jimmy related between bites. "I was new in the states and unsure I wanted to stay. It was a cold day, I was hungry and you guys crashed the restaurant with your big fight. I was this close to returning back to Haiti," he said after placing his index finger near his thumb with little space between them emphasizing his point.

"That's where everything got out of hand," Ti Zoot moved his coffee aside. "Up until that point, I could keep Ernse in line when he did something stupid. But that winter, he got into a situation, I had no answer for."

"I understand," Jimmy placed a hand on Ti Zoot's forearm. "And everyone knows you'd switch fates with him in a heartbeat."

"You ever hear the name Quico circulate in the neighborhood?"

Jimmy shook his head, "You know I stay away from all that street stuff."

"Well, that Quico is big on these streets," Ti Zoot explained. "Even the craziest street hustler will think twice before crossing Quico and his crew. That's exactly what Ernse did."

"Damn," Jimmy crossed his arms listening intently.

"I didn't even know it myself at the time but Ernse was having an affair with Quico's girlfriend. Quico's brother, Javier found out about the affair and confronted Ernse. That's when I found out everything myself which was bad enough, but then Ernse told me she was pregnant. That fight you saw in front of the restaurant that day was between Ernse and Javier."

"God," Jimmy whispered. "It's like Ernse had a death wish."

"All of that flashes in my mind all the time. I reexamine how I could've done things different, to prevent the outcome at least."

"I don't know if you could've really prevented that, not based on what you've just told me," Jimmy explained. "But what happened to the girl and the baby?"

"This is the crazy part," Ti Zoot leaned in. "She had the baby and she's still with Quico. I always wonder if he thinks that baby is his."

"Is it?"

Ti Zoot stared at his friend, "I wish I knew. I've never seen the baby myself. The only saving grace is that Nancy never found out."

***

Fiona walked into the apartment and found all the lights were off save for the light coming through the cracks of the bedroom door. She started in that direction but doubled back to the kitchen to grab two glasses and a bottle of wine. She kicked the bedroom door open, set the refreshments down, and placed her clothes on a chair.

"It's almost three o'clock in the morning," she said to Ti Zoot, who sat on the bed flipping through a deck of cards. "Are you up waiting for me?"

"Had a good time?" Ti Zoot ignored her question.

"Yes! At least people pay attention to me out there."

She stood before him hopingnude he'd turn in her direction. "Are we going to make love? If not, I won't shower tonight."

Again, he didn't answer. Sometimes he found her antics funny. Other times, he wouldn't entertain them for a second.

She slipped on her nightgown and headed to the bathroom to brush her teeth. There, she shouted taunts in his direction. "Un bel homme m'a propose de faire l'amour ce soir. Did you hear me? A handsome man offered me sex."

When Ti Zoot didn't respond, she continued the conversation with herself.

"Malheureusement, j'ai refusé l'offre. Au moment où je me suis dit, 'est-ce que l'homme avec qui je suis impliqué serait en colère ou jaloux?' Are you jealous…even though I refused?"

Still, nothing from Ti Zoot.

"Les hommes sont si gentils au début." She rinsed her mouth and reentered the bedroom. "Men are so nice initially." She pondered only to find he wasn't actually ignoring her this time.

"Poor soul, finally, you sleep," she removed his playing cards from the bed. "You never heard me. You never hear me no matter what language I speak."

CHAPTER 3

New Year's was still fresh in everyone's mind. Nancy decided to take care of some bills to ease her burdens, and she scratched the '93 date off a couple of checks since the new check book she ordered, had yet to arrive.

It was past 10:00 p.m. and Ernse hadn't reached home yet. His routine was to always come home between 6:00 and 7 p.m. to have dinner before stepping out again. Tonight, she couldn't shake the feeling something was wrong. He hadn't replied to any of her pages. It was one of those nights where the city felt more live than usual and promised trouble for guys like her husband. She kept the TV off, afraid she'd see a live shot of Ernse in handcuffs while being forced into a police car. Morbid though it may be, that was the good version of possible outcomes that ran through her mind.

Thankfully, Emily was already asleep after indulging in one of her kiddie tapes. Watching her daughter sleep serenely somehow raised her nerves. She couldn't shake the feeling that Emily's calm was a symbolic precursor to a storm heading her way.

A thud struck against the front door. She froze, and her heart raced. She couldn't make out the noise. Another thud followed as did another. Voices accompanied the ruckus. She cautiously walked to the door and immediately recognized Ernse and Ti Zoot's voices. There was no mistake they were arguing. Through the peephole, she saw Ti Zoot with both hands around her husband's collar pressing him against the opposite wall.

She returned to the living room, picked Emily up from the couch, and placed her daughter in bed. She didn't want Ernse and Ti Zoot's conflict to wake her up.

Back in the foyer, she quietly opened the door. Ti Zoot pressed a hand against Ernse's face. "You better stay low until I can clean this shit!" he screamed into his ear. "Stupid! Stupid! Stupid!"

Ernse looked up and saw Nancy at the doorway. Ti Zoot, realizing the same, released his grip and entered the apartment, heading straight for the kitchen where he grabbed a drink.

"What's going on here?" Nancy followed Ernse into the living room.

He took the remote and powered on the TV. Nancy shook her head upon noticing the red marks Ti Zoot's hand left on her husband's face.

"This guy is an idiot!" Ti Zoot burst into the living room. "If he steps one foot out of that door for the next few days, I want you to page me. I swear, Nancy, if he takes a bath, page me! When he wakes up, page me!"

"Okay. I know he won't tell me anything, but can you please explain what the hell is going on here? I have a three-year-old in that room!"

Ti Zoot set his drink down. "Please, just listen to me. Everything will be okay. You're much smarter than this dumb ass. I know you'll listen to me."

Frustrated, she took a step back to massage her temple. "I can't keep living my life in the dark. What happened?"

"Nancy, please, just keep him here until I can tell you everything."

"He's not going to listen to me. You know that."

Ti Zoot grabbed her shoulder. "That's why I'm telling to page about everything, and he better not test my will."

"So, no one is talking? You know what?" She threw up her hands.

"I don't want to know what mess you and Ernse are involved in. He's a grown ass man acting like a boy even though my child needs a father."

"You're right, he's still behaving like the same boy you met years ago. But listen, any move he makes outside of this apartment, I'll be on his tail."

Ti Zoot walked over to Ernse and slapped the TV remote out of his hand. "You hear me?"

"I hear you," Ernse responded slowly.

Nancy disappeared into the bathroom and slammed the door. Ernse picked the remote off the floor and resumed his channel search.

Disgusted with the situation, Ti Zoot decided against wasting time with Ernse. Nancy made better decisions than her husband anyway.

"Nancy, come out here now." He pounded on the bathroom door.

He could hear the faucet running but suspected she was only trying to drown her sobs. She didn't respond, so he retreated to the kitchen and refilled his glass with another shot of rhum. This time he sipped the liquid, savoring the taste, while he weighed having another talk with Ernse.

"You and your family need to get out of this neighborhood." Ti Zoot swallowed the last of his drink. "I'm not doing this again, I won't always be here."

Ernse kept his mouth shut. It was never a good idea to argue with Ti Zoot because his warnings were more than mere scare tactics. A moment later, Nancy exited the bathroom. She stood in the hallway and waited Ti Zoot to finish.

"Listen, you're my little sister. Unfortunately, that fool you call husband is also like a brother. I'll never let anything happen to you, but you'll have to trust me. You got that?"

"I trust you. You know that, but I just can't anymore. We have a child now. He wants a son. He doesn't know it, but this has been dominating my thoughts lately, I'll never give him one the way things are going."

The comment buried Ernse's heart into the pit of his stomach. At the same time, he felt a lump form in his throat and stopped minding the TV. He'd never sensed an aversion to having another child, but he was aware of the constant worry he gave her even though he knew his abilities as good father were in doubt. The remote slipped from his hand and landed on the couch, symbolic of the way his life had gone in recent weeks.

"I won't ask any more questions." Nancy stood with her arms folded. From the sound of her voice, tears weren't far. "Do whatever you have to."

"Don't worry." Ti Zoot forced a hug which she ignored..

The moment seemed surreal to Ernse—almost as if he wasn't in the room, and they were discussing something he knew nothing about.

"Page me," Ti Zoot told Nancy before exiting the apartment. "It's going to be okay."

She nodded and returned to the bathroom with the world on her shoulders. She couldn't help but recall the boy the boy from junior high, whom nobody painted him in a positive light.

Yet somehow, the handsome boy they called Ernse cut her off in the hallway before fourth period. He was visibly nervous but asked for her name and number. They made eye contact a few times, but she never thought much of him as she was hardly interested in boys at that age.

"Why?" she'd asked him. No one had ever asked for her number before. He exuded a little confidence when he explained how he had observed her for a while, developed a crush, and wanted to exchange numbers just to talk.

She politely asked what he wanted to talk about. Caught off guard, he mumbled something and then opened his hand, revealing a pen and piece of paper in his palm.

She scribbled down her name, and he told her that 'Nancy' was a beautiful name.

She responded by saying her name was plain and blushed as she finished writing the number.

"I'm Ernse," he smiled.

She had imagined this Ernse character as some big, ugly oaf. Instead, he was quite the opposite and even polite!

"Sorry. I'm going to be late for class." She rushed off.

He thought he'd knocked it out of the park until he looked at the paper saw that Nancy had only written first four digits of a phone number.

"Played," he said aloud.

He was ready to crumple the paper but tucked it in his pocket instead. He spent the rest of the school year pursuing Nancy, getting the final three digits on the last day of school. She would discover his good side a far cry from the reputation he earned in school. Their friendship grew fast as he was very open about himself and his difficult childhood.

Later that summer, tragedy struck. Nancy's father killed her mother then committed suicide.

Ernse was one of the few people who could connect with the girl who had suddenly become withdrawn. He became her best friend, her lover, and father to her child. But they struggled as husband and wife mainly because of his dedication to the streets.

***

April 20, 1996

It was early spring, but it already felt like summer. Jimmy tagged along with Ti Zoot, who took his car for detailing at the car wash.

"Papa, ou mankè yon kwen la," Ti Zoot criticized the man buffing the exterior.

"I'd like to get my hands on vehicle like this," Jimmy said.

"You're looking for trouble."

"A nice car like that? What trouble?"

"Nice cars attract nice trouble."

"Eh, I'll take that chance." Jimmy stared at the shiny fender.

"Start with a better home, less trouble."

The two continued back and forth while a sedan double-parked directly across the street from them. Inside the midnight tinted windows, Steve sat at the wheel with Fredo in the passenger and Max and Eddie filling out the rear.

"I'm telling you, that's duke." Fredo lowered his window for a better view. "That's duke. U-turn and pull up over there."

"Max, I'm telling you, don't let Fredo handle this shit," Steve pled.

"Fuck that! Let's go over there and put it on this dude!" Fredo shouted.

"Calm down," Max advised. "You had a run-in with him, we're going to talk to him so he understands there's a new set of rules now. But don't make me look like a clown, it's not good for my business."

"Fuck that, Max," Fredo replied. "I got a burner right here under the seat man!"

"See this is what I'm talkin' about? It's the middle of the day man!" Steve pointed out.

The words escalated between Steve and Fredo, but the exchange was mostly nonsense. Eddie sat waiting for Max's reaction in the matter. He preferred Max's temperament and thought Fredo was prone to unnecessary drama.

Still, Fredo pressed on. "Fuck this. I'm about show some balls in this joint."

Max leapt from the back of the sedan and pushed Fredo back into his seat. "Cut this shit out. We handle things my way. Understand?"

Fredo winced and agreed allowing Max to release the grip on his shoulders.

"Okay. Now," Max straightened his shoulders, "pull the car up in across the street."

They made a U-turn and parked in front of Ti Zoot and Jimmy who were both occupied with the job the detailer performed.

Max leaned into Fredo's ear. "You good? We wouldn't want this guy to see us at less than one hundred." Fredo fixed his shirt and composed himself. "I'm aight."

"Steve, Eddie, do me a favor, walk over there and let this guy know I'd like to have a word with him."

Steve took the lead with Eddie trailing. Fredo pretended to look straight ahead but followed everything from his peripheral view. Max sat relaxed and bobbed his head to The Lost Boyz's "Renee."

"Hey, what up?" Steve addressed Ti Zoot directly. "My man over there would like a word with you." Hs pointed to Max in the car.

Instead of looking where Steve pointed, Ti Zoot studied the two messengers, examining them from their bandanas down to their Timbs. He wasn't impressed.

They're probably a couple kids in their early twenties at best, but that meant danger. Eddie was rail thin and far from filling out the way men eventually do. Steve was more solid, but Ti Zoot knew he could take them both. However, the x-factor sat in the car. He'd seen that seen that same pearl E420 a couple of times in the neighborhood, but he never caught who rode inside. The neighborhood's make up was changing so fast, he couldn't keep pace.

"Over there in that car, partner." Eddie pointed again when Ti Zoot didn't answer. "He wants to have a word with you."

Jimmy nudged Ti Zoot, hoping to draw him from any conflict. "I think the car is ready."

Ti Zoot leaned in on the two young men. "Get the fuck out of my face!"

Steve did a double take. "What's your problem, homie?"

"What's my prob—lem?" Ti Zoot's palm caught Steve flush on the jaw.

Eddie's reaction was to look back at the car for a cue from Max. Before he knew it, he found his face on the cement, not even aware Ti Zoot had struck. When he looked up, Ti Zoot was hovering over him yelling, but Eddie couldn't make sense of it all. The next thing he saw was Steve in a series of exchanges with Ti Zoot, but even that was over quickly as Steve keeled over and remained low gasping for air.

Jimmy tried to grab Ti Zoot with hopes of leaving the scene, but he resisted.

"What's going on here?" Max was now standing between Ti Zoot and his fallen deputies.

Max's six-foot three frame cast a shadow over Ti Zoot, but that didn't faze him one bit. He stood toe-to-toe with Max. Steve and Eddie rose from the ground and flanked each side of Max.

"What's going on here?" Ti Zoot repeated Max's words. "I'm what's going on!"

"I think you're misunderstanding something. I'm not some pushover. In fact, I do all the pushing."

"Oh, okay...new sheriff in town. I didn't know." Ti Zoot threw a left-cross that Max mostly dodged. The two scuffled for a moment and locked arms with no clear advantage. Steve and Eddie started for Ti Zoot, but they were intercepted by Jimmy, who shoved Eddie off and struggled with Steve.

"Fuck this. I got heat for this clown!" Fredo stormed into the melee.

Jimmy noticed the .32 low in Fredo's right hand.

"Yo, man. Remember me? Yeah, how this shit feel now?"

Max backed off and put a hand in front of Steve to do the same. He then positioned himself between Fredo and the weapon, shielding it from view as much as possible. "Homie, I just wanted a word with you, but you took this in another direction. We'll be seeing you again. That's my word."

"Me? Whatever you got, I can handle it now!" Ti Zoot yelled for everyone within an earshot.

Jimmy's eyes were fixed on the gun and Fredo's every move. Still, he managed to tug at Ti Zoot's elbow so they could leave, but his charged up friend didn't budge.

"All right, if that's how you want it." Max tucked the .32 under Fredo's T-shirt and directed things back to the car. Fredo looked Ti Zoot in the eye and raised his T-shirt displaying the .32. He followed that by spitting on the ground then parted with a message. "Ya old ass is done, homie."

Several blocks away, Steve pulled the car over into a side street per Max's request.

"I like your fire," Max told Fredo. "But you have to work on discipline. I see why this dude is a problem. He probably thinks it's 1985 and "La Di Da Di" is still playing in his head. We're going to take care of him and anyone else having a hard time gripping with reality." Max stared at Fredo. "But it has to be my way."

***

"I can't believe you hardly unpacked anything." Nancy looked at the pile of moving boxes still sealed in Marie's living room.

"No time." Marie lay back on the rug. "It's work, work, and more work. I wish I had time to unpack everything and enjoy my place. You're more than welcome to come and set things straight for me, couz."

"As busy as I am? Not going to happen."

"Oh, that's right. Mr. Man has all of your attention these days," Marie cracked.

"Uh, no. There's a certain six-year-old who dominates my time. I squeeze Max in where I can."

"Does Max squeeze back?"

"Shut up," Nancy joked.

"When do I get to meet this Max?" Marie placed a hand over her eyes to shield them from the ceiling light. "You know I have to give my stamp of approval."

Nancy didn't respond. Instead, she maneuvered around some boxes and sat on the love seat.

Marie peaked through her fingers. "Oh my God, you really like him. I can see it in you!"

"That's just it. Everything feels so right. It's scary," Nancy confessed.

"Look at you. You're open." Marie sat up with excitement. "I have to meet him soon."

"You will." Nancy assured her, but segued into another topic. "How are things between you and Claudette?"

"There's nothing between us. Leave that alone. I've been stress free for days now, I'm good."

"Marie, you're living in your own space now. I get the fact the two of you can't coexist in the same home, but bury the hatchet. You're her only child. This is hard on her, despite the front she puts on."

"I'm in a pleasant mood, Nance." Marie rose from the rug. "Don't kill that by talking about me and my mother's bullshit."

"Couz, I can sit here and tell you I'm not getting involved in your business, but you know I always get pulled in the middle of everything."

"Just how your aunt likes it." Marie rose to grab some water from the fridge. Nancy followed her lead but also munched on celery and carrot sticks she pulled from a Ziploc in the empty fridge. Taking opposing ends at the table, they continued the conversation.

"Ugh! How can you eat these things?" Nancy cried after biting a celery stalk.

"Then put my snacks back," Marie ordered.

"You have a birthday coming up," Nancy moved onto the carrots.

"Hmm. I'm not feeling it. Not feeling anything."

"Come on Marie, we should do something."

"I don't have any plans or anyone."

"Oh, so that's it? You need to be in a relationship to have a party?"

"Party? Whoa, whoa." Marie held up her hands. "I want nothing, no surprises, nothing."

Nancy threw a carrot stick that pelted Marie's cheek.

"Ay pa derespektè mwen. Don't disrespect me! I'm older than you and this is my house!"

Before that last word escaped her cousin's mouth, Nancy doubled over with laughter. Marie's impression of her mother was always dead-on because they were so alike.

"Don't make fun of my aunt." Nancy tried to contain herself.

"How's the job going?"

"They're taking advantage. They've got me teaching this email stuff to the staff."

"That's great," Marie said.

"I barely know the damn thing myself."

"I'm sure you're doing great. Use that on your resume when you move on."

"Amen," Nancy said. "I keep having this recurring dream that I'm a receptionist at that place for the rest of my life."

"That's subconscious motivation," Marie explained.

"Huh?"

"Yeah. I always get this one where I'm late to a class and I never get inside."

"That's weird. You finished school a while now."

"Our dreams are trying to tell us things about ourselves," Marie explained.

Nancy rummaged through the bag careful to avoid the celery. "By the way, I'm enrolling in school. Hopefully I'll start during the winter semester."

"You see!" Marie cried. "That's probably what that dream was telling you. That's great, Nance."

"I hope I can manage it all."

Marie took her hand. "Of course, you can and will!"

"Honestly, it's not only getting a degree, but I want to be an example for Emily."

"That's beautiful." Marie squeezed her hand. "I can't promise every night, but I'll play my part and have Emily over while you study."

"Of course, you will. That's nothing new," Nancy laughed.

"Hmm. Finish up and graduate quick. My sitting service is limited."

"I'll be sure to remember that." Nancy bit into a carrot as she studied the kitchen. "You know, it's a shame you don't like to cook. This is a nice kitchen. You have all these cabinets, and it's so spacious."

"Yeah, you don't see kitchens this size in New York City apartments. I struck gold."

"Just a waste for the takeout queen."

"You're more than welcome to come over and cook dinners for me every night, couz," Marie sipped her water.

"But seriously, I want to have something for your birthday."

"No. I'm not in the mood right now."

"It's six weeks away! You'll be in the mood the closer we get."

"No, I won't."

"Come on, couz. It's been a long time since we've done anything together. It'll be like old times."

"Nance, the old times are gone. Just keep the fond memories. Don't relive anything good. It never works out."

Nancy quieted. Getting her way got harder the older they got, but Marie would inevitably give in after a series of rejections. "Couz, the last party we had was Emily's Christening…"

Marie shot her back a funny look. "Was it that long ago?"

"It was." Nancy sensed an opening.

"That was a great party," Marie remarked. "Feels like so long ago. Yeah, that was a hell of a party…until Ti Zoot, cracked a bottle over some guy's head, right? No thank you!"

"Aww, come on, Marie. That guy walked in off the street and was acting all kinds of crazy."

"The only Christening party where the baby's godfather gets into a bloody fight. No, I'm good. How are you going to pay for a party, anyway?"

"Come on, couz. You know we can get everyone to potluck everything. Margot will cook something. Ti Zoot always brings the alcohol."

"Yeah, then he has a sip and wants to fight."

"Marie, stop. You know he has to be there."

"Well, he can be there all he wants. I'm not showing up."

Nancy grabbed a few more carrot sticks and followed Marie into the living room. "Couz, please. This would be a great event for me to introduce Max to everyone."

The comment stopped Marie in her tracks. "Oh, my God. Is it that serious?"

"No…yes. Maybe."

"Come here." Marie sat on the couch and placed a cushion under her arm. "My baby cousin has fallen for a man. It's my job to make sure you don't end up hurt like me all the time. Let's talk."

Nancy lay her head on Marie's lap and shut her eyes while she spoke her mind. "I feel awkward. I have no idea how to behave. Not everything I've experienced with Ernse will apply in a new relationship, but he's all I've ever known. We started so young. I have no idea how to deal with anyone else."

"They're all the same sweetie, especially the ones that try to be different."

"It doesn't feel that way. In fact, it feels like he and Ernse are so different. I can't connect many things between them. I'm starting from scratch."

"Maybe it's better that way. Toss out everything you thought you knew and try a new angle."

"Couz, I'm not sure I understand, but he makes me feel special again. Maybe I'm one of those people that needs to be in a relationship. I mean, my last relationship started when I was fourteen."

"You're overthinking, Nance. Take it for what it is. He's a nice guy showing you a good time."

"You're right. It seems like it's been a long time,longer than the two years since…"

"I know you miss him. We all do." Marie stroked Nancy's hair. "Just make sure you're not transferring your feelings for Ernse onto this guy."

Nancy reflected on her words. There wasn't a lot of similarity between Ernse and Max, both were undeniably charming.

In Ernse's case, that charm could be a negative. He could be too callous and wild with it. He never knew when to contain himself. Ernse was still in her heart, but she had enough of an unstable world.

The verdict was still out on Max. It would be awhile before she peeled the layers. He was more of a slow burn.

"So, we're having that party for you?"

"Woy, pitit," Marie shoved Nancy's head off her leg and stood up. "No party…no!"

CHAPTER 4

April 27, 1996

The weekend brought dreary weather. Sporadic rain kept the skies gray, but the heavy storm the news promised never came, missing its target and veering east.

The barbershop on Beverly was full, but only a few patrons were getting shape-ups and cuts. The shop's owner, Antoine, was the senior spokesman in the neighborhood for Haitians in his circle. He enjoyed an audience, so he rarely chased folks out—even those who just hung around and never got a haircut. Antoine always made sure to mention to anyone within earshot, he came to the U.S. in 1962 to escape Duvalier's Regime and often had a story or two to back that claim.

Anyone who knew Antoine, even in passing, called him 'Lulu.' He enjoyed socializing with young folk and kept himself as youthful as his seventy-three years allowed. He sported a jet-black afro and maintained a row of perfect dentures that people often compared to Chicklets. He also stayed current with the fashionable lingo, but his Kreyol accent had all but disappeared. His cadence was a mix of a Harlemite from the 1960s and Rudy Ray Moore's scatter pace, making his background hard to decipher.

Lulu rented the large backroom in the barbershop to Biembo, a Dominican man who ran numbers from behind a picnic table. Between the political parley and the numbers clientele— foot traffic was always brisk in Lulu's Barbershop.

Steve and Max had barely stepped inside the shop when Lulu, sitting with his back to the entrance, saw their reflection in a large mirror and greeted Steve in familiar fashion.

"Stevie, Steve." Lulu welcomed him with a smile fit for an Ultrabrite ad. "My young blood, my young blood."

"Lulu. What's good, O.G.?" Steve's voice reverberated across the railway shop.

"Whoa...what happened to your face young blood? It looks like you went three rounds with Tyson."

"Eh, all that street shit, Lulu. Squash it."

"Aww, man, you gotta break it all down for Lulu and let me know who you beefing with, young blood."

"Nah, Lulu. Consider this shit in the past. We'll talk another time."

"I got you, Stevie." Lulu eyed Max who stood by the entrance. "Too many ears in Lulu's shop, but I'm glad you brought new business for me today."

"Oh, my bad." Steve approached Lulu. "I never introduced you?"

"No, young son."

"Lulu, this is Max. Miami Maxwell."

"This is Miami Max?" Lulu grinned and extended his hand for a firm shake.

Lulu was always in the know and keeping tabs. The latest he'd heard was that Max was making all kinds of waves.

"Good to meet you." Max glanced at the long pinky nail on Lulu's right hand. "I hope my reputation is good so far."

"All good," Lulu cackled. "I'm glad young Stevie is hanging out with someone like you. Too many knuckleheads running around these streets now."

"I'm keeping it low-key, Lulu," Stevie winked.

"What can I do for you?"

"Just a shape up. Mustache and goatee," Max answered.

"Don't worry. Lulu will have you looking clean, crisp, and classy. Ain't that right, young Stevie?"

Steve chatted with someone on the sidelines and ignored Lulu.

Max sat as Lulu placed a thick lather on his face. Every so often Lulu noticed someone walk in the shop and head straight to the back acknowledging no one. Even though the business done in the back was far more lucrative than the barber on most days, Lulu wasn't concerned since he collected money either way.

Grabbing his blade, Lulu lowered his head and whispered in Max's ear. "Young blood, to be honest, I've seen you around a couple of times."

"Oh?"

"Was that Ms. Nancy I saw you with in front of Medina's the other day?"

"It had to be." Max shut his eyes. "Why?"

"Oh, no problem with that, young blood. She's a fine young thing. Good girl." Lulu navigated the blade around Max's chin. "In fact, after her husband died, old Lulu favored her a little. But she was so distraught with grief, she never understood my advances. Sweet girl."

"So you're still very much in the game?" Max asked. This old fool had nerve.

"Young blood, I'm always on the hunt. S'why old Lulu never let himself get tied down or married. I like them young and pretty. Old and pretty? That's when I exit the scene."

"Did you know her husband?" Max wondered.

"Yeah, I knew the knucklehead. Steady running around with people even more foolish than he was. He could've had everything! But you know the type, they have to live it up harder than the next man. The knucklehead didn't respect anyone...didn't respect his own life. Always spat in the face of danger. Never understood how he got someone as nice as Ms. Nancy."

"Things are always like that." Max rolled his eyes. This O.G. was full of bark and swag, but he'd seen too many summers. No matter how much he tried to hide it with bottles of Just for Men, his winter had arrived.

"You know, young blood, you're wise. Miami prepared you well. You'll do well with Ms. Nancy by your side. Keep her there. Have you met that cousin of hers, Marie? I think her name is…yes, Ms. Marie. She's every bit as fine as Ms. Nancy. Let me tell you that family is full of fine women. Old Lulu would get in a lot of trouble messing with that family." He paused mid-shave. "I had a thing for Ms. Marie too. One time she caught me staring at her beaver and never spoke to me again."

Max let him cackle at his own joke. His shape up was complete. He looked in the mirror and was impressed more than he expected. Maybe that was Lulu's trick, talk smack while doling out sharp cuts. Those old hands were good for something. He didn't mind the old clown and looked forward to more time in the chair even if it meant putting up with a few lousy stories.

"Young Stevie!" Lulu shouted across the room. "Come check this cut out. I got your homeboy looking clean, crisp, and classy."

"Yeah, that's sharp," Steve agreed.

"I got young blood looking like that boy on Orlando…Hardaway… Penny Hardaway," Lulu mused. "Young blood you ready for an NBA contract!"

"Thanks," Max handed Lulu his fee plus tip.

"Young blood, keep coming through. Old Lulu will treat you right."

Max didn't respond. He merely moved toward the exit with Steve in tow, dropping goodbyes on the way out.

With Max and Steve a good distance out the door, Lulu walked to the center of the shop. "Always some new motherfucker walking these streets thinking he's the new sheriff. We'll see how long this one wears the badge."

***

Nancy hated rain, especially on weekends. There was too much to catch up on Saturdays for the complication rain brought. She had already taken care of half a dozen items on her list and was headed back out when the phone rang.

"Mom...phone!"

"Emily, I told you never pick up the phone! Now who is it?"

"Mr. Jimmy."

Nancy took the phone. "Hey, Jimmy. I'm on my way out, what's up?"

"Whenever you get back just call me," Jimmy said.

"Important?"

"Not urgent," he said.

"All right, I'll call you later." She grabbed her keys.

"Okay, later."

"Jimmy, wait! I'm going to pick up a table. I can use some help. I can pick you up in ten minutes. Can you tag along?"

"Uh, yeah, that works."

"We can talk on the way. Cool?"

"Okay, see you soon."

***

"What's that old fool's game?" Max asked Steve as they approached Cortelyou Road. He didn't take the old man seriously, but he still hated the way he was probing with regards to Nancy. He had to wonder, if Lulu been a younger man, would he have been more aggressive about the matter?

"Ah, he's harmless. He thinks his old ass can still hang with gun clappers."

"Yeah, he does," Max pulled under a red light, "but he wants me to know he's got the lowdown on everything."

"Oh, yeah. Lulu knows everything," Steve laughed. "Amazing, considering how big the neighborhood is, but he knows it all.""That's not good. He talks too much."

Steve turned, confused by the implication.

"I don't mean like that," Max smiled. "He's no threat. I just don't like people who talk. He said he saw me with that chick Nancy and started giving me all kinds of details. It's like he's fishing for something."

"He's a character," Steve explained. "So, how's it working out with her?"

"Nancy?"

"Yeah."

"She's all right."

Steve let it slide but wasn't buying his nonchalance.

"She really got a homie thinking about her," Max gave in and laughed, "but I'm just getting into this New York shit. Too much already looking my way."

"You ain't lying," Steve said. "They're always asking 'who's the new guy you're hanging out with?'"

"Hmph. Anyway, more important things to do than kick it to shorties all day. I needed a change from South Miami for a lot of reasons. No matter how much I'm feeling these New York chicks, business comes first."

From the first time they met, Steve found Max agreeable. In Max he found an associate with a likeminded business first attitude. He seldom cared for the Fredo and Piks he found himself aligned with because of the trade they were involved in. Though only slightly older, Steve often deferred to Max as if the age gap was greater than the couple of years it actually was.

Their connection was brokered by Pap, a gunrunner who worked from the Carolinas back up to New York for close to a decade. Steve, Eddie and Fredo were a generation younger than Pap who kept the then young kids at an arm's length until he was ready to reel them in his business.

But Pap's inner circle got careless and sloppy, which resulted in a thirteen-year sentence. Business cooled down until Fredo brokered a run through Steve, who Pap was willing to open doors for. Pap then summoned Max from Miami, moving him to the forefront in New York.. Filling the void after Pap's indictment, Max was adamant exercising better judgment would render a better fate than his predecessor.

Not everyone involved was a Max fan or believed in him the way Steve did, but they all agreed he was effective. He also earned praise from Pap, whose wife still received a personal kickback from Max once in a while. Despite the recent Disneyfication of New York City, Max believed he could still maintain a sizeable profit moving metal if he kept the operation conservative and flew under the radar.

"So far, I've been surprised. I didn't expect things to move so smooth in the Big Apple," Max admitted. "Except for that incident with that old fool at the car wash."

"He's been in the hood forever living off an old rep," Steve explained.

"Maybe," Max glanced at the bruise on Steve's face. "Rep or not, he made you guys look bad."

Steve nodded his head in agreement.

"O.G.'s might slow down," Max continued, "but they always have the streets in them. They get a little wiser, make sharper decisions. They don't get to be O.G.'s for nothing." He pulled along the curb, set the car in park and turned to Steve. "Even though I'm in this business, I'm not a killer. I'm providing and facilitating a service. Again, I'm not a killer, but I'll protect my business. Fredo is an idiot at times, but I guess he's proven himself to Pap, so he's good for business. This O.G., if he's got a problem with Fredo, that's going to impact business."

***

"Oh, my God." Nancy opened her car trunk. "Thanks for helping me out with this, Jimmy. I don't know how I would have handled this by myself."

They were inside the parking garage at the mall. Jimmy had wheeled Nancy's table on a shopping cart to the section where she parked.

"I would have helped you, Mommy." Emily smiled and took the last bite of the double scoop ice cream Jimmy bought.

"Of course, you're always helpful." Nancy beamed with pride.

"Emily, can help me put the table together?" Jimmy joked as he struggled to fit the box in the trunk. "Nancy can you push the other end down?"

"Oh, yes." She tucked the box under the trunk's hinge.

"Thanks." Jimmy repeated the effort on his end and settled the box inside before they drove off.

"So what's on your mind Jimmy, or is it something I have to make sure Emily isn't around for?"

"Nothing risqué," Jimmy laughed. "Just worried about our friend."

"Ti Zoot? Why did I think this was about Marie?"

"Jimmy shook his head and looked in the rearview mirror to see if Emily was keyed into their conversation. She wasn't. Her attention was focused on using her fingers to trace raindrops as they slid down the back window.

"The other day, he got into an altercation with some thugs."

"I'm not surprised. I can't believe he's still behaves like he's seventeen!"

"It wasn't his fault. These guys were out of control."

"Doesn't matter, Jimmy. Don't you see? Ti Zoot is always the common denominator?"

"I was there, Nancy, it wasn't his fault," Jimmy pointed out. "The thing is, Ti Zoot's world is far apart from mine. What seems monumental to me, might just be posturing. I have no idea. I've hung out with him. He's slowed down, but things like that incident follow him. They just do."

"There's no talking to him," she explained. "He's a stubborn blockhead. I hope time will force him to grow." Her hand twitched with concern on the steering wheel, so she changed the subject. "You know, Jimmy, I'm glad you helped me out. I have an invitation for you."

"Invitation?"

"I'm throwing a birthday party for Marie." She pulled a card from the center console. "A month from now. Last Saturday in May, Memorial Day weekend."

"Thanks. Is it a milestone birthday?"

"Other than number twenty-seven? No, it's been a while. We used to have parties in my aunt's backyard all the time. Legendary stuff."

"Looking forward to it then."

"She hasn't agreed to it yet," Nancy admitted, "but I'm throwing it anyway."

"Okay." He smiled at her determination.

By the time they reached Nancy's place, the rain had slowed to a drizzle. Emily, eager to help, held the door to the building while Jimmy lugged the box and her mother followed with shopping bags.

"What year did you come to the states?" Nancy asked after they loaded everything inside the elevator.

"March 8, 1993." Jimmy dragged the box down the hallway with Emily acting as a guide.

"Okay, it was a little before that we stopped having parties and get-togethers. The last one was for Marie's graduation. Responsibility started to dictate life. You know, adult stuff."

"The best of times," he remarked.

"Yeah, yeah. Seems like such a long time ago. I used to think things were so difficult back then. Didn't matter, though. We had great times with family and friends."

"Do you want me to set this up for you?" Jimmy placed the box inside the apartment.

"Uh, yeah. I wasn't going to let you leave without putting this table together."

"So, is this party supposed recapture your yesteryears?"

"Maybe. And build new memories," she responded. "I guess I'm nostalgic, Jimmy."

"Nothing wrong with that."

"At least I'm thinking about good times now." She closed the apartment door. "Before this, for a while, all I could do was feel sorry for myself."

***

"Ay, big man in the house!" Fredo greeted Max as he and Steve strolled in the tiny apartment that served as a place to rest at night and conduct business round the clock. Six guys were cramped in a small living room. Fredo and Pik shared the apartment, but their compadres visited so often and at all hours of the night that neighbors quietly complained to the landlord about the noise and activity.

The furniture was bare save for a table in the middle of the room and a collection of mix-matched chairs. A lone floor-model television sat heavily before a huge couch with empty beer cans and liquor bottles finishing the décor.

Max scanned the room, but his attention kept coming back to the sweaty walls and stale air. Even when the windows were open, the air remained fetid. A product of too many guys in a cramped apartment. He rubbed his nose to dull the scent.

"Why does this place always smell like a dog in heat?" Steve said.

"Well, look around." Pik shuffled some cards in a stained wife beater and boxers.

"But you don't have any dogs." Max grabbed a chair to sit.

"What's new, Max?" Fredo joined him with a bottle of malt liquor.

"What's new? We have a run."

"That means money," someone hollered from the couch.

"You're right," Max replied. "And if you're smart, it'll be a load of cheddar."

Fredo dipped into the kitchen and moved a floor cabinet to reveal an old-style dumbwaiter. He opened it and pulled out a semi-automatic, which he inspected and polished.

"Gimme the loot!" Fredo screamed as he placed the weapon in the middle of the table and took his seat. Max looked to Steve, who then inspected the tool.

"How much?" Steve asked.

Fredo raised a hand then his pointer finger.

Steve eyed the metal like candy. "Yeah, this is will be money on these streets!"

"Okay," Max clasped his hands. "We roll then."

***

"That was quick," Jimmy said, noticing Emily asleep on the couch.

"Oh, yeah, long day. She hasn't napped yet," Nancy said.

"Usually, she's asleep as soon as the car takes off but not today."

"Here you go." He handed back the screwdriver and Allen key he used to put the table together. "Goodnight."

"Where are you going? I ordered Chinese."

"Oh, then I'm staying," he laughed.

"Please, I can use the company some time."

"I'm sure Emily is good company."

"The best," Nancy smiled. "Although I find myself too wrapped up in Elmo and cartoons from time to time."

"You make it all look so easy."

"Excuse me?"

"This…everything," Jimmy said.

"It's not. It's far from easy, Jimmy, but I thank you. If it looks easy, I must be doing something right, I guess."

"You are. It couldn't be easy after—"

"After losing my husband? You can say it. I had to learn to deal with it. I remember after it happened for weeks…months. I refused to let myself smile, enjoy a moment with my daughter, share my thoughts. I refused to live. Ernse was my world. I came to that realization after he died. The irony is I thought I anchored our family. Once he was gone, my rock floated away. The two hardest things I've had to do was watch his casket lowered and find strength to continue on with my daughter."

"I remember. It was just after I met you all," he said. "You've come a long way."

***

Max, Steve, Eddie, and Fredo remained hunched over the living room table, where poker games and business transactions usually took place. The overhead light glinted off the black steel of the weapons spread there. It made the place look and feel like something out of a movie despite the spartan décor.

"I'm looking forward to this road trip. My man down there got this tricked out AMG," Fredo said, nursing his malt liquor.

"Nah, you stay here," Max countered. "This trip is only me and Steve."

"What? I brokered this!"

"You did, which is why you're off the hook."

"Max, this ain't making sense." Fredo rose from his chair. "I put this together."

"Relax, Fredo. I'm sure there's a good reason," Steve interjected.

"I'm saying, how am I going out of my way making the initial trip down there getting a good deal for us, and I'm not in this?"

The room got quiet, save for the TV in the background. Some of Fredo's clique drew closer, paying attention to their words, waiting for whatever exchange came next.

"I gotta be in this, son. I gotta be in this."

"Have a seat," Max ordered.

Fredo was burning inside, but he sat with his eyes fixed on the deal laying on the table. His deal. Max checked his pager several times before addressing the room.

"I think that Pap incident is still fresh on our minds. I know it's fresh in his. Fredo you and Eddie are fortunate. There was heat directed your way, but Pap being the man that he is just ate that up. God bless him. Every day you walk outside these doors, thank Pap. This deal you brokered…beautiful. We couldn't ask for better. But knowing the heat you carry, it's not wise for you to be on this trip. Besides, the fewer people we have making this trip, the more likely we'll fly under the radar. But you brokered this, so something is coming your way."

"Thanks, Max." Fredo extended a hand, only to be ignored.

"I'm not finished," Max replied. "Your head is too hot for this game. You cool off, or we'll all be reuniting with Pap. Understand?"

"I got it. I wasn't thinking straight. You know I'm a soldier, and I love being out there."

"I get that, but my job is to lead, and that's the only way things will succeed."

"Man, you're always right," Fredo capitulated. "You're never wrong."

Max rose from the table and gave Fredo a pound. He kept his visits brief and purposeful. Steve nodded in Eddie's direction and the three exited.

Max stopped in the lobby. "That's the second time he did that shit. I can't let this operation go down like it did with Pap. If homie upstairs keeps this up, we'll lose everything."

Yeah," Steve agreed. "You're right."

"I'm reasonable," Max continued. "But if his behavior poses a threat, what am I going to do? The shit he pulled the other day at the car wash, that's not the kind of thing we need. E-Flow, you with me?"

"I'm with it," Eddie said, trailing the two.

***

"She'll sleep through the night." Nancy looked over at Emily on the couch. Jimmy was still working on his chicken satay.

"Thanks for dinner."

"I should thank you…you made today a lot easier for me," Nancy picked at the food in her plate. "Drink?"

"Some wine, please."

"Coming right up." She cleared the table and returned with a Malbec and goblet.

Jimmy grabbed them and poured into the glass. "You're not joining me?"

"Nah." Nancy sat on the other end. "I'm good."

"I don't get how you always have wine and liquor, but you rarely drink."

"I keep drinks on hand out of habit. Ernse bought drinks on Fridays, so we always had a bar in the cabinet. In fact, a good portion of what's there now, he bought. That was him and Ti Zoot's thing. They'd drink on any occasion, for any reason."

He was enjoying the wine and her conversation. She was a good listener. He figured she would be a great person to vent to if the occasion ever presented itself.

"So, are you going to talk to our friend?"

"I guess so," she relented. "I just don't think it matters. Ti Zoot has never listened to anyone. I talk, he pretends to listen. He'll do the first stupid thing that comes his way. Wash. Repeat. Same cycle."

"Yeah, but if anyone can reach him, it's you."

She positioned herself lotus style on the couch before responding. "No I don't think so Jimmy. The days of reaching Ti Zoot are gone. At least for me. You saw his behavior towards me last time you were here."

"It wasn't towards you," Jimmy countered. "I mean, it's more than that, I think. You'll always be like a little sister in his eyes."

"Maybe. I know it's painful, but even I have to move on from Ernse, no?"

"Yes, of course you do," Jimmy quickly said, feeling a bit of guilt and hoped Nancy didn't think he was also judging her willingness to turn a new page. "Either way, just talk to him. I'm sure he's ready to listen."

"I'll do it, but only because you helped me today," she admitted. "Make yourself comfortable and finish that bottle. I'm going to change that little girl into her pajamas and tuck her in."

"Oh, I was about to head out."

"So soon? Guess I took too much of your day."

"Not really. It's not like I had plans. I thought maybe you'd want to call it a night and get ready for church tomorrow."

"Yeah, but the truth is I won't fall asleep until late," she said. "Well, don't rush that drink. I'll be back."

Nancy grabbed a towel from the bathroom. When she returned to the living room to collect Emily, Jimmy wouldn't allow her. He kindly carried the child to her bed with Nancy leading the way.

Once Jimmy left the room, she undressed Emily, wiped her down, and slipped on her pajamas. She nudged a stuffed teddy between the girl's arms. "So much your father's child," she mused. "My aunt disagrees, but my genes had no part in this. You're every bit as beautiful as he was handsome." She kissed the child and wished her a good night.

"What's on?" Nancy wandered into the living room where Jimmy sat staring at the TV screen.

71

"Just flipping through the channels and this was playing."

"Oh, my God. *Mahogany*. I love that movie! Have you this before?"

"Nope," Jimmy said. "You're forgetting I wasn't born here like you."

"Well, you're going to love this movie. It's great."

"Isn't that Diana Ross?"

"Yes and Billy Dee Williams," she explained.

"Doesn't look like a good action movie," he sighed.

"Just watch. Action movies are silly anyway."

The rough, southside Chicago 1970s scenes reeled him in as did the iconic theme song. Every so often, he found himself staring across at Nancy. The light bounced from the TV and created a soft hue on her profile, which he found captivating.

Luckily, she didn't notice. For her, Diana and Billy's onscreen chemistry was always a perfect escape.

***

Ti Zoot stashed a handful of lottery receipts in his pocket as he left the bodega. He had walked in and spent thirty minutes over numbers he hoped were a complete match, box or straight, but none of the numbers lined up for a win.

The rare times he was able to sleep, he found himself lost in an odd dream. If he remembered the dream, he had the task of figuring out what it symbolized. Specifically, he had to translate the dream into a series of numbers. These turned into a routine set of playing numbers for both the state lottery and street numbers.

His most recent dream gave him one, six, seven. In that dream, he was hiding, but it was never clear who he hid from. What he recalled "hiding" were numbers one, six, seven in his ch'alla, a little pamphlet style booklet Haitians who gambled were all too familiar with. He double checked the book to confirm one, six, seven. When he'd thumbed through the book, he'd decided the dream could be interpreted in other ways and played a set of other numbers in every combination as backup.

Despite his scientific gamble, he was out thirty-three dollars. "Ay primo, since this is Dominican lotto, you should charge me in Dominican currency." His joke was lost on the man behind the counter. He just wasn't used to humor from Ti Zoot.

"What came out?" An elderly woman crossed into Ti Zoot's path.

"Five, nine, four. I played that all January of last year," he said regretfully. "Can you believe it?"

"Five, nine, four?" The woman looked puzzled. "Those are Marie-Jo's numbers. I should have known!"

Ti Zoot was amused. He had played every combination and lost everything, and this woman thought luck should have been in her corner because of some Marie-Jo.

"Good night, Mamie." He walked off shaking his head and turned the corner, dipping into a Spanish restaurant. The place was empty— odd for a Saturday night—but their bouyon bef, a hearty beef stew soup, was always good. He spoke with two women behind the counter. They didn't bother taking his order as it could be set by an automatic timer at this point. Elva, the younger female, went to the kitchen and poured the piping hot soup into a large container.

"No action tonight?" the older woman asked.

"No action." He removed the lotto receipts from his pocket, hoping five, nine, four was buried somewhere in the bunch.

***

"How you feel about that shit Max said earlier?" Pik dusted lint from his wife-beater and jeans as he strolled to the liquor store with Fredo.

"I'm not feelin' that or Max." Fredo shouted. "And who the fuck is Max coming up with all this shit like Pap put him in charge?"

"But he is," Pik explained. "He's got Steve, E-Flow, and a few others buying his shit."

"I don't like the way Max is flexing on me. I'm not feelin' that." Fredo crossed the street and Pik followed. "The way I see it, fam," Fredo continued, "Pap is doing a bid and that's unfortunate, but there's nothing that says we have to cut paper with Max."

"I wonder what Pap really thinks about all of this? It might not be a bad idea for you to visit Pap."

"I ain't doing that. Fuck that!" Fredo eyed his companion. "But on the real, I don't see myself staying patient dealing with Max. Steve, E-Flow, and anyone else will have to take sides."

"We got the real soldiers in our camp son." Pik entered the liquor store.

"That's what's up. A, yo, remind me we gotta check something on Edgecombe this week."

"Yo, I hate going up there. That shit is like a fucking war zone."

"A, yo, Pik. Pull your skirt down homie." Fredo teased then turned his attention to the row of liquor behind the plexiglass.

"That Absolut right there. That shit is fire." Pik went into his pocket and tossed a wad of crinkled bills on the counter. "A, yo, money. Give me that bottle right there!" He barked at the man behind the counter, demanding a few more bottles for good measure.

"You know something, Pik, I may just visit Pap like you suggested. It's not a bad idea to have a direct convo about how everything is going down. We may be going upstate soon."

***

An elderly gentleman spotted Ti Zoot in the middle of the street still shuffling lottery receipts.

"Ti Zoot," he called out. "I just lost a bundle too."

"I've been having a nasty streak, misfortune after misfortune," Ti Zoot said grimly.

"Well, better misfortune with numbers than in life, par la grâce de Dieu," the elderly man smiled with an all-white beard, contrasting sharply against his ebony complexion.

"With the grace of God to you too." Ti Zoot stared at the man. "Although it's all one and the same."

Before the gentleman could respond, Ti Zoot's pager went off. It was Fiona. He fished in his pocket for a quarter and walked to the nearest pay phone.

"Hello, what happened?" His greetings were always gruff.

"It's your cousin from Haiti. He called again," Fiona said.

"What does he need this time?"

"He wouldn't say, but it sounded urgent."

"It's always urgent," he sighed.

Just across the street, stepping out of the liquor store, were Fredo and Pik, brown bags in tow. They walked a good yard before Fredo looked up and spotted Ti Zoot, who too busy in his conversation with Fiona to notice anything. Fredo had a word with Pik and they casually walked over.

Fredo took the lead, stepping into Ti Zoot's line of sight. "Yo, money. Remember me?"

Ti Zoot, absorbed in his phone conversation, did not bat an eye, prompting Fredo to take a step closer.

"Yo!" he shouted even louder.

Ti Zoot didn't look up.

Fredo turned to Pik. "You believe this motherfucker?" Fredo gripped the bottle in his hand tighter. "A, yo, fuck this shit, man. It's on." He swung the bottle at Ti Zoot who countered by hammering Fredo with the payphone before the bottle connected.

The blow caught Fredo flush below his nose, pummeling his front teeth. Without missing a beat, Ti Zoot grabbed Fredo's T-shirt by the neck and struck the phone onto his head. Helpless, Fredo went down.

Pik, frozen from the attack, watched Fredo struggle on the ground with his arms aloft to protect his bruised head. To his right, Fredo's bottle, still in its brown paper bag, rolled off the sidewalk onto the street where a passing car crushed it.

Pik charged Ti Zoot with his own bottle but tripped on Fredo, who screamed something unintelligible. Both he and his bottle went down. The glass shattered upon impact, sending bits of glass into his face.

But Ti Zoot didn't give him much time to recover, stomping Pik with the heel of his shoe. "You think it's that easy?" he barked. "You think I'm that easy? Ask around motherfucker!"

Each time Fredo and Pik tried getting up, they got another blow from Ti Zoot's heel. Finally giving up, Ti Zoot blew his nose in their direction, popped his collar, and turned his attention to the buzzing phone, dangling back and forth on its line. He gently placed the receiver back onto the hook and checked his pocket. His lottery receipts were still intact, so he walked off as if the altercation had never occurred.

***

"It was good," Jimmy said.

"Don't say it like that."

"Like what?"

"Like you're being forced to say it was good," she explained.

"It was good. That's all."

"Mahogany is a great movie! After watching, every woman wishes they were Diana Ross and every guy wants to be Billy Dee!"

"No way. Too much love story for me," he joked.

"Typical man. If there isn't a gun shooting scene every two minutes, it's no good."

"You forgot sex scenes," he teased.

Playfully offended, she grabbed the remote and powered off the TV. "Another drink?"

"No! I've had enough. It's eleven o'clock. I better get going."

"Thanks for everything today, Jimmy."

"It wasn't like I was busy. Thank you."

She walked him to the front door and hugged him. He returned the gesture with a snug cuddle, which he held a little longer than normal before finding her lips. The sensation was as smooth as he imagined, but something was off. Her body language didn't signal a rebuke but it also didn't welcome the gesture.

"Sorry, Jimmy, but I'm involved…"

"Oh, my God. I'm so sorry." He backed away embarrassed. "I lost my mind."

"It's okay. It happens."

"Nancy, sorry. And you just went on a date the other day! How stupid of me."

"Jimmy, it's okay. I'm not offended. Sometimes friends confuse their emotions."

He tilted his head against the wall. "I guess the alcohol got to me."

"Don't worry. We had a great day together. Emily and I enjoyed the time."

Jimmy eased his way to the other side of the door, exiting the apartment. "I'm stupid."

"Stop!" she said. "It wasn't bad at all, and if I wasn't involved, who knows."

He forced a smile. She watched him walk past the elevator and take the stairs instead. She shut the door then slid down behind it and sat down.

***

Fiona opened her eyes. The clock on the nightstand read 3:28 a.m. Turning to her right, Ti Zoot was, of course, wide awake staring at the ceiling. Some nights he was mesmerized by the opposite wall. The routine also took its toll on her sleep and woke her most nights.

"I've been dreaming…" He took a long deep breath. "I've been dreaming I've been hiding from someone."

She sat up and placed a pillow between her legs, waiting for him to finish.

"Tonight, I dreamt I was trying to open a crate. I try, but I can't open it. I use a crowbar and nothing opens. Finally, someone comes from behind and throws a key in the air. I look up, waiting for the key to land. It never lands. I glance over, hoping to see who threw the key, but they move too fast. I never see their face."

It was the first dream he had detailed. He was serene, but she knew it bothered him. In fact, all the dreams bothered him. She lost count how many times he tossed or blurted out something in the middle of one. Once, she woke him in the middle of a dream. He protested, claiming his heart could fail on the spot if she did that again.

She waited for more details, but he never spoke past his initial account. It was closing in on 4:00 a.m., and her eyes were giving in. At least, she could sleep a little since they were getting somewhere.

CHAPTER 5

April 29, 1996

Max looked at his watch. It was 5:47—same as it was thirty seconds ago when he last checked. He was standing before Paramount Plaza on Broadway. It seemed like the entire Times Square neighborhood had left their offices and headed for home except Nancy. Again, he stared at the swivel doors until she made her way through.

"Sorry." She placed a warm kiss on his cheek. "I had to prepare a conference room for a meeting in the morning."

"I thought you forgot I was picking you up," he pouted.

"Of course, not." She took his hand and led him down Broadway. "Did I tell you I hate my stupid job?"

Max marveled at the skyline. "How can you hate working here?" The few times he'd visited Manhattan, the experience never failed to leave an impression.

"My job is stupid. I don't want to be there half the time."

"Well, make do until you can move on."

"I don't have a choice," she agreed. "I've got bills and a little girl."

A herd of tourists suddenly came their way resulting in Max accidently elbowing a tourist's camera. It was a nice spring evening and they were moving at a leisurely pace in contrast to the sidewalk traffic.

"So, what did you want to talk about?"

"Nothing important. I'll be out of town for a couple of days," Max said.

"Oh, are you going home?"

"No, just a little business," he answered. "I'm leaving tomorrow midday, but I'll be back before you know it."

She stopped, but continued to grip his hand, which broke his stride. He looked back. She had her serious face on.

"Are you playing games?"

"Games? I'm not sure what you're trying to say, but I'm going out of town for business with my homie Steve." He planted a kiss on her forehead. "Look, let me page him right now and you can ask him yourself."

"No, that's not necessary." She playfully swatted his hand and resumed their walk. "I just don't want to be played. I'm not in anything to play games. I hurt easily."

"I'm not here to hurt you. It's just business," he reassured.

"Well, it would help if I knew what business you were in."

"Nice try," he laughed. "We've already discussed this. I'm not selling drugs or anything like that, but the less you know about my crazy business the better off you'll be. It's just dumb stuff, nothing all that serious."

He seemed genuine, so what could she say? Everyone had their own hustle from bootleg CDs to knock-off Louis bags.

She prayed to God it was something more in that vein.

***

"What the hell are you doing at my job?" Marie asked.

"I have to talk to you."

Rudy stood with a bouquet in hand which Marie had already refused twice. She looked around the reception area hoping no one passed by or, more specifically, could hear their conversation.

"Wait, are you drunk?" She winced. The smell of stale alcohol suddenly struck her nose.

"I just want to talk Marie-Carmelle."

"That's not necessary. I told you that already."

"Thirty minutes."

"Goodbye, Rudy. Get out of here or I'll call security."

He placed the bouquet in front of her again. Whatever she was saying did not register. She hadn't noticed it, but he was uncharacteristically disheveled. Untied laces, stains on his suit, and the aroma of heavy liquor pointed to someone in desperate need of a shower. She had avoided his calls for months and disregarded any message he relayed through their circle of friends.

"Go ahead. Call security!"

He was serious, and she knew it. He had that look in his eyes.

"Okay, give me five...no, ten minutes. I'll listen to what you have to say over coffee. You need it."

"I'll wait over there." He pointed to a couch in the reception area.

"No! Downstairs in the lobby," she said. "In fact, make it outside."

After waiting so long for a face-to-face, he didn't push it. "Fine."

She made sure he entered the elevator before she returned to her desk. A flashing light on the phone console indicated a voicemail.

"Couz? It's Nancy. Are you still able to head home with us...with me? Page me."

"Oh shoot! Totally forgot." She opened her drawer and pulled out her pager. Nancy had already sent two messages. She read their location and paged back '20 min.'

She powered off her computer, grabbed her bag, and dashed to the elevator. Once she arrived in the lobby, she found Rudy sitting in the courtyard. The bouquet was gone. Somehow, he looked worse than he did upstairs. Daylight had a way of doing that.

"I spoke to your mother the other day. She was upbeat."

"She has good and bad days," he confessed.

"Yeah, she told me the same."

"I can't believe we haven't spoken in so long."

"I don't have much time. I need to meet someone, so whatever you have to say, say it fast."

"But you said we'd have coffee."

"I did, but I forgot I had an appointment." She looked around the courtyard hoping co-workers weren't around.

"I just wanted to see you," he smiled. "I'm hoping you accept my calls again."

"That's it? I have to go. I'm not up for social chit-chat."

"Who are you meeting?"

"Excuse me?" she snapped. "Gotta go, Rudy."

"Marie come on. That's not fair. I didn't even get five minutes."

"Look, I'm headed downtown, but I'm late. Walk along if you really have something to say." She caught herself staring into his eyes, which never worked in her favor.

"How far are you walking? My feet hurt."

"What's happening to you?" She stared at his scuffed-up shoes and walked off.

"Marie, wait. I just want to talk." He did his best to keep up.

"I don't see what we have to discuss."

"All right...all right. This is how you want it."

"I don't want anything," she snapped. "Except maybe the peace I've been fortunate enough to experience lately. I don't mind that at all."

"That's my doing." His tone was contrite.

"Rudy, the day you told meyou impregnated another woman , that was enough for me. I was done. I won't relive the past. I think it's best you do the same and move along with your life."

He thought about stopping but walked despite her jabs and his foot pain. Blocks later, he was lost in his thoughts. When he looked up, he saw Nancy across the street with an unfamiliar face. For a second, he thought the person was there for Marie, but the gentleman took Nancy's hand. Thank God.

"Hey, couz." Nancy beamed. "Max, this is my favorite cousin, my sister, Marie."

"Hi, Marie. I feel like I already know you. Nancy is always talking about you."

Marie extended her arm for a handshake, but Max drew close and pulled her into a friendly embrace.

"My cousin has a big mouth." Marie welcomed the gesture. "Don't listen to anything she says about me."

"That's too bad," Nancy interjected, "because I've only told him the good things."

"Max, listen to my cousin," Marie joked. "She's not just gorgeous but smart too."

Max laughed and turned to Nancy. "I like her already."

Nancy finally noticed Rudy standing off to the side. In fact, she almost didn't recognize him. Gone was the confidence and meticulous wardrobe. She wondered if his mother's illness played a part in that.

"Hello Rudy, I didn't know you were joining."

"He's not," Marie cut her off. "He's on his way to...wherever. Somehow he got the idea that he should sneak up on me at work."

"Oh, this is Max." Nancy tried to diffuse the awkward moment. "Max this is Rudy...uhm Marie's..."

"Ex," Rudy said and extended a hand to Max. "What's up? Nice to meet you."

"How's your mom doing?" Nancy asked.

"She's holding on. Being strong...being strong."

Nancy felt Marie's stare, so she kept things short. "Please send her my regards. We're headed to a lounge."

"Have fun." Rudy never took his eyes off Marie. "Enjoy the night."

Marie walked off without a word, leaving Nancy smiling awkwardly at Rudy. With nothing left to say, Nancy followed her cousin and Max trailed behind with a "later" that was muffled by the noisy street.

"Can we finish our conversation another time?" Rudy yelled in Marie's direction.

She was far enough away to ignore the comment but responded anyway. "I thought we were finished. We're good, Rudy."

Marie took a step, only to stop and ask, "How's the baby?"

They had never spoken about that. It was a simple question, but her tone said it all. He understood—she was still hurting.

But Marie didn't really wait for his response. Instead she grabbed Max and Nancy each by an arm then sprinted off and disappeared in a horde of pedestrians.

Rudy swore he could hear the laughter in her heart.

***

"Drinks are on me." Max announced. "What will it be, ladies?"

"He's a keeper," Marie laughed. "I'll have a Long Island iced-tea."

"Apple martini," Nancy chimed in.

"Only a few drinks," Marie advised. "I don't want you-know-who throwing shade your way later."

Nancy smiled at the comment. She had begged Claudette to pick Emily up after school, telling the matriarch she was forced to work overtime. Even though it was Claudette's day off, it was a routine struggle to get her aunt to babysit, especially weeknights.

"Ladies' room." Marie set her bag on the table beside Nancy and stood.

Nancy studied the lounge. She was glad to be around so many happy faces. She rarely got opportunities to indulge. If it took some manipulating to get this moment, it was worth it. She had been desperate for them share some social time after Marie adopted her new work schedule.

But she also hoped to use this occasion to get her cousin's take on Max. Her opinion always mattered. That was true even when they were Emily's age.

For Marie's seventh birthday party, Nancy wore a little pink dress with a matching bow. She looked like a toy doll come to life. She didn't know it at the time, but her mother, Veronique, did in fact pattern the dress after a porcelain figurine she had as a child in Haiti.

Veronique often wore matching colors and styles with her daughter and that birthday party was no different. She sported a one-piece dress, in a lighter shade of pink, that her husband argued was too much for a child's party.

"This is my little cousin," Marie announced to the other kids at the party.

"She's so cute." A nine-year-old grabbed Nancy's hand, pulling her into their group.

Claudette, who was working hard in the kitchen, stepped out when she heard that her sister, niece, and brother-in-law had arrived. "Marc, come. I have something special for you."

Marc's eyes widened. "Soup tet-bef! I've said this a dozen times, I should have married you and not your sister."

Veronique ignored him and instead continued into the living room greeting family and friends.

"You know you married the right sister," Claudette insisted in the kitchen. "You always loved Veronique and everyone in Jacmel knew it."

Marc grabbed a ladle and bowl and helped himself to the soup before planting himself on a chair.

"Where's that nosey friend of yours?" he asked. "I didn't see her in the living room or yard."

"Margot?"

"Who else?"

"She's working the weekend shift."

Nancy wandered into the kitchen. She couldn't help but notice how her father was engaged with his meal. "Daddy, what's that?"

"Soup princess. Come here." He placed her on his lap just as he'd done hundreds of times after his typically long shifts. Sometimes she'd fall asleep on his lap, other times sleep claimed him first.

"Try some."

"Mmm, it's yummy daddy."

"Your tattie Claudette is the world's best cook," he beamed.

Elsewhere, Veronique insisted she hang a piñata, suggesting the thing should hang on a hook in the living room ceiling that once supported a Trailing Jade plant.

"That will be perfect," she told those helping her. "Let me just loosen the cord and make it a little longer."

"Let me help you," said François, a handsome, well-groomed man in his twenties.

"Thank you." Veronique batted an eye in his direction.

Veronique and a couple of women looked on as the muscles on François' forearms flexed with every knot he loosened.

"Here it is. The length should be just right." François handed the cord back to Veronique.

"Yes, that looks about right. I hope it's strong enough."

"Oh, it's plenty strong." He tugged the cord to demonstrate.

François grabbed a folding chair and placed it below the ceiling hook. Just as he was about to stand on it, Veronique motioned him aside. "No let me," she smiled.

"Are you sure?" he asked, fearing she'd forgotten how short her dress was.

"Veronique, you'll fall," a female guest cried.

"I'll be fine," she insisted, removing her heels. The men in the room stopped politicking and watched Veronique's next move. She hopped up on the chair in one stride, mostly because of legs that seemed to go on forever. Half the women looked on with envy, while the others watched with admiration.

"Tattie Vero, be careful," Marie called from below. "Please hold her chair tight, François."

"It's not going anywhere," François grinned.

"This ceiling is higher than I thought." Veronique admitted as she glanced down at her audience. "If I can just tippy-toe…"

Back in the kitchen, Marc placed his bowl in the sink. "That was divine, as always."

"That's just greed, right down in the pit of your stomach," Claudette said refuting his compliment.

"I wish I could summon a similar appetite for your sister's meals."

"My sister is a fine cook."

"She's many things, but a cook of your caliber, she's not."

The hook was still a half-inch from Veronique's fingertips.

"…I can almost reach. François, you tied this part of the cord too small." She announced when she couldn't lasso the hook.

"You should let me handle this," François repeated.

"You aren't tall enough, François," she replied. A roar of laughter rose up from the men in the room. She then hopped an inch, clearing the cord over the hook to a round of applause. But on her way down, she lost footing and slipped off the chair. Luckily, François was positioned perfectly and broke her fall by grabbing her thighs in a huge bear hug. He then placed her on steady ground, which Marc witnessed upon making his way into the living room.

François took his handkerchief out to wipe his forehead. When he finished, all he could see was Marc's jaw and fist tightly clenched.

François uncomfortably backed from where the piñata hung, blending in with the rest of the onlookers in the room.

"Are you okay?" an older woman asked.

"Just lost my balance. Thank God François reacted so quick."

Veronique hadn't noticed Marc. She simply inched her dress down and thanked François once more as she placed her heels back on.

Unable to contain himself any longer, Marc stepped to the center of the room.

"Veronique!" His shout seemed to rattle the windows and silence everyone in the room.

Veronique looked his way, rolled her eyes, and dismissed him. She gathered the kids, attempting to start the piñata festivities, but Marc did not budge.

"VERONIQUE COME HERE NOW!"

Nancy stood behind Marc watching the exchange. She was used to frequent screams between the two, but fracases always unsettled her.

Claudette, appalled by the public display, hurried from the kitchen. François broke the silence hoping to shed light on the situation. "She was only hanging the piñata—"

"I did not speak to you," Marc shouted.

Veronique couldn't hide her embarrassment. She walked up and confronted Marc face-to-face. "How dare you?" she yelled before turning to exit, but he snatched her elbow.

A struggle ensued, shocking the guests. The more aggressive Marc got, the more Veronique resisted, shoving and scratching him whenever she got an opening. Marc eventually lost his balance and bumped into the wall, knocking down the picture of Claudette holding newborn Marie in her arms. Veronique took advantage and dug her nails in his left cheek and scraped off skin.

Claudette shook her head and rubbed her temples. "Mother Mary, why?"

Marc regained his footing, lunged at Veronique, and struggled to trap her in a bear-hug. Her strikes were wild, randomly pounding him here and there, but her efforts were futile since he was eighty pounds heavier and more powerful. She soon lost her wind, and the fight inside her faded a bit. He hauled her off to the bathroom in a tight bear-hug. But even then, she wouldn't give in, struggling to inch her way out, throwing insults along the way.

Once inside the bathroom, the yelling continued. Veronique ordered Marc out of her way so she could exit while he accused her of deliberately trying to embarrass him. She fired back calling him jealous and pathetic.

François and another man, Bobby, approached the bathroom door to intervene. Francois rolled up his sleeves, and Bobby nodded in agreement.

"No!" Claudette jumped in before François rammed the door. "You'll only make it worse. They have to calm down on their own. They will eventually. They always do."

An older couple suggested the adults move the party to the backyard. François and Bobby watched as everyone except Claudette filed out of the room.

Somehow, no one noticed Nancy in a corner of the living room. She was trembling, shocked by the incident. Her eyes were red and full of tears.

When Marie saw her cousin's heartbreak, she hugged her in hopes of shielding her from additional grief.

Finally, the bathroom door opened. Marc walked out, the lacerations from his cheek had dripped blood all over his canary shirt. He stopped for a moment and eyed François and Bobby, who were still standing by. Fearing another altercation, Claudette raced over and stood between Marc and her two guests. She took Marc's hand and pointed to the kitchen. He had no fuss left, so he followed her and sat calmly in the corner where he'd eaten his soup earlier.

She handed him a glass of water, but he was non-responsive, almost in a trance. So she placed the water on the table, hoping he'd come around.

François approached the kitchen and stood just outside the entrance. Once she noticed him, Claudette led him out to the yard to join the rest of the party. She grabbed his arm and stopped short on the stoop. "Thank you, François."

"I'm sorry, Claudette. If I knew things would turn out like this, I would have avoided even speaking to your sister."

"No, no. This is something much bigger than what happened today. It's been this way for a long time now."

"How sad. Good evening, Claudette."

She saw a couple exiting the gate with their son, so she cut them off and begged them to come back. They were reluctant, but the little boy wanted to stay. She reached in the bushes in front of gate, pulled a branch and stripped the leaves off.

"Gregory, go inside," she handed the stick to the boy. "Please, we are starting the piñata. Go play."

His parents felt bad and went back to the yard, leery of Marc and unsure what to expect.

"Children, let's go into the living room and do the piñata!"

The kids were joyous with the announcement. One by one, they lined up behind Gregory and reentered the living room. It didn't take long, but soon the room was filled with smiles and laughter after one kid tried a roundhouse swing that missed the piñata entirely. He smiled it off and blamed it on the tooth he had just lost that morning.

On the side, Marie still had her arms around Nancy whom she hadn't released since rescuing her earlier. Claudette walked over, gave Nancy a warm kiss, and asked Marie to make sure they each had a turn at the piñata. Marie planted an equally warm kiss on Nancy's cheek and assured her mother everything would be okay.

"Finish up inside," an older woman advised Claudette, steering her to the kitchen. "We'll take care of everything out here."

"Thank you," Claudette said.

Two of her friends, Danielle and Anne, tagged along to help. When they reached the kitchen, she found the glass of water, untouched on the table, but Marc was gone.

"He left through the front door," Anne explained.

Claudette paused for a second and decided it would be good to check on Veronique before starting anything in the kitchen. Truthfully, she was afraid to see what state her little sister was in.

The bathroom door was slightly ajar. She pushed it wide and found Veronique on the floor with her arms folded over her knees just as she did when they were kids.

"Are you going to be okay?"

"I don't know, Claudette. I don't know."

"Nancy will ask for you."

"I'll be there, but I need a moment."

"Okay, I'll be serving food soon." Claudette stepped toward the door.

"Is he still here?"

She never had reason to before today, but Claudette felt pity for her little sister. Her confident, beautiful, and intelligent sister sat on the bathroom floor fearful of stepping out to face embarrassment and her insanely jealous husband. How did a fairytale romance quickly turn to this?

"He left. Go up to my room." Claudette brushed Veronique's hair away from her face. It was a habit she had from the time they were kids. She loved Veronique's long, curly mane.

"Go up," Claudette repeated as she helped her sister up from the floor. "I'll check on you—"

"Can you believe what we witnessed today?" A voice floated in through the open bathroom window.

Heat flushed Veronique's skin at the comment. She broke from her sister's grasp and dashed upstairs. At the top of the stairway, tears poured, but she made sure it was momentary, wiping her eyes dry. She wasn't going to give in. Ever.

She opened the door to Claudette's room. It wasn't big, but her sister did a good job outfitting it with simple but vibrant accents. She locked the door and removed her dress, folding it neatly on the bed. She hadn't noticed the bruise on her side. Marc always left a reminder. She kept a mental list of every one of them.

She moved the comforter over to the side and snuggled into the bed. It didn't take long before she was fast asleep. Exhaustion and pain took their toll.

"Oh, wow!" a kid yelled from the living room. His swing busted the piñata wide open causing a downpour of candy on the hardwood.

Claudette peeked into the living room. Her spirits were lifted. The frenzy of kids and adults scurrying for candy brought a smile her face. She watched Marie ditch her birthday hat for her share of candy but also noticed Nancy off to the side. The girl didn't seem to have fully recovered from the earlier incident.

Claudette grabbed a cup from the birthday table and scooped some candy off the floor before the other kids snatched it all up. She offered the contents to Nancy, who grabbed the cup then wrapped her arms around Claudette's waist.

"Nancy...Nancy."

Max struggled to get her attention while he balanced a screwdriver, Long Island iced-tea and apple martini in his hands.

"Were you dreaming?"

"No. Where's Marie?"

"You were dreaming. She went to the ladies' room, but here she comes now."

"What did I miss?" Marie asked and then thanked Max for her drink.

"Not much. Except Nancy daydreaming here."

Marie took a sip. "My cousin. She'll never change…a perpetual dreamer."

***

Eddie walked into the Fredo and Pik's apartment and wondered why things felt strange. Normally, it was full of banter during all hours of the night, particularly on weekends. Even though it was Monday, things were still unusually quiet.

He had been visiting the place since he was fourteen. The unit once belonged to Fredo's grandmother, who willed him the apartment before she passed away. Fredo's parents were rarely in the picture. In fact, the only time Eddie saw Fredo's mother was at his grandmother's wake. She looked to Eddie like someone who'd had a rough life.

In the kitchen, the only movement was a roach rummaging through the usual stack of dishes in the sink.

"Where is everybody?" He turned and called out into the living room. "What the—" He did a double take.

Fredo and Pik were on opposite ends of the room, but it was very apparent they had just gone through the same ordeal. Eddie was floored. They looked like victims of an Iron Mike fight circa 1987.

"Man, what the fuck happened here? Did you two go at it?"

"Duddde…beef…ehch…" Fredo tried to explain, but he was nursing a loose teeth along with swollen gums and a bruised upper lip. Every so often he spat blood into a Styrofoam cup.

Pik wasn't much better, but it was at least easier to recognize his words. "That motherfucker Fredo's beefing with…dude snuck up on us and rolled hard." He limped across the room to give Eddie a better view.

"Damn!" Eddie's eyes bulged. "Did he beat you with a toolie? Ya'll look fucked up!"

"Shud…f-fuck up…man," Fredo managed, followed by another wad of spit in his cup.

Pik kicked over a crate full of CDs and loose tapes. "Where's Max and Steve, man?"

"I don't know," Eddie replied. "They never told anyone when they were leaving."

"Das bullshit!" Fredo pounded his fist into the wall.

"But I'm thinking they had to leave by now. I know they're meeting a connect in two days. Max wants to case things out before they do business."

"E, your man Max moves shady." Pik massaged his jaw with an icepack.

"He does shit a little different," Eddie admitted.

"Well, we gonna have to take care of this situation right away," Pik explained. "That O.G. is gettin' bodied!"

Eddie shook his head. He knew they talked that way in Max's absence. From the get-go, they resented and viewed him as an outsider. "That Miami Mofo," they often said behind his back. Nonetheless, they followed things the way Pap laid them out because he had everyone's respect and loyalty, even behind bars.

"We're going out later to take care of this," Pik explained. "You with us?"

"Tonight?" Eddie stalled. "Shouldn't he get his teeth checked?"

"This motherfucker right here." Pik turned to Fredo, who rushed over and got in Eddie's face.

"Look, you know I'm down." Eddie stepped back. "But don't you think he needs to see a dentist?"

"Man, what the hell you know about fucking teeth?" Pik asked. "First, we take care of this, then he can go to the fucking dentist."

Eddie knew he was stuck. Once they took care of Ti Zoot, Max would flip because he didn't okay it.

"I'm with it, man. You know that."

***

"He's hot! Are you kidding me?" Marie said. "And he's a spender too! Don't hesitate on this one, couz."

Nancy smiled on the other end of the phone. "He's too mysterious about how he earns a living. I'm not comfortable with that."

"I knew it was too good to be true. What is it, drugs?"

"No! He says it's nothing like that, but he has his own hustle."

"Well, that can be anything, Nancy. You may not want to get serious. Could he be selling bootleg tapes?"

"That wouldn't be his style."

"How do you know what he's hustling? He's probably selling knock-offs from a suitcase down on Canal."

Nancy laughed at the thought. "Shut-up, couz!"

"Maybe they're high quality knock-offs. I may want to check them out!"

"Shut-up!"

"Everyone is into some mess these days, but be careful," Marie cautioned. "I wouldn't get too involved."

The words stuck in Nancy's head, but a blissful memory was also on repeat—the night she pinned Max down and had her way with him. Even if this relationship didn't work out long-term, she was going to need a few more moments like that before she could purge him from her system.

CHAPTER 6

January 29, 1994

The zipper on the suitcase looked like it could break open with the slightest tug. Ernse had joked Ti Zoot shouldn't have packed half of his apartment in it. Ti Zoot ignored him and knotted two scarves, a red and blue, around a strap on the suitcase. He lugged the heavy bag onto a scale.

"Nintey-three pounds! Damn!"

He stared at the overtaxed zipper and debated whether he should remove some of the load. Ultimately, he ruled against the trouble that would cause. He would have to pay the difference.

"I don't understand how you can travel with so much crap when this is a last-minute trip." Ernse skimmed through a Vibe magazine. "I mean, you bought your ticket less than a week ago."

They were in Ti Zoot's living room. He disregarded anything Ernse threw his way. Many conversations between the two followed this pattern. Ernse spoke at length. When Ti Zoot had enough, he'd suggest his young friend relax. Meanwhile, he went over to each window and checked if the clear plastic was tightly sealed over each pane, so he wouldn't find a cold apartment when he returned.

"Let's go." Ti Zoot checked the stove, shut off the lights and picked up his keys. He pointed Ernse towards the oversized suitcase.

Ernse, slow to get up, grabbed it, and forced the thing to roll on wheels that weren't up to the task. "I can't take this big-ass suitcase down four flights by myself, man!"

"Come on, get out." Ti Zoot ordered and grabbed his coat of the rack in the foyer. "And don't break it."

Outside, the thirty-six degree cold found its way right through Ti Zoot's open coat. A particularly sharp gust of wind pushed right against his chest. When he reached the end of the corner, he cased the block and waited on Ernse who struggled with the suitcase. Save for a pair of stray cats in the alley, the street was empty as it was dawn.

"Here." He tossed Ernse the car keys. "Do me a favor. Alternate side on this block is Monday, Wednesday and Saturday. Be responsible for once. I don't want to come back owing tickets. And don't lose my damn keys again! I don't have a spare anymore thanks to you!"

"You know I got this, man."

Ti Zoot stopped in his tracks. "You say that bull every day, but you always find trouble."

"Come on, Zoot," Ernse said. Everyone and everything had piled on his shoulders in recent weeks, it seemed.

"You're already messing up. Today is Saturday." Ti Zoot pointed at the street sign. "Take my car. Your car is good on that side."

"Man, you're really scared of tickets," Ernse teased. "I rip mine up! Fuck it."

"You're a clown."

Ti Zoot watched him force the suitcase in the trunk and then sat in the car.

"Zoot, I know I mess up, but come on. You have to start treating me like the man I am. I'm not that kid anymore!"

"You're a man? You don't know the first thing!"

Ernse started the car and peeled out. Since the day Ti Zoot intervened in the beat down Ernse administered to street bigwig

Quico's brother Javier front of the crowd, the two had little dialogue In fact, anything Ti Zoot relayed to Ernse, he did through Nancy.

"Look man, I fucked up…"

Ti Zoot pulled his ticket out and double-checked it. The travel agent got everything right, except for the price.

"Look, I'll fix this. I'll fix everything."

"Fix everything? You're stupid! You mess with this dude's woman, get her pregnant, and bitch slap his brother. I don't think you know who this guy is, Ernse!"

"I know…" Ernse realized how much he screwed up after hearing the way Ti Zoot laid it out.

"NO, YOU DON'T!" Ti Zoot slapped the dashboard.

Ernse let his objections go and remained silent.

After they hit the Belt Parkway, Ti Zoot resumed. "Look, for you to be here in this position, it means I've failed so many ways. I let you run around like nothing would ever go down. I did a horrible disservice to you, Nancy, and the baby."

"Zoot man—"

"Let me finish. I can't run around like it's still the 1980s and babysit the block anymore. You're a man now whether you want to be or not. You have a beautiful wife and an adorable baby girl…everything I would kill for right now. It's eating away at me that you'd jeopardize all of it. For what?"

Ti Zoot checked the gate number for his flight. "And now this? These people murder everyday like it's nothing! I know their moves well." He slipped the ticket back into his pocket. "On top of it all, you pick the worse time to start beef with me having to leave for Haiti. My mother hasn't been well in months. Things can take a turn for the worse any day now, I have to be there."

"I'm sorry, man. I remember your mom well."

"Cancer," he blurted. "But you know Haiti; so much superstition, my aunt swears it's something else."

"Like I said, I want you to stay home the next seven days. Don't even go to the corner store. Nothing! I'll figure this out. I have to."

From where he sat, Ti Zoot didn't couldn't see the tear that coming down the left side of Ernse's face. Everything Ti Zoot said was true, it always was. The love he had for his family was undeniable, but something always forced his worse instincts to surface.

"Zoot, you know what's crazy?" he choked. "I appreciate everything you're saying. I appreciate everything you're doing even more. But out of all of this craziness, what I fear the most is telling Nancy about getting another woman pregnant. I can't believe I took it this far. I love Nancy and Emily so much."

"She's been through so much in her life. I can't tell you how to handle your marriage, but however you break this to her, have some thought and sensitivity. She'll need it."

The stench from the Belt entered the car, forcing Ti Zoot to shut the vents. He had a lot on his mind. His mother, Ernse, and the everyday drama in the neighborhood stressed him like no time before.

"Zoot, I'm going to pull through this."

Ti Zoot shook his head. "You have a lot of faith."

"Well, when I get through this, I'm changing my game, changing my life. I swear. I don't care about anything on these streets, only my family and that's it!"

"Look man, I don't need a solemn oath. Let me think about the situation and come up with a solution."

Ernse knew Ti Zoot was pissed but he had to speak his piece. "You've been that big brother I never had. I've looked up to you ever since I could remember. We hang tight. We wear the same jewelry. We even drive the same fucking cars!"

"Is that my chain you have on?"

"Listen Zoot, please. What I'm trying to say is, thanks for everything you've ever done. Thanks for everything you're doing now. I'm a total fuck-up but you keep grinding it out with me. I respect that and everything you've ever stood for."

"Prove your words have meaning. If you say it, you have to live it."

He let that sink in. Everything Ti Zoot was saying bothered him because it was all true. "You think I'll be able to save my marriage?"

Ti Zoot ignored him, and they were soon on the departure ramp. Ernse handed the suitcase to a porter as Ti Zoot took his coat off and tossed it in the back seat. Despite the cold dawn air, he felt Haiti's sun ready to welcome him.

"All right, Zoot, send your mother my love."

Ti Zoot hugged him, but it was more to get in his ear than anything. "Remember what I said, stay out of trouble and stay off these streets. I'll figure this out."

"You always do." Ernse looked around, avoiding eye contact.

"Focus. Remember what you just said in the car. Focus."

Ernse extended his hand. Ti Zoot shook it firmly and said goodbye. He waited on the ramp's curb and watched Ernse drive away.

April 29, 1996

"No!"

Fiona raced into the bedroom. "What is it? What's wrong?"

Ti Zoot was drenched, his face pale. His heart raced much too fast.

"Another dream?" She planted herself next to him. "No, no. This wasn't a dream. This actually happened."

She placed his head on her chest, caressed it, hoping he could forget whatever it was. "I'm making tea. That should calm you."

"No," he rose from the bed, "I need a walk."

Fiona pulled her hair. "How can you go out?"

NO MOLASSES IN RHUM

He washed his face, dressed, and left the apartment without a word.

When Ti Zoot's feet hit the curb, he didn't really have a destination. Something was bothering him, but he couldn't pinpoint it. He thought about returning home and discussing the images he had just relived in his sleep, but he decided Fiona had no connection to any of it and wouldn't understand.

Instead, he walked to the night and continued a journey to nowhere.

***

April 30, 1996

Emily ran from her bedroom into the living room. She had just set the world record for changing into her pajamas. She wasn't going to miss the beginning of her favorite show.

"What about your teeth?" Nancy wondered. "You still have to do that."

"I know, Mommy. I will."

"Soon Em. It's getting late sweetie."

Nancy picked up the pager, hoping she'd missed a message, but the screen was still blank. Again, she paged Max. He hadn't called except for a moment the night before. Wherever this trip was, he was too busy or didn't care enough to talk. Frustrated, she sat down on the couch and dialed the phone.

"Hello."

"Hi, Jimmy."

"Nancy?"

"Yes, it's me. I haven't heard from you in a while."

"Just a lot of overtime at work." The awkwardness of their last encounter was fresh on his mind.

"I see. Everything else okay?"

"I'm fine. How's Emily?"

"Em is good—a handful of course."

"Of course," he chuckled.

Neither was sure what to say next. "Okay. Good night, Nancy."

"Well...goodnight." She listened to the line go dead then redialed. "Jimmy, don't get all weird on me. I enjoy our friendship. You're a very nice person. I need that in my life."

"I don't plan to change. It's just...I got a little crazy last time."

"Jimmy, come on! That's no excuse for acting strange. We kissed. So what? If I stopped talking to someone every time that happened, I wouldn't have any friends."

"Oh, wow." His voice softened. "I guess I never thought of that. Why'd you have to be so damn perfect?"

"I'm far from," she corrected him.

"You are. Everyone thinks so."

"Maybe perfection is what people choose to see. I'm a very flawed person."

He took a deep breath. "Can I share something?"

"Please, I'm all ears." She nestled into the couch.

"I've felt guilty since the first day I met you. I knew you were a recent widow, but I found myself attracted to you."

"I don't understand. I always thought you had feelings for Marie."

"Marie has never noticed me," he said. "And I can see why. I'm not her speed. You were always so down to earth. I always imagined something could happen between us."

"You kept those feelings well hidden. I had no clue."

Jimmy quieted. "I feel terrible now, but truthfully, it was in the back of my mind.

I saw an opening during your most vulnerable moment, but I shouldn't have taken advantage of that."

"My marriage had its problems and there were times I was lonely. But I don't think I could've been anything but loyal to Ernse. And yes, that loyalty extended well after he passed.

Through our ups and downs, I adored him, and I knew he adored me despite his vices."

"I envy what Ernse had—a family, Emily, you."

"No, Jimmy. It's easy looking on the outside and thinking everything would've been great. Like I said, I'm flawed."

"Still, it would be worth finding out."

"I'm involved with someone, Jimmy. If things were different, who knows? But I value our friendship a lot more than something that can crash at any time. Understand?"

"I do. It was embarrassing more than anything. "

"Wait. What's so wrong with me that you'd be embarrassed to kiss me?"

"Absolutely nothing."

"Oh, okay. Just checking."

"Nancy, thanks. You're a sweetheart."

"Yes, I am...I am," she giggled.

***

"Hold up, E," Pik directed from the backseat of the car. "Let me go in there and grab the Dutch."

Eddie pulled over in front of a bodega and let Pik out. Fredo rode shotgun. The swelling had gone down some and his speech had gotten better, but he couldn't stop spitting. This was the second night they drove around looking for Ti Zoot.

Tonight was turning into another failure, but the truth is Eddie drove around random places he hoped Ti Zoot wouldn't frequent. The idea was to stall until Max returned. He had taken part in beat downs and was comfortable with that level of violence because catching bodies wasn't his thing. The way Fredo and Pik talked, murder was inevitable. He was glad they were mostly concerned about their smoke and Ti Zoot was on the backburner.

"Ay, man, who's that chick with Max?"

"I see her around, but she don't really fuck with the hood," Eddie explained.

"Fuck you mean? She's in the hood!"

"Yeah, but she goes about her business," Eddie replied."She don't fuck with dudes out here."

"She's fucking Max."

"Max ain't from around here, is he?"

"Yeah." Fredo tilted his head back. "That's why I'm not comfortable with that motherfucker. He fucks with my comfort zone."

"Well, he's getting us paper."

Fredo side eyed him unsure if Eddie was really in his camp. He was adamant on involving Eddie, ensuring his loyalty and getting rid of his Ti Zoot problem simultaneously.

Once he returned, Pik didn't waste time moistening and slicing the Dutch after removing the butt.

"You roll that shit too tight!" Fredo shouted as he watched from the rearview mirror.

"Purple Haze," Pik said to himself, sparking the joint. He took a long pull, and the back of the car became a smog fest.

"Pass that shit." Fredo's tone was impatient.

"How you smoking with your mouth jacked up like that?" Pik asked.

"Man, pass that and stop the bullshit! Plus, this shit will make the pain go away."

Eddie got a tinge of déjà vu. A third night with these two would be unbearable.

***

"…and you know I'll need your help for Marie's party, so don't disappear on me," Nancy said.

"Hey," Jimmy laughed. "I'm here, you know that."

"Uh-huh, if I hadn't set you straight tonight, I'd never hear from you again."

"Not true," Jimmy teased. "Maybe for a few days."

"Don't play, punk." She glanced at the pager beside her.

"Okay. I'm behaving."

"Jimmy, have you seen Ti Zoot?"

"No, I haven't seen him much."

"I'm not surprised." She flipped the pager over. "He hasn't been himself for weeks now. I never hear from him. I wonder if that Frenchie girlfriend is taking up all of his time?"

"Fiona? I doubt it. Any time I've been over there, all she does is complain about the lack of attention she's getting. He barely speaks to her—at least when I'm around."

Marie grabbed the pager again. The screen was still blank, so she tossed it deep into the love seat. "Then I don't have any answers when it comes our friend. He's just not the same anymore."

***

A car screeched down the avenue as Ti Zoot waited at a crosswalk. He assumed some kids were stunting or up to something worse. The vehicle stopped then take off in a hurry. Another driver approached the intersection and slowed down to let Ti Zoot cross. When he stood there and failed to cross, the driver honked his horn. Ti Zoot looked up and glanced at the woman driving then stepped into the road to cross. He glanced up at the sky, and a raindrop smacked his forehead, but he was too preoccupied with the past to be concerned.

He recalled the day he stood, beaming with pride, by Ernse and Nancy as they baptized Emily. Afterward, they celebrated at Claudette's backyard. Attendees joked Emily's baptism was Ti Zoot's first time in church. He corrected them by explaining church was all he knew as a boy and further shocked them by schooling them on sacrament.

Once he made it to the other end of the block, another memory came into focus.

This time, he was at Claudette's side on the day she buried her sister, Veronique. He couldn't feel his legs under him, as he helped carry the coffin, his limbs numb from the raw emotional strain.

He was standing in a corner alone in a hall during Veronique's repass when Claudette spotted him. She was inundated with family and friends giving their love and well wishes, but every so often, she looked his way. When she had a free moment, she made her way to him.

"Ti Zoot—"

"You want me to leave?"

"No. In fact, your presence is one of the few I find comforting here. Why would you ask that?"

"You know…Marc's service is tomorrow."

"Yes, I was told."

"I'm considering attending."

"Considering?"

"Yes. I'm hearing talk that doing so is an insult to your sister's memory."

"Ridiculous!" She snapped. "You were friends with both of them. You're friends with his family too. You should attend. I'm happy you stood by our side today, but you should do the same for them tomorrow. What happened between him and my sister can't be explained or judged. A moment of madness can't define who they were or how we move in their aftermath."

She took his hand. "Please attend and say a prayer…for both of their souls."

"Thank you. Thank you Claudette." He pulled her into a hug. "How is Nancy doing?"

"She's going to be okay." Claudette exhaled deeply. "We'll see to that."

"I'm here for anything you need," he stressed. "It's a good thing she's not here today."

"I couldn't allow that. Not after all she's been through. Too much for a twelve-year-old."

Again, he embraced her. She was emotionally spent and nothing could hide it.

The very next day, he attended Marc's funeral. The contrast between the two ceremonies was striking. Hundreds of people came to Veronique's wake and funeral. Even those who had never met her felt compelled to attend after reading about her death in the papers. On the other hand, her abusive husband's sendoff, was attended only by his mother, a couple of siblings, and handful of friends scattered in the funeral parlor.

That bitter feeling of loneliness echoed in Ti Zoot's bones as he continued on in the rain and let his mind wander to another day. This time to a street in Port-Au-Prince where he played marbles with Ti Jean. Both both boys were fresh faced, but Ti Zoot's thin frame made him appear even younger than his years. Their game, however, was cut short when a commotion broke out in the intersection.

A crowd quickly formed, but Ti Zoot maneuvered himself into a good position as folks overhead stepped onto their balconies to get a bird's-eye view. A woman in a flowery dress, accompanied by an officer, forced her way through the horde and ultimately stood between Ti Zoot and Ti Jean. The two boys eyed each other when they noticed the officer's revolver sitting in its holster.

The crowd was now fired up. Peeking through, Ti Zoot saw the fender of a big black 300SEL 6.3.

"It's the President," a young man yelled. "Long live His Excellency."

The woman in the flowery dressed stepped in front of Ti Zoot, blocking his view as the car slowly made its way through the mass. He nudged a little and wedged his bony frame between the officer and the woman. Both looked down and glared at him but said nothing, allowing him to keep his position.

It was hard to believe, but he had a clear view of the young President, whose image adorned hundreds of homes with 'His Excellence' written in big black and white letters on the poster.

Ti Zoot was momentarily distracted by the officer placing a hand on the woman's inner thigh. No one else noticed, as the packed crowd was fixated on the President, allowing the officer to caress her with abandonment.

"That's him. That's him." Ti Jean shouted.

Ti Zoot's focus shifted to a quartet of military officers directing the crowd away from the vehicle as its engine roared to life. He fixated on the sound as the shiny 6.3 started a slow crawl.

A girl started jogging behind the car. "My aunt is gravely sick. Can you help her, Your Excellence?"

Two of the military men turned to face her, and their stares forced her to a halt. The President casually waved goodbye but failed to extend his hand whenever someone reached for it. Ti Zoot was in great position to catch one of these waves, but the woman in the flowery dress suddenly took a step eclipsing his view. He looked up at the woman, who was maybe two heads taller, tugged her skirt aside, and again stuck his head between her and the officer. This time he had a direct view of the President's profile.

The small company moved at a snail's pace and the military officers became agitated as the increasing crowd made it harder to manage the convoy. The President stopped waving and spoke to someone accompanying him in the car. Ti Zoot stared at the size of the man. He wasn't used to seeing people this size. This man was well kept and had the best meals at his beck and call. His face was bright and round. He looked like he never worried a day in his life.

One of the military officers, a Léopard, shouted something as the

6.3 reached a corner, made a left turn, and sped off leaving a trail of dust in the hot sun engulfing the crowd.

"Ti Zoot, Ti Zoot! Did you see him? Did you?"

"Of course, I saw him." He gazed through the cloud of dust and wiped his eyes. "He even waved to me, Ti Jean."

"He waved to you?"

"Yes, he waved and then smiled. His sideburns were magnificent."

Ti Zoot laughed at the recollection barely aware he was at the edge of the crosswalk.

"Are you going to kick it?" An elderly woman asked pointing to the can that had just been blown into Ti Zoot's path. "You're never too old to kick the can, young man."

Lost somewhere between that distant memory in Port-Au-Prince and where he stood in the present, he didn't respond to the elderly woman, but instead looked down at the rain puddle he stepped into.

"You remind of something I saw long ago," she resumed after noticing the scar on his face. "I was a little younger then, but it's the sort of thing you don't forget even with time."

"Was it a stabbing?" he asked after angling his face so she could get a better look at his scar.

"Good day, sir," she moved down the block not wanting to pursue the conversation any further.

Ti Zoot looked on debating whether to return home and get out of his wet shoes. He knew the elderly woman was of course referring to something that took place in 1983.

He had initially migrated from Haiti in spring 1981 to Miami, and found himself in the middle of a drug infested city and culture. A year later, he moved to Brooklyn where family and friends told him he'd find better work than what was available in Little Haiti.

But a major recession in America later that year meant Brooklyn wasn't all that different from Miami when it came to opportunities.

While cocaine satiated Miami, a new form, crack was making New York an unstable environment.

What the elderly woman had witnessed was only a snapshot of that instability which Ti Zoot found himself caught in. One afternoon, a neighborhood dealer fired a round of shots after him on a busy street. Ti Zoot escaped, unscathed that day and refused to discuss why those shots were fired. But he thought about it deeply and concluded he had to confront this hustler, Sweets, or he would eventually be a body on the street.

Days after the shooting, Ti Zoot saw Sweets roll up to a stoplight. He knew Sweets' daily movements on the block, so he waited for him to do his routine circle around the block. Ti Zoot also knew Sweets had a habit of planting his left elbow on the doorsill as he slowly drove down the street.

Hiding between two parked cars, Ti Zoot leapt, grabbed Sweets' left arm and started shanking him with an ice pick under his armpit. Sweets struggled, trying to reach inside his center console, and pull his chrome piece with his free hand, but Ti Zoot was relentless. Desperate, Sweets hit the accelerator but met a busy intersection ramming full throttle into another car.

A trail of blood littered the asphalt, with the final drip falling off the ice pick and landing on Ti Zoot's pea-soup Bally's. Sweets lay headfirst on his 944's steering wheel, as a trio of air fresheners rocked back and forth from the rearview mirror. Ti Zoot calmly slid the ice pick back up his sleeve and casually walked off.

He went into hiding until word got out that Sweets was arrested at King's County on a myriad of unrelated charges. The ordeal was sloppy but effective, giving him the reputation of a loose cannon. From that moment, Ti Zoot garnered respect whatever circles his stone-face frequented. But a lot had changed since that summer 1983 incident. He was now in his late thirties, the neighborhood was gradually changing as the crack epidemic eased its grip.

He looked up and realized he walked all the way to Crown Heights. He side-stepped the can the elderly woman suggested he kicked and did an impromptu U-turn home.

***

"A, yo, E. You drive too fast." Fredo yelled from the passenger seat. "I can't see in this rain."

"It's not raining hard," Eddie said.

"I still can't see outta this shit. Slow the fuck down."

Pik sat patiently in the backseat, only giving a cursory glance to the blocks which they sped through. He was tired and wanted to head back, but he knew if he even suggested that Fredo would blow his top. He'd rather play it cool, hoping they would find Ti Zoot within the next five minutes or return to their spot and drink the night away.

"Where does this motherfucker hang out?" Fredo wondered. "I bet his ass is hiding from us."

"I bet," Eddie repeated with little conviction.

"I thought you said dude was from your block, E?"

"I said he was. I don't know where he stays now. I don't know O.G. like that."

"Whatever," Fredo dismissed. "Something about Duke I just don't like. It's like the motherfucker thinks he's better than the next man or some shit like that."

"He's an O.G. That's how they think," Eddie explained.

"And he ain't no O.G.," Fredo corrected. "That motherfucker is an Old G."

With that Fredo, hit the down button on his window. He did a double take. "Wait...stop!"

Eddie stomped on the brakes and the car skidded through the intersection.

"That's him right there!" Fredo jumped. "He just went down 21st. Back up and turn!"

"I can't tell…"

"A, yo, Pik. Ain't that him walking over there?"

"Bam, that's him!" Pik confirmed. "Back up."

Eddie reversed the car and made a left turn down East 21st.

"Aight. He didn't spot us." Fredo drew closer to his window. "Drive nice and slow. When we pass Kenmore Terrace, we'll corner him there. He won't be able to get away. That's a dead-end."

"Hold on," Eddie cautioned. "I can't tell it's still wet out here."

"Yo, don't pussy-out on me right now. Just handle yours. Me and Pik got this motherfucker."

The two pulled out their weapons and removed the safeties. Fredo's eyes locked on his target while Pik alternated between the .38 in his hand and their pursuit.

"He's walking faster." Fredo leaned closer to the windshield as if that would clear the raindrops the wipers failed to clean. "He spotted us! E, go, go!"

Eddie hit the accelerator, causing the tires to spin on the wet asphalt. When they caught traction, they were already a car length ahead of their subject, who took off running.

"Cut him off at the corner," Pik shouted.

A garbage can, knocked over by the wind, rolled into the street impeding the man's path. He jumped it like a track star, but slipped on the wet street upon landing. Even then he rose and continued his run, but the momentum created an advantage for Fredo and Pik, who sprinted from the car.

The man heard their steps splashing through the water and knew they were tailing him. He made the mistake of looking back, and Fredo fired a shot that missed. Another shot came, but that also failed to hit anything. Then another and the man screamed, but he couldn't hear his own voice. In fact, he no longer heard Fredo and Pik's footsteps or the car that also chased him down. He couldn't hear anything, but he felt water on the side of his face, followed by the feel of hard concrete against his cheek. A searing sensation shot across his back and legs. It was heat like he had never experienced, but the pain would last only seconds.

Fredo and Pik walked up to the man just as Eddie stopped the car and ran out shouting, "That's not him! Fuck!"

"What the fuck are you doing out of the car? Get the fuck back." Fredo screamed as he fired a single shot into the man's temple. He then froze a moment, studying the mess caused by the bullet. In his excitement, he hadn't noticed the blood that splattered his pants and boots.

"Shit!" Eddie screamed. "Shit!"

"E, get back in that fucking car and let's roll," Fredo waved his gun, but Eddie didn't respond.

Fredo raised the gun slightly in front of his friend's face. Eddie backed away and looked around to see if anyone in the neighborhood saw what just went down even though Pap's advice rang in his ears.

"Always keep your head down. You can change a haircut but you can't change your face."

Eddie dropped his head and studied every crack and puddle on the sidewalk until he re-entered the car.

***

As soon as the key turned the lock, Fiona pulled the door open and let Ti Zoot inside.

"Were you waiting by the door?"

"Maybe." She stepped away from him and flopped on the couch.

"The rain forced me to turn back."

"Maybe you'll sleep. The sound of raindrops helps me sleep. I hope it will do the same and keep your dreams at bay."

"No dreams tonight." He loosened his shirt. "I did enough of that during my walk."

CHAPTER 7

May 4, 1996

"Aren't you happy to see me?"

Nancy didn't answer. She looked in every direction except for Max's. They were exiting Prospect Park after briefly attending a local music performance.

Max had arrived back in town the night before. After he'd called Nancy, she informed him of the performance at the park. They'd agreed to attend, but she'd kept to herself from the moment he picked her up—except to point out he'd only called her for a total of five minutes when he was away.

"Did you have fun on your vacation?"

"I wasn't on vacation." He shook his head. "Told you it was business."

"Hmm. Vacation, business, whichever."

He grabbed her arm and hooked it under his as they walked. "Want to check out this place down on Dean Street for dinner?"

"Not today. I want to spend the rest of the day with Emily after I pick her up from that birthday party." She loosened her arm from his clutches.

"I know I'm in the doghouse." He kissed her cheek. "I have some making up to do."

"No need. After all, you've got nothing to put you in the doghouse. You're not guilty of anything, right?"

"Right. I have no reason to be guilty except I should've tried calling you more often even though I didn't have many chances."

She rolled her eyes and sighed.

"Come on, Nancy—" From the corner of his eye, he caught Steve, Fredo and Pik in the middle of a group of neighborhood flunkies. He had the good sense to veer left to another exit trail in the park, but it was too late. The clique had already spotted him.

"MAX!" Fredo's voice echoed through the park.

"Look at this." Pik beamed with surprise.

Max grabbed Nancy's hand. This time she did not fight it.

"Maxwell," Fredo hugged him. "We got briefed by your man here." He motioned to Steve.

"What happened to you?" Max studied Fredo and Pik's broken faces.

"Long story with O.G. my dude." Fredo said as he focused on Nancy. "Pardon my manners. I'm Fredo."

"Hello." Nancy extended her hand.

"Max, are you hiding this lovely? I didn't think you were smooth like that."

He ignored Fredo. "Where you guys headed?"

"There's a cypher in the park," Pik answered. "You rolling through?"

"I'm leaving. We just saw a group perform."

Fredo's eyes were all over Nancy. "Miss, I have to say you do wonders for Max's image."

"All right. Later." Max nudged Nancy to the exit.

"What's the rush?" She asked enjoying the attention and his nervousness.

"Yeah, what's the rush?" Pik added. "She got a sister?"

"Parnell?"

Pik froze, hung his head down. He thought her face was familiar, but he couldn't place where they crossed paths.

"Parnell?" Steve was puzzled. "That's his name?"

"Fuck. I know," Fredo answered. "But Perry is funny as shit."

"Parnell," Nancy corrected him.

"You know him?" Max's eyebrows revealed his surprise.

"Of course, I know him," Nancy smiled. "His big sister Dion and I were best friends in grade school. It's been a long time, and he's even taller than me now."

"That's you ,Nan?"

"Yeah." She embraced him. "He was the cutest little boy in grade school."

"I bet Parnell was adorable," Fredo cracked.

"How do you all know Max?" Nancy wondered.

Max gently tugged her hand, but she didn't budge.

"He and an old buddy introed us." Steve replied. "We just started playing ball when he moved up north. I'm Steve."

"Oh, this is Steve," she said. All of a sudden Max's discomfort made sense. "The whole time I thought you were the only friend Max had here. You're the only person he ever mentions."

"Max, you never mention me?" Fredo pretended he was hurt.

"We're cool, I guess." Steve explained. "You know Max, he doesn't say much."

"True, true. Max doesn't say much," Fredo said.

"Parnell, how's your sister? I ran into her just before I had my daughter. I can't believe it's been so long."

"She's good. She moved to North Carolina with some dude."

"Oh wow, good for her," Nancy said. "But what happened to your face Parnell? Are you still getting into trouble?"

"All right, later, y'all." Max was not happy about the chance meeting and where the conversation was heading.

"Well, glad to see you're all grown up Parnell. Nice meeting you all." She waved and smiled to the group.

"Nice to meet you," Fredo stressed. "For real though, Max is a lucky man."

They barely walked a foot when Nancy stopped. "Parnell, why don't you and your friends come to a party I'm having for my cousin at the end of this month?"

Max was ticked, but he wouldn't allow anyone to see him ruffled, so he kept quiet.

"I'd love to see Max and his friends in a party environment," she added.

"Say word?" Fredo's excitement was apparent. "I'm definitely in."

Nancy made all kinds of promises of a good time at the party before they parted in the wake of the young men's banter.

She turned to Max. "I can't wait for you to meet my family and friends".

"Why'd you do that?"

"They're your friends." She enjoyed her newfound advantage. "I'm sure things will be okay."

"I'm sure they will. You can tell me all about it. I'm not coming."

She grabbed his elbow before he could walk off. "What? Stop playing, Max!"

"I'm not playing. I don't like crowds. This thing sounds like a crowded affair."

"Max, come on. Just because I invited your friends? You really don't want me to know anything about you."

"They're not my friends."

"Oh, yeah. Well what are they then?"

"Acquaintances."

"Well, you always talk about Steve. He has to be a friend," she reasoned.

"Nancy, that's not the point. I'm very selective about who I hang out with—especially who I introduce you to."

"What are you ashamed of? Maybe you didn't want your friends to meet me?"

"Come off that. Besides, if this party is so important to you, why would you invite them?"

"I think it's perfect. You won't feel alone at the party when I'm with my guests. Plus, I knew Parnell when he was knee high, so I'm extending my friendship with him. This is not about you."

"I think I just got played," Max grieved.

***

"This dude is like two different people." Pik watched Max and Nancy in the distance.

"He sure put an act on in front of shorty, didn't he?" Fredo turned to Steve. "Is that how your man plays it out here?"

"How should he act?" Steve asked. "Straight thug?"

"You right," Fredo nodded. "I mean if I had a shorty like that, I'd be a sucka for love too. You're a good soldier, Steve. You see both sides even when shit don't look right."

Fredo turned to Pik, "You should've introduced me to shorty a long time ago."

"I haven't seen her in years. I didn't even know E-Flow meant her." Pik scratched is head. "Well, E-Flow was definitely right. Nancy was always a bad shorty."

"Yeah," Fredo conceded. "Max handles it all so well."

"Everything. Business, the women…he's definitely someone to examine."

"What are the chances we run into her and Max like this?" Pik gave Fredo a sharp-eyed look.

***

"This is the new girl?"

"Not new," Ti Zoot answered. He didn't smile often, but watching Claudette interrogate Fiona—forced a grin.

"How old is she?"

"Ask her," Ti Zoot said.

"How old are you? Twenty?"

"I am twenty-nine-years old." Fiona blushed, unsure if the question was sarcasm on Claudette's part.

"Oh, an accent." Claudette looked Fiona up and down.

"Je suis, Français."

Ti Zoot eased over to the stove and raised the lids to all four pots only to find each shiny but all empty.

"I didn't cook." Claudette broke from her conversation with Fiona. "There's no one to cook for anymore."

"You can cook for me every night if you're looking for someone."

"Tiup." She sat down and motioned for Fiona to do the same. "You're are not my husband. I'm too old for you with your twenty-year-old girl. She cooks for you, and a lot more than meals I'm sure."

Ti Zoot perched himself on the counter. "She doesn't cook. It's takeout every night."

"He dated this Haitian girl," Claudette turned to Fiona, "great cook, nice personality. She had beautiful, strong calves. What did he do? He drove her off, and she rushed into a bad marriage."

Fiona looked back at him. Finally, someone was willing explain this enigma.

"I didn't even know he had friends other than Jimmy," Fiona admitted. "He never told me about you just that we were stopping by a dear old friend's house."

"I told you. This is Marie's mother. Nancy's aunt," he replied.

Claudette side-eyed him. "Are you going to do the same thing to this one? Or does she have a chance?"

He wasn't having it and tinkered with the menu on his pager instead.

"Men never mature," Claudette opined. "I married my husband at only twenty-two and gave him my best years. He didn't mature one bit during that time. He chased everything in a skirt and those women were just as immoral, always ready to lay down with him."

"One day, I gave him a choice: me or the women. Can you believe that pig left? Well, I got him back. I never gave him a divorce. He's stuck for the rest of his life. I had a good part in making that man who he is. Even if he got his divorce, no woman in their right mind would marry him."

"He hasn't stepped foot in this house in seven years," Ti Zoot jabbed.

"You see," Claudette pointed, "they never mature."

"If Wesner thinks the milk is free, he will have to find another cow," Fiona said.

"I like her." Claudette turned to Ti Zoot. "You need a someone who isn't docile and speaks her mind!"

"Claudette, please with this talk, I stopped here hoping you made some pain-patate."

"I don't do that anymore. Who will eat it? It's an empty house."

"Pain-patate on Sundays was an institution," he explained to Fiona. "Some things should go on forever."

"No," Claudette countered. "Everything is just a moment in time. Sometimes it lasts weeks, months, maybe even years. But once it's gone, that's it. There's no return."

Ti Zoot nudged Fiona. Claudette only had philosophy or frustration to share. He could tolerate it with a meal, but he was hungry and all too familiar with her grievances.

He planted a kiss on Claudette's forehead and moved toward the door. "So, there's a party here in two weeks?"

"Tiup. So I hear. That's Nancy's business. As long as no one asks me for anything, I don't care."

"It's Marie's birthday."

"Again, that's Nancy's business. I celebrated enough birthdays. they can take the baton."

"I'll be here," he said.

Claudette rose to lock the door as they stepped onto the stoop. She gave Fiona a final once over. "I hope you don't waste this one's time. She has decent calves too."

"I hope you're handling things at this party," Ti Zoot called from the door to his car. "The girls can't work a kitchen like you."

"Flattery." Claudette shut her door.

Ti Zoot backed the car out of the driveway and shook his head. "She's too young to behave this old."

***

"All Haitian guys want to do is screw me," Marie proclaimed. "I think I'm through with them for a while. Maybe forever."

"Um, well, that's not always a bad thing." Nancy laughed and looked at Max, who turned away to avoid the conversation.

Nancy and Max had stopped by Marie's place after the park as a way to kill time before they picked up Emily from the birthday party. Marie tidied up as she chatted with them. She had made decent progress unboxing her household items since Nancy last visited.

"I'm serious," Marie continued. "Either they're too Frenchie or they're trying too hard to get in my pants."

"She's so difficult." Nancy turned to Max.

"I'm not. You see all the losers out there?"

"Okay," Nancy agreed. "The selection is slim, but there were some good ones you probably overlooked."

"I don't have time." She walked over to the ringing telephone.

"Hello? Wait. How did you get this number?"

She checked the caller ID, but the screen was blank.

"Don't use this number again, please." She slammed the phone down. "I can't believe this."

"Who was that?"

"Rudy!"

"Rudy? Why is he calling you?"

"Is that the guy we met a couple of weeks ago?" Max asked.

"That's the one," she shouted.

"Touchy subject." Nancy whispered in his ear.

"We're discussing losers, and he calls...his timing was always impeccable. Now how did he get my home number?"

"Don't look at me," Nancy said.

"Has he been to my mother's place recently?"

"Oh, come on, couz. You know my aunt wouldn't do that, especially the way Rudy broke up with you."

Marie looked at her as if she had grown a third eye. That last statement came out wrong. "Of course, she would do that. That bitch is crazy, and you know it."

"That's my aunt," Nancy said. "She never acts crazy with me."

"Sure. Just don't bring back any wet umbrellas. Other than that, she's completely sane."

Caught off-guard, Nancy found it hard to contain her laughter, prompting Marie to giggle.

Max was amused. "What's so funny about a wet umbrella?"

"Okay. You got me on that incident, but I love my Auntie," Nancy said, catching her breath.

"What's the joke?" Max pushed.

"Nothing." Marie played it off.

"That woman can play sweet one minute and change her demeanor in a split second. I used to always tell Nance that, but she swore that it was just with me and her aunt was an angel. One day, Nancy was stepping out, and it started to rain hard. Nancy goes to Claudette for an umbrella. Claudette was all too happy to hand her favorite niece an umbrella. So when Nancy finally comes back and hands Claudette the umbrella, she is livid. What did you do to my umbrella? I lend you my umbrella you come back with it like this?

"Nance is like, what do you mean Auntie?"

"Claudette goes into a diatribe about how she's had that umbrella for six years and kept it nice and tidy, but Nancy borrows this umbrella and, in just one day, brings it back misshapen and…wet."

"It was a what-the-fuck moment, Nance needed to see who her aunt really was. Crazy bitch and all."

"One of the few times she went crazy on me," Nancy stressed. "And it was one of those colorful rainbow umbrellas."

Max looked at them, waiting for a punchline. "I'm not sure I understand this," he said. "The umbrella got wet…in a rainstorm?"

"Exactly," Marie went on. "I'm looking on the side like, 'what the fuck?' Nancy has the same look but wouldn't dare say it. Claudette just keeps rambling on about the umbrella."

"There had to be more to it than that," Max said.

"I'm afraid not," Marie explained. "That's Claudette. Her stuff can be completely random. And to be honest, I was happy she went off on Nance like that. Until that point, all my life, I was unsure;. I always assumed Claudette was sane and it was me, that my elevator didn't reach the top floor but that incident confirmed Claudette was the nutty one."

"Well, I wouldn't say that. She's stressed at times," Nancy pleaded. "It wasn't always easy for her holding everything down alone. And yet, she still managed to do right by us."

"See how good natured my cousin is, Max? She can find good in the devil."

"Just saying," Nancy continued. "Other than a handful of incidents,

I don't have issues with my Auntie. I just keep quiet and everything blows over."

Marie went back into the kitchen and placed her cleaning items in a cabinet but quickly returned to her guests. "And by the way, Rudy didn't break up anything. I broke it off!"

"I didn't mean it like that." Nancy regretted her slip-up.

"Damn. Old boy must have wronged you bad," Max said.

"Uh, yeah. How about getting a good friend pregnant?"

Nancy pinched his arm, but it was too late. The cat was already out of the bag.

"And that bitch started bad-mouthing me! I don't want to go there."

"Yes, couz. No need to," Nancy responded. "His life is screwed up now. I told you the stories about him out there. His new woman has him on his ass financially."

That brought a smile to Marie's face and her eyes danced. "Max, you want to have a beer with me?"

He welcomed the offer, so Marie keyed open a couple of Coronas and handed him one. He slid the bottle in Nancy's direction for a sip, but she brushed it aside.

"No wine left." Marie kicked her feet up on the coffee table. "It's 1996, and I don't need headaches. All a man can do for me now is eat me good and keep it moving."

"That's a hell of a visual," Max laughed.

"Shut up," Nancy elbowed him. "This is serious. She's hurt."

Marie took a swig. "You know, couz, it gets easier every time I break up with a man. I figure next time this happens, I'll just laugh it off. If a man's feelings for me aren't enough to keep him honest, I really don't need relationships. Sorry if I'm offending you Max, but that's just how I see men."

"No offense," Max replied. "In fact, I get what you're saying."

"Why can't men control themselves?" Marie took a swig of her beer.

"The ladies should start giving the guys a taste of their own medicine."

"I think they already have."

"Please, Max," Nancy interjected. "Women aren't doing a fraction of what guys do. That's why it makes it so hard to open up to a guy. I don't need anyone playing with my heart."

"I think it's a *Boomerang* night." Marie grabbed a tape from the TV stand.

"But I'm picking up Emily in an hour."

"That's just enough time for us to watch the best parts and hear, 'Love should have brought your ass home last night.'"

"*Boomerang*?" Max wondered.

"Yeah, the movie." Nancy looked at him funny. "You never saw it?"

"Never."

"What rock does this guy live under, Nance?" Marie hit play on the VCR.

"I'm wondering the same thing, couz."

"Hey, I told you I was a homebody," Max laughed.

Marie side-eyed him. "I bet."

CHAPTER 8

May 25, 1996

It was early morning. Fiona had coffee brewing. Ti Zoot always complained the coffee was weak, but he always drank the last drop, so she figured he was just yammering.

She thought for a moment how she ended up here, mostly wrapped in his world or more accurately the little he shared with her. On occasion he would ask about her history and how she grew up. She appreciated the fact he genuinely cared about her past.

From Rennes, she sought the big city and found herself in Paris at nineteen. A few years in, she thought Paris was too pretentious. Escape came in the name of Robert, an older gentleman she encountered on a trip to Madrid. He fell for her and invited her to visit New York and stay with him. Once there, she partied from the West Village all the way up to Washington Heights on a nightly basis.

One night at the Latin Lounge, she noticed one of the patrons on the dance floor. He sported a tan suit and one unwavering expression of annoyance. He never smiled or let on he was having a good time. Yet, the way he moved and danced told another story. She spent a good part of the night watching him, finally walking up to him, and asking him to dance. They did so until the place closed.

Neither said a word the whole night but left the lounge together with a group that took their gathering to an all-night diner on Seventh Avenue. There, they spoke their first words since she had asked him for a dance. The casual breakfast conversation led to a Sunday sunrise in Manhattan. She immediately decided she wouldn't return to Robert and New York was going to be her permanent home, she mused.

"Coffee is ready," she called out, leaving her memories behind.

"Merçi," Ti Zoot entered the kitchen with a loose towel around his waist, fresh from a shower. He pecked her cheek and reached for his coffee.

"You slept well last night." She tipped some sugar into his mug.

"Did I?"

"You snored the entire night."

"I heard myself," he ribbed.

She snatched the towel from his waist and wiped the areas still wet on his body.

"What time is that party tonight?" He sipped his drink.

"I don't know. She's your friend." She fastened the towel tightly around his waist and grabbed hold of his penis so that he couldn't walk away. "Does it have a problem? Maybe a therapist will help?"

He wasn't in the mood to entertain her.

"Shameful. You leave me for weeks at a time."

"Are you finished? Can I get dressed?"

His response was deflating. She squeezed him until it was too much for him to bear.

He slapped her hand causing her to bump into the counter and topple the coffeemaker.

"You touched a woman?" she screamed. "Abuse!"

He stared at the coffee leaking from the counter like a waterfall. "You made a mess, clean it up!" He stomped out.

"Coward!" She chased him down the hallway. When she caught him, she dug her nails in his back. He responded by pinning her against the wall while she struggled against him. "You're not a man. Fraud! No one knows the truth." She bit his forearm. "Is that the only way you can touch me?"

"Wench!" He shoved her away.

"I'll tell everyone you're not a man. You're a gelding." Her accent grew thick with anger.

"Pack your things! You can go!"

"I'm not going anywhere!" she yelled. "You need me!"

"Get out!"

"No." She grabbed him, hoping to deescalate things.

Neither realized how excited he'd gotten during the ruckus. The towel had fallen to the floor, and she found him as alive as she could ever recall. The room was quiet, save for heavy breathing, mostly hers.

She planted kisses on his pectorals, along his collar bone, and slowly rose to kiss his lips. Suddenly, the room felt warm. She let her robe fall to the floor, and he pulled her down along with it. He gently brushed her mane aside, and their eyes locked.

"Dieu," she whispered gripping his shoulders. There was the man she had sat with and watched the sunrise over Manhattan early one Sunday morning. The irritated, sleep deprived zombie was gone, at least for this moment.

***

"But Auntie, it's 7:00 a.m." Nancy was still groggy from her slumber. Emily was next to her deep in sleep.

"Aren't you having your party tonight?"

"Yes, of course."

"Well, this party is you and Marie's idea, not mine. Except for some beer Jimmy dropped off earlier this week, I don't see anything. When are you coming to set up? Where's the food? No one came to clean the yard."

Once Claudette started a diatribe, you just had to let her finish. Nancy dropped her head on the pillow. She already had a miserable night. Emily had crawled in her bed then tossed and kicked her the whole time.

"Don't expect me to do everything for you two. This is not my party."

Nancy rolled her eyes. "Auntie, I'll be over soon. Some of my girlfriends and Jimmy are helping me."

"Jimmy?" Claudette came to a halt. "You've been spending a lot of time together. Are you two—"

"No, Auntie. It's not like that, Jimmy is a very nice guy. In fact, I've been seeing someone. I'll introduce you to him later tonight."

"I don't need to meet anyone. When you have problems with your men, no one better call me. I don't want to be involved."

"Oh, Auntie," Nancy sighed. She knew Claudette was bluffing. If she didn't introduce Max to her aunt, she wouldn't hear the end of it. "Let me get ready, we'll be over there soon."

She wanted to sleep another hour, but if she did that, Claudette would ring her phone off the hook. So, she grabbed her pager and sent Jimmy a message. A minute later, he called.

"I can't even get five minutes of sleep. Hi, Jimmy. Why'd you have to call me right away?"

"You paged me." He sounded confused.

"I know, I know. Rough night. I hardly slept, and my aunt calls me first thing this morning yelling all kinds of nonsense."

"Well, we should get an early start. Pick you up at eight?"

"Eight thirty. No, eight forty-five."

"Okay, bye."

She didn't put the phone down on the cradle a full second when it rang again. "What is it, Jimmy?"

"Jimmy? It's Marie."

"Hi, couz. Not you too with the early morning calls."

"Huh? I thought you just paged me from Claudette's number," Marie explained. "When I called, she said you weren't there and everything is in disarray."

"I didn't page you, Claudette did."

"Apparently. I didn't even know Claudette knew how to page," Marie laughed. "So why didn't she tell me she was the one who paged me?"

"I think she wants us over there bright and early to fix the place up."

"Us? Nuh-uh. You're putting this party together. It's in my honor, so I can't help."

"Fine." Nancy frowned. "Jimmy, Myrtha, and Frances are giving me a hand."

"See, you're good. I'm just going to show up in my fabulous dress to cut my cake."

"Just be on time," Nancy warned.

***

"Why do I have to insult you to get affection?" Fiona wrapped her herself around Ti Zoot.

"I don't know," he exhaled. "That's the nature of our relationship and I don't know why."

"Do you love me?"

"No."

"Have you ever loved before?"

"No…yes." His gaze drifted toward the wall.

"You have me around for no reason at all. I'm here, but not a part of your life. No different than the laces on your shoes or a button on your shirt. Is there someone else you love?"

When he failed to answer, she sat on his chest forcing him to look at her. "You know there are many men who would want me, and I'm not even sure I'm in love with you. But the fact that you don't adore me is sickening."

He caressed her arm. "And you love me. Even if I'm disgusting." He pulled her closer.

***

"How old is she now anyway?"

"Auntie, she's twenty-seven today," Nancy groaned. "How can you forget?"

Nancy and Jimmy were lugging party goods onto Claudette's back porch in between her questions, rants, and concerns. She did her best to answer and keep her aunt calm, but the effort was working on her nerves.

"I'm barely lucid these days. What do I know?"

"Auntie, you're only fifty and look incredible. I'm not buying that talk."

"Once you sacrifice your life for a child, you lose everything. Your beauty, your mind—"

"You should stop talking like you have one leg in the grave. You're much too young and vibrant."

"Anyway, why'd you get all this stuff? How big is this party?"

Nancy let out a sigh of frustration. "We talked about this already."

"Well, how are you able to afford this?"

"Some friends contributed," Nancy answered.

"Jimmy, are you the one buying all of this stuff?"

"Auntie!"

"No ma'am." Jimmy struggled with a crate. "I bought just a few drinks. That was all."

"Jimmy, you're a young man. I'm sure you have responsibilities, a family back home. I don't know what business you have going on with Nancy and Marie, but you can't be spending your little money on them."

NO MOLASSES IN RHUM

"Auntie, please!"

Claudette left the two in the yard and went back into her kitchen. Nancy turned to Jimmy. "Does she just have to know everything?"

"It's okay," Jimmy laughed. "My mother behaves the same way."

"Sorry, I love my aunt, but she can be a major pain."

***

It was almost noon and Marie needed to get going. She needed to get a manicure, pedicure, and handle a bunch of last-minute details before the party.

She was unsure this party was a good idea, but she was feeling down and warmed up to it the more her friends talked about it. And of course, Nancy was relentless about having one, so she gave in.

The Weather Channel was on, but she stepped to the window anyway, parting the curtains, looking for signs from the clouds. She didn't recall many rainy days on past birthdays and today looked like another safe bet.

She walked to the closet, pulled out a dress, and set it against her body. She imagined how fabulous she was going to look once her hair and nails were done. It was a one-strap citrus yellow affair that fell just above the knee with mid-thigh slit. Imagining how hot she'd look suddenly made the party seem like a great idea.

The sound of the telephone disrupted her good mood, and she picked up the line despite the number on the caller ID.

"Why are you—"

"Happy birthday." Rudy rushed the words out.

She wasn't expecting that. But if there was one thing, he was good at, it was celebrating her birthday. He had a knack for making the occasion big by inviting her friends to dinners or clubs.

"Thanks." She wasn't sure what to say next.

"I just wanted to wish you a Happy Birthday and all of God's Blessings."

"Thank you, Rudy." She mulled over his words, unsure of his motives. "That's very nice. But when I said no calls, I meant it. That includes birthdays, especially birthdays."

"No biggie. I just remembered the date and wanted to send my regards."

She forgot how good he could be. He'd actually coordinated a surprise party for her last year. Everything was flawless. There was also a birthday trip to the Bahamas on year and, at one point, they'd talked about a trip to Rome. She figured that would've been their honeymoon destination the way things were progressing. The problem was when he was bad, the act was usually something unforgivable like his infidelity.

"Why do you keep doing this? Every time I erase you from my thoughts, somehow you worm your way back in. I hope you're not trying to attend my party tonight by calling now."

"Marie, I don't know about any party. Like I said, I'm just wishing you happy birthday."

Was he sincere? She was about to thank him and hang up when the dress caught the corner of her eye. "You know, why don't you come to the party? I mean no hard feelings, right?"

"Are you for real?"

"Yes, come on through tonight. Claudette's backyard." She imagined herself in the dress and smiled. "It's a celebration after all. The past is the past."

"I don't know. I'd be ashamed to show my face," he was frank.

"Well, that's on you, but I'm cool with you being there if you change your mind."

"Thanks," he said feeling better than he did at the start of the conversation. "But a birthday wish is all I can manage these days."

"Oh well, have a good day," she shut the phone placed the dress in the closet.

Every time she comes close to forgetting...he does it again, she thought.

***

Ti Zoot and Fiona had retreated to their bed and remained there all morning. In between naps, they spoke about many things. In fact, this was the most she'd ever got out of him. His responses were always short as if words cost him money and air. There were hours and sometimes days when he just wouldn't talk except for a word here and there.

She had gotten used to it. But for whatever reason, having seen him interact with Claudette painted a different picture from what she saw when he interacted with Jimmy, Nancy, or Marie. Even with the little time they'd spent at Claudette, she started to accept that maybe his treatment of her wasn't personal. Perhaps, life had forced him that way.

"What was your childhood like?"

"It's been so long. I don't remember any childhood."

"Mon Dieu, you are so difficult."

A minute passed, and she looked up to find his eyes shut. He was napping again. She rubbed his chest, hoping to wake him. Instead, he tried to turn over, but she planted herself on him so he couldn't quite make the turn.

"You're not sleeping. No games."

He sighed and halfheartedly nudged her. She dug her nails into his chest, and he found himself aroused again.

"You're sick." She panted, wrapping her arms around him.

"You met me this way." He pulled her closer, smothering her with kisses.

"...frustrating...this is the only way.... you get...off!"

Drenched in sweat, the room became a sauna. She was happy, the moment was burying some of her angst. She clawed harder and when she was too tired to even do that, she just held his shoulders.

***

"A, yo. It's Max." Pik looked through the peephole.

"And?" Fredo sat in a chair in the kitchen as a young woman braided his hair. "Open up!"

Pik jiggled the lock, unchained the door. "Max, what up?"

Max hardly acknowledged him but entered. He looked in the kitchen and saw Fredo and a young woman. He nodded her way as if tipping an imaginary hat.

Fredo was all smiles. "Big Max, what you got for me, homie?"

"Not a lot." Max stood in the hallway that bridged the kitchen and living room.

"Max, you gotta get me that paper, homie. You see what I'm lookin' at." He raised a brochure and spread its pages revealing a car. "Gold on gold, Max. GS, this is it right here. You gotta get me that paper, big homie."

"That's that wheat joint. It'll match my Timbs."

Max looked at the car on the page. "Work on that." He turned in the direction of the living room. "Steve here?"

"Yeah, he's back there." Fredo waved the brochure hoping to get a reaction. "Right there, Max. GS. Gold on gold."

Before Fredo finished the thought, Max bolted to the back end of the railroad apartment.

Pik grabbed the brochure from Fredo, "I don't think Max is crazy about this GS. Maybe you should be lookin' at a five?"

Fredo slapped the brochure out of his hand. "I'm getting tired of this motherfucker," he whispered.

Pik looked at the young lady and they shared a laugh. "Max is a funny dude yo."

"This shit ain't right. This shit ain't right at all," Fredo complained.

"So, what," the young woman said. "Why do you have to agree on a car anyway? I like that gold one."

"It's not the car!" Fredo explained. "This whole setup is wrong. I should be making major decisions."

"You all need a woman to help run this. Braiding hair ain't making me any money, put me down." The young woman smiled.

Meanwhile, Max walked to the room on the far end of the apartment. It was hard to make Steve out from the thick haze in the room. Steve and another guy sat on chairs playing *Madden* as five people sat on a king-sized bed adding their play-by-play.

Too many people in this tiny space, he thought. The place was always a mess. He wondered how a female could hang out in this sty, but the females were often every bit as grimy.

"Oh." Steve paused the game when he realized Max had enter the room. "What's good?"

"Not much," Max studied the faces on the bed. "Just wanted to check something with you."

"Got you." Steve stood and the two returned to the kitchen.

"I'm sorry," Max said to the young woman still braiding Fredo's hair, "I don't believe we were introduced."

"I'm Celine. Fredo never talk about me?"

"Hi. I'm Max."

"I heard so much about you and not just from Fredo," she offered a warm smile.

"Celine, please excuse us. I just want a word with Fredo and Pik outside."

Celine dug the comb into Fredo's mane and the four stepped out into the building hallway where a couple of teens sat on the stairway.

"Fuck outta here," Fredo screamed. "I told y'all don't hang out in front of my crib."

The kids quietly raced down the stairs.

"Sorry, Max." Fredo motioned for Pik to check the stairwell to see if anyone was within an earshot.

"Heads up, I have a local deal coming our way. Something in

Newark," Max pulled out a tiny paper and showed it to the three.

"Aight, that's good shit, but Newark though? That's a hotbed," Pik said.

"That's why we do everything low-key, under the radar," Steve explained.

"Keep your shit on point and everything will go right," Max added. "I can't stress that enough."

"Hey, Max, no worries. We're with this program one hundred." Fredo tugged on a finished braid.

"Glad to hear," Max replied. "No bullshit at that party tonight. And just you, Steve, and Pik. None of those knuckleheads in that bedroom. Got that?"

There was a momentary pause as Fredo looked over to Pik and Steve. "Of course, Max. We wouldn't do shit like that. Respect."

"Cool." Max started down the steps. "We'll talk about the Jersey details later. Also, I have something I'm going to hook you two with later."

Max was about halfway down the flight of stairs when Pik called his name.

"Yeah?"

"That shorty, Nancy, good move there," Pik said.

"And? What the fuck does that have to do with anything?"

Fredo busted out laughing at Pik's expense. "Pik, you stay corny!"

"That's all?" Max asked.

Pik's face was red from the awkward exchange. "Yeah Max, that's all."

"Go ahead man," Fredo called to Steve who had followed Max downstairs. "Go do your boss's errands."

Steve looked at him cross but continued downstairs.

"You stupid," Fredo turned to Pik. "Get off Max's jock man."

"Ain't no one on his jock," Pik complained. "Dude think his shit smells like roses."

"I told you. Max ain't shit!" Fredo sat back in his chair. "Celine come and finish my shit! I got some thoughts in my head I need to process."

CHAPTER 9

May 25, 1996

The streetlights had just come on and some kids were playing touch football on the street. A car drove down the block and the driver had to honk his horn several times before players, excited by the game, cleared his path. They hurled some words in the driver's direction to protest the interruption. Just as the game resumed, Claudette dashed from her front door heading to Margot across the street. She just missed getting hit by a lateral pass but didn't even noticed the play in motion.

"Margot, open up." She knocked then rang the bell. "Margot, I need cinnamon sticks quick!"

"Oh." Margot opened the door in her undergarments.

She was just a couple of years younger than Claudette and one of the few people living on the block when Claudette's family moved in the fall of 1975. At the time, Margot was a new bride who just had a big wedding over the summer. She and her husband Lelio were living in her current home with her parents back then. Margot and her family welcomed Claudette, her husband Jerome, and six-year-old Marie with open arms as they were the only other Haitians on the block in the mid-1970s.

Both couples became fast friends. When she could get away from Marc, sometimes Veronique would join them. Jerome, Claudette,

Margot, and Lelio soon traveled in the same circles. Claudette, Veronique, and Margot shopped big at A&S, Macy's, and Gimbels.

Jerome and Lelio often escorted the three women to a host of Haitian night clubs en vogue in that era. The staff at Chateau Royale knew the clique by name. They danced to Skah Shah, Tabou, and any band traveling the circuit from Port-Au-Prince to Miami to New York City. On multiple occasions, they took their friendship on the road for weekend trips to big events in Montreal.

But both marriages ended up having the same shelf-life as disco. Claudette noticed little changes first, things like Jerome routinely pulling out a stick of Doublemint gum and popping it in his mouth just before he entered their home. He was out three or four nights a week, coming and going like clockwork. On more than one occasion, she swore his tweed jacket reeked of strong perfume.

One day, in early December, a friend phoned and told her Jerome was frequenting a club in Queens every Thursday evening after 8:00 p.m. with a hot bitch from Petion-Ville. A lump lodged in her throat. Jerome had lots of explanations why he came home late, but a club in Queens was never mentioned.

"You are a gossiping, lying bitch!" Claudette screamed into the phone, but the reveal struck a chord and connected some dots.

Despite her hurt, she never let Jerome know about the conversation or that she was onto any club in Queens. She searched for clues and one day, found a stash of prophylactics in his sport coat.

She had enough evidence to confront him, but she wanted to visit the club. For her peace of mind, she had to see for herself. She wasn't about to go alone, so she invited Margot but never clued her in on any of her motives and intentions.

"I've never been to this club." Margot looked around. "Why are we here?"

"Enough with the questions," Claudette replied. "We need to visit different places, I'm tired of the same clubs, same people, and the same bands."

Located off Springfield and Linden, the club was far different from the ritzy places they frequented on weekends. Still, Margot went along and took in the cheap cigarette smoke in stride.

"This place is worlds apart from Chateau Royale. And why did we have to come here so early?" Margot wondered aloud as they walked to the back of the venue and sat in a booth.

"I have work and you have school in the morning," Claudette explained.

"That never forced us into a club this early in the past. Maybe it's a sign we're getting old."

"Calm down, we won't be here long." Claudette looked around and hoped none of the men in the small venue came in their direction. She wasn't up to dealing with pick-up lines.

She looked at her watch and wondered if this was a wild goose-chase. It was almost eight thirty with no sign of Jerome.

"Maybe we should order drinks." Claudette flagged a server. "Two wines,"

"Red or white?" the waiter asked.

"Two Manischewitz," Margot replied.

"I'll see if we have that." The waiter smirked and strolledback to the bar .

"Next time you can come here by yourself," Margot said.

"There won't be a next time."

"Can you believe it's almost 1980?" Margot studied the poster on the wall promoting an upcoming New Year's party at the club.

"I can." Claudette wasn't really paying attention. "This place is a turnoff."

"Here you are." The waiter set the drinks down. "Two Manischewitz."

"Who would welcome the 1980s in this dump?" Margot was still fixated on the poster.

Suddenly, Jerome walked in the club. Claudette had a hard time believing it even as he stood there under a bright light in the otherwise dim club. She'd imagined the confrontation before, but it never played out this way in her mind. The ambience of this wretched place was throwing her off.

"Tuck in." She pulled Margot into the booth and glanced in Jerome's direction. "Don't say a word."

"Oh, my God!" Margot explained as she caught a glimpse of her friend's husband.

"Quiet, not a word." Claudette pressed Margot's hand down on the table.

Jerome wore his maroon leather jacket with the wide collar. Under that was a polyester shirt, tucked into one of his side-strap leisure pants. Now she understood his recent wardrobe expansion.

On his arm was a woman with a white fur stole. The two greeted the bartender and several patrons. After a minute, Jerome motioned to the bartender and headed to the back of the club.

Claudette kept her head down, but her eyes followed every move Jerome and his lady made. "I knew it!"

"What are you going to do, Claudette?" Margot asked even though she know realized the evening's destination was far from random.

Jerome's date placed her lips against his and then parted them with her tongue. Margot watched in shock, her eyes alternating between the couple and Claudette.

The bartender placed two drinks on the table, interrupting their foreplay. As the couple came up for air, Claudette locked eyes with Jerome.

"Claudette!" He gasped and pushed away from his date.

"This is what you do every night?" She ran over to their table. "With this bitch?"

The woman rolled her eyes, dismissing the comments, and escaped to the bar. Margot unsure what to do, took a gulp from her wine and joined Claudette's side.

"This is not the place." Jerome reached for her arm as if to escort her out.

"This is not the place, Jerome? Where should we discuss it? At home in front of Marie?"

Claudette walked over to the bar to confront his date."Did you know he has another life with a daughter and wife?"

"Claudette, please, let's leave." Jerome's tone become calm as if talking to an unreasonable child. "We'll talk about it."

"We won't talk about anything. I don't want you at the house. Stay with your bitch tonight!"

"Tiup!" The woman smirked.

Claudette was in disbelief. "Wait, hold this." She tossed her handbag to Margot then strolled to the table where she once sat, confusing Jerome and his mistress, until Claudette returned with her wine. Cornered, the woman had no time to react as Claudette poured the Manischewitz all over her fur stole.

"Oh, my God! Oh, my God!" the woman wailed. "She destroyed my mink! She ruined it!"

"Bouzën Petion-Ville, that's not mink!" Claudette shouted in her face. Jerome froze in shock, and Margot avoided eye contact with him as chased after Claudette.

Outside, Claudette stood motionless the sidewalk. Everything that had just transpired replayed in her mind. The way the tramp's lips touched Jerome. The interaction as intimate as any kiss she shared with Jerome in all their years together.

That passion was the reason Jerome shoved Doublemint into his mouth before entering the house. The first time she saw him was a coincidence, an innocent look through the living room curtains when he hesitated too long on the porch. But as she monitored his arrival on subsequent weeks, she found it was an ongoing routine. How many times had he kissed his wife or made love after doing the same to that Petion-Ville bitch?

"Let's go, Claudette." Margot pulled her friend's arm and found it trembling.

"Get the car, please." Claudette's voice as soft. "I'll wait here."

Margot complied but never let Claudette out of her sight, afraid her friend might jump into traffic or do something equally crazy. The car was a block away, but when Margot pulled up several minutes later, Claudette was still oddly quiet.

"He never came after me," she said. "That says it all."

"I'm sorry, Claudette. That was horrible."

"It's okay. Someone told me about Jerome and this place. I just wanted to know for sure/ I had to know. He wasn't mine for a long time now. Maybe he never was."

It wasn't long after this incident, Margot's marriage took a turn for the worse. Lelio had constant issues living with her parents and soon found comfort from a woman willing to listen to his grievances.

By the summer of 1982, both women had hit the dating scene hard, frequently double-dating. But it wasn't all fun and games since Claudette had to singlehandedly raise Marie while holding down a mortgage. Plus, Marc and Veronique's aftermath made picking up the pieces difficult. However, she kept her home as solid as possible, mostly for Nancy.

By the 1990s, her interest in dating waned, the laundry list of untrustworthy men had dimmed her spirit. Luckily, Margot, who had also failed to find her prince charming, was always across the street as a shoulder to lean on—a watered-down substitute for her lost sister, Veronique, or at the very least, someone whose refrigerator she could raid in a pinch.

"I need cloves and cinnamon sticks!"

"I think I have some. Check the cabinet." Margot rushed back to her bathroom. "You can also grab the macaroni on the counter."

"I have no time. I'll send someone." Claudette scanned the cabinets.

"No time?" Margot shouted. "You're across the street. Take the macaroni!"

Claudette ignored her. She found cinnamon sticks along with some other tidbits. "Where are the cloves? No cloves! No cloves, Margot!"

"You don't see any in the cabinet?"

"No, I don't. What am I going to do with my ham?"

"You don't need that for the ham. It does nothing, just decoration."

"It gives it flavor. Why don't you have cloves?"

"You didn't buy me any," Margot explained. "Besides, it was just last week you swore you wouldn't help with this party."

"Okay. I'm leaving. I'll send someone to pick up the macaroni." She dashed out of the house into the street.

"Mamie, mamie." A young man shouted from a car full of passengers.

Claudette paused in the middle of the road to see who it was. The sun was setting so she couldn't make out who was behind the wheel until the young man poked his head out of the window.

"It's me mamie, Bigga!"

"Big who? Listen, whatever you think your name is, go into number 1208, and tell Margot you're picking up the macaroni for me."

"Are you sure we're invited to this party, Bigga?" asked the woman driving the car. "It doesn't look like she even knows you."

"Of course, she knows me." He stepped out and trotted his heavy frame over to Margot's. "Anyway, if I'm bringing the macaroni, then I'm in the party."

"Oh, boy. Bad sign," said a man struggling to get out of the backseat. "Are you sure you know these people, Bigga? I don't want to get kicked out."

"Everybody knows Bigga," he stressed. "Bigga is international."

Inside, Claudette set the cinnamon sticks down and started rummaging through the fridge. In the backyard, the DJ had "Shook Ones" on which was giving her a headache.

"Play some Haitian music," she shouted, furthering aggravating the pain.

***

"I got these for you," Max handed Fredo and Pik matching cellular phones.

"Oh, shit." Pik couldn't contain his bliss.

"We shouldn't be doing that pager shit anymore." Steve pulled the heavy device from its plastic cover.

"An official Motorola," Fredo gushed. "Is this the hook-up you told us about? I thought it was some bitches."

Max bit his tongue as the four huddled around the hood of Max's car going over plans taking place later in the week. A couple of times Max was forced to bark a word or two to get Fredo and Pik inline as they were distracted by their new devices.

"I don't know anything about Jersey except they steal cars like a motherfucker out there."

"Relax," Steve said. "It's just like Brooklyn, only across the river. You two need to get out this borough some time."

"Stop being a bitch, Pik," Fredo said. "This is business."

"Dump those pagers," Max advised. "Feds know all the codes on those things. That's why I got us phones. Feds don't speak hood."

"My girl got me this beeper for Christmas." Pik pulled his pager out.

"Just dump it," Max reiterated.

"Okay," Pik sighed.

Fredo snatched the pager from Pik's hand, dropping it on the ground in one motion. A quick kick launched the pager across the street, whereupon it skidded into a gutter.

"Fuck!" Pik cried out.

Fredo let out a loud laugh.

"You're fucked-up," Pik replied.

"Man, fuck you care about that shit?" Fredo got serious. "Max just hit us off with fucking cellular phones!"

"Kill that noise." Steve tugged Pik's elbow. "Let's roll."

***

"Bigga!" Nancy screamed from across the yard. "You came!"

"Of course, I came darling. You know Bigga loves you."

Nancy smiled at the comment and ran into the kitchen where Claudette was handling a hundred different things at once.

"Where is she?"

"It's still early Aunt Claudette."

"Early? This party better not finish late. I have to go to church in the morning."

"Oh, come on, Auntie, when was the last time you went to church early?" Nancy grabbed a pack of napkins.

"It doesn't matter what time I choose to go. I need my sleep."

Nancy kept quiet. The last thing she wanted to do was incite her aunt into killing the party early.

"Will this DJ play that music all night?"

"No, Auntie. He's saving the Haitian music for later," she assured.

Nancy collected as many packs of napkin as she could handle and took the stack out to the yard. Outside, the party started to take shape. It felt just like the old days. Sure, there were new faces, but people she went to high school and junior high school with were all here. It was a pleasant surprise, almost perfect. She would note the final tally after Max arrived.

"Oh, my God," Myrtha, an old friend from high school, stopped

Nancy. "Emily is so frickin' cute."

"Thank you," Emily smiled as she shook Myrtha's hand.

"I can't believe how fast she is growing," Myrtha said. "I want one just like her!"

"You know what she asked me the other day?" Nancy looked down at Emily. "Mommy, was there color when you were young?"

"Too much!" Myrtha laughed. "Sweetheart, you have a young mommy."

"I don't think she understands how young and hip her mom is." Nancy handed Myrtha the two packs of napkins. "Help a sister out."

"I guess that's why you invited me," Myrtha joked. "Where's Frances? She's not doing any work."

"Find her. I have to take care of a few things. I'll be back." Nancy rushed over to the DJ.

"Bradley, you have to play some kompa or my aunt will start flipping."

"Got you, Nancy." He removed his headset. "In 20 minutes. But I have to play this to keep the young-heads here."

"Young-heads my foot," Nancy said. "Play some kompa before that woman drives me up a wall."

Jimmy ran the bar located opposite the DJ, next to the steps that led to the kitchen. He wasn't a mixologist, but luckily, most of his requests was basic rhum and Coke. He was serving a drink and noticed Nancy could use one too. He did his best with a kamikaze and walked it over to her.

"Jimm-yy." Nancy happily took the cocktail. She motioned over couple of friends who had just strolled into the party. "Joelle, Maureen. This is Jimmy."

"Hi, Jimmy," Maureen greeted him with a handshake. "Nice to meet you."

"Same here," Joelle chimed in and turned to Nancy, "Is this the guy?"

"Jimmy is my brother," Nancy said. "He's too smart to get involved with me."

"Anyway, enjoy the drink." He smiled and returned to tend the bar.

"He's a sweetheart." Nancy commented to her friends.

A woman leapt from a lawn chair, her drunken momentum almost causing her to trip in front of Nancy and her two friends.

"Where's Marie?" the woman asked, regaining her balance.

"That's a great question," Nancy replied. "She hasn't returned my pages. I'm sure she's waiting to make a grand entrance. You know Marie."

A huge arm draped across Nancy's shoulder. It was Bigga again.

"Where are you going with that Haitian shirt?" Maureen pointed to the guayabera he was wearing.

"Do you know how expensive this shirt is?" Bigga snapped. "I bought this at Bloomingdale's."

"No, no, no. They don't sell those at Bloomies," Joelle replied. "Maybe Conway's!"

Nancy's pager buzzed, and she checked it hoping to see a message from Marie. The text indicated it was Laurel, the woman who made the cake for the evening. She excused herself and went into the kitchen to return the call.

"Hi, Laurel. It's Nancy."

"Nancy, I have a problem. The cake is ready, but my husband's car broke down on Atlantic and Pacific."

"Oh, gosh," Nancy winced.

"Can you have someone pick up the cake? We'll have to get the car towed."

"I'm so sorry to hear that, Laurel. I really hoped you could be here."

"I know dear, but you're going to have pick up the cake before a tow truck arrives."

"Okay, Laurel. I'm sending someone to Atlantic and Pacific, right now."

She ran back out to the yard and went straight to Jimmy, who was still mixing drinks.

"Jimmy, I need another huge favor from you."

"You're about to use up all your favors in a single month," he smiled.

"The lady who made the cake has car trouble. So can you pick up the cake at Atlantic and Pacific? It's a blue SUV."

"What about the bar?"

"I'll get someone to handle that."

"Party has to have cake." He shrugged and rounded the table.

"Jimmy, you're the best!" She pulled him into a hug.

"Better be a Haitian cake," he winked.

Looking for a bartender, she stopped in front of Barbara, the friend who invited her to a lounge back in January where she met Max.

"Barbie, I need help. Can you please tend the bar?"

"As long as I stay sober, yeah."

"Thanks. I think." Nancy sighed with relief. "Jimmy will be back soon to relieve you."

She spun around to return to the kitchen when she saw Max and his friends entered the yard.

Her heart skipped a beat as they approached in what felt like slow motion.

***

Ti Zoot studied the tie around his neck. He decided against it since it was a backyard affair, but he was determined to attend in his new suit. It was conservative, but the tan color was perfect for spring and summer. His merlot-colored wingtips were a gift from Fiona. She hated the Bally's he favored and wanted him to try something new. He hadn't cared for them after unboxing them months ago, but Fiona got him to try them on again and he liked the way they looked with the suit.

"This is perfect," Fiona said.

He nodded in the mirror, admiring his reflection.

"I mean, this day is perfect," she wrapped her arms around his waist. "Do you realize we've never spent an entire day together except during that one snowstorm? We're always going out in different circles."

"Yep," he agreed. "Perfect."

***

Max stood in a corner talking to Steve while Fredo and Pik hung at the bar with Barbara, who seemed to enjoy their rough, sophomoric humor.

"How old are you"?" Fredo asked.

"How old are you two?" Barbara countered. "Either way, I think you are too young for me."

"Please," Pik said. "I bet you're about twenty-four."

"Hmm. Thank you," Barbara said. "But I'm a little older than that, closer to thirty."

"Wow. Either way, we can do this," Fredo propositioned.

"Do what?" she laughed. "Are you sure those drinks aren't getting to you?"

"We just started drinking, ma," Pik countered. "We'll drink you under the table."

She was curious. Guys her age or older were never so direct. "So, do you two live with your mothers or your grandmothers?"

"Hell nah!" Fredo replied. "I got my own crib."

"Well, we share a crib," Pik corrected.

"It's my crib! I just let you stay there."

"Do you really have your own place? For real, how old are you guys?"

"I'm twenty-three," Fredo said. "He's twenty-two." He grinned at having adding two years to both their ages.

"Well, you're younger than what I'm used to," she told Fredo.

On the other side of the yard, Max watched the three at the bar. He was particularly dumbfounded as to why the woman hadn't sent them away. It took him a minute, but he finally recognized Barbara, the friend Nancy was with the night they met. She appeared upscale, why would she be interested in a couple of hoods wearing T-shirts and Air-Force Ones?

"What's going on with those two over there?" He nudged Steve in reference to Fredo and Pik.

"You never know with them," Steve said.

"I'm going to talk to Nancy. Do me a favor, see what those two fools are up to."

"Cool." Steve walked over to the bar. He was always babysitting Fredo, Pik, and the rest of their tiresome clique.

"Trust me," Fredo sipped his drink. "I attract older women all the time."

"Oh, so you're a player?" Barbara asked.

"Nah, I gave that up." Fredo smiled.

"What's good?" Pik called as Steve approached. "Need a drink?"

"Yeah, a refill."

"Stand in line," Pik said.

"I don't see no line," Steve smirked.

"Ha! Me and Fredo got the bar on lock, homie."

"Don't listen to them," Barbara interjected. "I'll refill that. What were you drinking?"

"J&B on the rocks, please."

"Good, I like easy drinks. I'm just filling in for the real bartender," Barbara explained. "Is this a friend?"

"Yeah, he's part of my crew," Fredo responded. "This is Stevie-Steve."

"Oh, what sort of crew is this?" Barbara poured the whisky.

Steve gave Fredo a sharp look. "Yeah, we're associates."

"Aw, he's playing it down. We're tight," Fredo laughed.

"How do you guys know Marie?" Barbara asked.

153

"Who?" Pik asked.

"Marie-Carmelle? This is her birthday party," she explained.

"Oh, her cousin Nancy invited us," Pik replied.

"You guys know Nancy too?"

"Yeah," Fredo said. "She knew Pik when he was a little Parnell in diapers. Plus, our homie Max is talking to her."

"Oh, Max is he here?" Barbara perked up. She saw nothing connecting Fredo and Pik to the Max she met at the lounge that night, their personalities and styles were in sharp contrast.

"Where Max at?" Pik turned to Steve. "I know ya'll tighter than tighty-whities caught between the crack of a fat man's ass."

"Thanks." Steve nursed his drink and ignored Pik's comment.

"My man." Fredo nudged Steve and pulled him aside. "I'm definitely rocking her to sleep tonight." He nodded his head toward Barbara.

Steve wasn't impressed with his wishful thinking and removed himself from the scene.

On the other side of the house, Max gripped Nancy's hand. "You kind of ignored me when I walked in."

"I got nervous," she admitted.

"Nervous, why?"

"I don't know. You caught me off-guard the way you came in with your friends."

"That's on you." He squeezed her hand. "You insisted on those guys coming tonight."

"I don't mean because of them. Just seeing you in this element took me by surprise. Plus, I got turned on."

"Damn." He looked her up and down. "We can handle that right now."

"Shut-up." She twisted her hand away.

"Anyone ever pass by those bushes over there?" He looked over to the patch hiding the side barrier.

"You're not helping." She gave him a playful shove.

"Sorry, but you look gorgeous."

"Thank you, but we have to get out of here," she advised.

"Where's your cousin?"

"I don't know. She hasn't returned my pages. She better come soon though."

He leaned in for a kiss, which she accepted. Her movements were slow and deliberate for fear further contact would fan her urges.

A roar came from the crowd in the backyard. "HAPPY BIRTHDAY!"

"Why did she have to come at this moment?" Nancy pried herself free from their embraced.

"Damn, guess you have to go?" Max tugged her toward the bushes, hoping she'd change her mind.

"Later." Nancy backed away. "I have to welcome her."

***

"Who's that?" Fredo wondered when Marie walked in the yard. As the chorus of birthday greetings arose, he connected the dots. "Oh, so that's the cousin?"

"Oh, yeah. I remember her," Pik said. "She was always with Nancy back in the day."

"She's hot, huh?" Barbara said. "Place your tongues back in your mouths, fellas."

"Hah, not even," Fredo said. "I'm more concerned with the bartender right now."

"You're definitely the player type." Barbara sipped her beverage.

As Marie approached the center of the mob of well-wishers, Nancy signaled DJ Bradley.

"All right, party people." Bradley voiced over the mic. "She's here. The fabulous, the radiant Marie-Carmelle. We are all here to celebrate this special day...this anniversary."

"Anniversary" by Tony! Toni! Tonè! played over the loud speakers. "That's her song!" a woman shouted.

Marie took everything in and proceeded to dance. A few couples got up and joined her. Nancy stood on the sidelines proud of a job well done. She'd missed Marie's arrival, but everything was going even better than she imagined. She knew Marie had to be impressed. This party was the perfect remedy for a lot of things their family endured the last couple of years.

Max made his way from the side of the house and planted himself near the backyard's entrance. He didn't take his eyes off Nancy until he noticed a gentleman in a linen suit arrive and stand near the fringe of the festivities.

Halfway through the nine-minute song, a tear came down Marie's cheek. Nancy was unsure at first, unable to get a clear view, but she nudged through the crowd in her cousin's direction anyway.

"Come here," Nancy opened her arms and welcomed her cousin. "I love you. Happy Birthday."

She was touched. "Thank you, Nance...love you too."

Nancy grabbed her by the waist and the two danced together just as they did when they were kids. A round of cheers circled them as camera lights flashed. At the end of the song, the DJ passed Nancy the mic. Emily joined her mother, holding her hand.

"Thank you all for coming to my cousin's, my sister's, Marie's birthday! It's been a long time since we've celebrated. We're all grown-ups now and have a different set of responsibilities, so my cousin and I have not been able to spend the time together that we'd like. But we still connect and always will. She's the older sister I never had. My aunt Claudette and my cousin took me in and never let me feel anything less than welcome."

"Thank you," Marie whispered. On the side, she noticed her mother step out of the kitchen and into the yard.

"Marie, you are my best friend," Nancy continued. "Your wisdom and advice have always guided me. And if you all know my cousin, she is always right."

"Yup, that's Marie-Carmelle," Bigga yelled from the crowd, who nodded and laughed in agreement.

"I want to thank you all for celebrating this night with us," Nancy said. "My cousin is one of the few people I can always lean on, but I can tell she is emotional with you all here, so I won't force her to give a speech."

"Aww," Joelle chimed up from the rear. "I think I'm going to cry. I love you girls."

"Hold up, Nancy. You can't let her off the hook like that," Bigga said. "Marie, give a speech."

"Speech! Speech! Speech!"

Nancy walked over and handed Marie the microphone. "Take your time, couz."

"Love you so much!" Marie squeezed Nancy and Emily.

"Leave her," Joelle called. "She's not giving any speech, too much emotion."

Nancy motioned for Claudette to join them. The matriarch hesitated at first but slowly made her way through the crowd.

Nancy took the two by the arm and led mother and daughter to an embrace. It was a long, emotionally charged moment, but the crowd waited quietly until the embraced.

"I'm okay. I'm okay." Marie muttered to her mother and Emily over the crowd's applause.

Nancy took the microphone and handed it back to Bradley as a signal to restart the music.

Max watched the entire scene play out from a distance, but still found himself caught up in the emotion of the moment. Nancy was the kind of girl he like to have in his life long term, but he feared having to tell her about his business as they got closer…and there was no way to avoid getting closer.

He made brief eye contact with Nancy who had just finished with the DJ and noticed that the gentleman in the linen outfit hadn't joined the party but instead turned to leave. Max couldn't see his face because of a shadow created by the house's overhang. But once he turned into the light, Max realized it was the same guy he met weeks ago, Rudy. The man had introduced himself as Marie's ex-boyfriend. Old boy really tried to come here tonight? Max found himself half-impressed by his brazenness.

The DJ livened things up with kompa, much to Claudette's relief. She greeted some family and friends on her way back to the kitchen. Even though she swore there was no way she would help, coordinating events was her element. She always took things over whether she was initially involved or not.

"We love you." Emily and Nancy announced from behind, catching Claudette off-guard.

"Thank you," she blushed. "I have to go back to the kitchen."

She embraced Nancy the pulled Emily into the hug fest. "Everything turned out beautiful." She surveyed the happy faces filling her yard. "Let me get back. I have to make sure everything is okay in the kitchen."

Nancy smiled at Max across the yard. She knew she should signal for him to come over and meet her family, but she was avoiding having to introduce him to Emily. It was much too early and his reticence about his business made him too much of a wild card.

***

"Big party." Ti Zoot drove down the block for a third time. "I can't find a parking spot anywhere."

"Wait, I think that gentleman is going to his car." Fiona pointed to a man walking in the street toward the end of the block, prompting Ti Zoot to speed up and position himself for a possible spot.

"Ti Zoot?" the man asked upon Ti Zoot's approach.

Ti Zoot stared at the figure through the open driver's side window, but the bright streetlight above did not permit him to see beyond the shadow created on the man's features.

"How is it going?"

"Rudy?" Ti Zoot recognized the voice. "Are you going to the party?" Ti Zoot was confused, considering his break-up with Marie.

"Oh, no." Rudy dangled his car keys. "Actually, I was contemplating going in, but I stopped at the entrance."

"I see," he said. "I was looking for parking spot."

"Yours man." Rudy pointed to his car. "Good to see you."

"Same here," Ti Zoot reached out and shook his hand.

"Enjoy. It's a special night. A lot of people there."

"Nancy invited you?"

"No, actually, Marie did." Rudy said.

"Marie?"

"Yes, I think she was being nice," he explained, "but I don't have a place there. It's family and friends."

"Maybe she wanted you there," Ti Zoot said. "Are you sure you won't go inside?"

"I'm sure. This is too much for me. Not only did I hurt Marie with that mess, but I hurt myself in the process."

"I see. Good luck with the baby, Rudy." Ti Zoot rolled up the window and positioned his vehicle to take the man's space.

"You never told me he impregnated another woman." Fiona's voice trembled.

"You never asked." Ti Zoot extended his arm to help her from the car. "Besides, you don't hang out with Marie. You hardly know her."

"It does not matter, Ti Zoot. Include me in your life." She nudged his shoulder as they walked to Claudette's. "I've met Marie dozens of times. I like her style. Très chic."

"Well, that's what happened, so they broke up."

"And they should. No woman should accept that."

His eyes narrowed, and he wondered if the statement was more warning than causal conversation.

***

"How's my bartender handling things?" Nancy asked.

"Trying to stay sober and dodge the advances of these two." Barbara pointed to Fredo and Pik.

"Are you guys causing trouble at my bar?"

"Not at all, Nancy." Pik slurred his words.

Max watched Nancy approach Fredo and Pik,, so he made a beeline in their direction. "Hey, what's good?"

"Pretty much everything," Nancy said.

"Well, hello. You probably forgot me," Barbara said.

"This is our homie Max we were telling you about earlier," Fredo replied.

"I've already met Max." She winked Nancy's way.

"Hey, Barbara." Max shook her hand.

"Sounds like she's been mixing some fabulous drinks," Nancy smiled.

"I don't know about that. The real bartender better return soon. I'm getting drunk here. Nice to see you again, Max."

"Same here," he replied.

"I'll be back," Nancy said. "I have to page Jimmy and see if everything went okay with the cake. You all mingle."

"Hold on." Max trotted after her. "Bathroom, please."

"Of course, come." She hooked her arm in his.

"Actually, me too," Steve said.

"Okay, but you'll have to go at different times," Nancy joked.

The commend cracked Fredo and Pik up, which made Max cringe.

In the distance, he could hear Fredo's crass take on the matter.

"I bet Steve is probably going to hold it while Max takes a whiz."

Nancy led them through the crowd and toward the deck leading to the house. Before she got there, she felt a tap on her shoulder.

"Hey, Margot."

"How is my beauty?" Margot kissed her cheek.

"I was wondering where you were. You only had to cross the street."

"You know me," Margot admitted. "That was beautiful earlier. I was in tears."

"Thanks, love," Nancy replied.

"Who are these two handsome young men?"

"Oh, these are two friends, Steve and uhm…Max."

"Hi, Steve. Hi 'uhm' Max," Margot teased.

"Nice to meet you," the two replied almost simultaneously.

"Well behaved." Margot raised an eyebrow at Nancy."Like soldiers."

"By the way, thank you for the dish." Nancy nodded to the fellas. "Marie and I adopted Margot as our aunt a long time ago!"

"My pleasure, baby girl."

Back at the bar, Fredo pulled out his massive mobile device, gaining the attention of everyone nearby. "Gotta make a call."

"Wait, you have a cellular phone?" Barbara's words dripped with curiosity. "I was wondering what was so bulky in your pocket?"

"Yeah, we keep business like that," Fredo said.

"And what kind of business are you in?"

"We sell stocks down at Wall Street," Pik chimed.

"Come on. You two don't look like Wall Street brokers to me."

"What we look like?" Fredo asked.

"Anything but brokers," Barbara laughed.

"Yeah, all right. Gotta make a phone call, but it's too noisy here."

"Go over there on the side of the house," Barbara directed.

"Cool. We'll be back," Fredo crossed the lawn with Pik in tow.

Meanwhile, Claudette and a couple of women were hard at work in the kitchen. She had already heard a few inquiries about food the second the DJ introduced Marie. She ready to place pans on Sterno racks outside when Nancy entered the house with Max and Steve.

"Ay, you can start serving this food once I place them on the rack," Claudette told Nancy. "We did everything so far, I'm going to sit after this."

"Of course," Nancy said. "Auntie, this is Max and Steve. They're using the bathroom." "Okay, hi," Claudette greeted them. "Once you two finish, make sure you wash your

hands and help put these trays on the table outside."

"Auntie," Nancy twisted herself and looked at Claudette funny.

"Auntie what! I don't care whatever princes they are, they better wash their hands after touching their balls, then place these trays out there!"

"Yes, ma'am," Max responded.

"Steve, head through the kitchen. There's a bathroom on the right." Nancy pointed at the foyer between the kitchen and living room. "Max, since you can't wait, you can use the bathroom in the basement."

"Why do I have to use the one in the basement?" Max asked.

"All good," Steve said. "I'll go down there."

"Okay, fine. Whatever." Nancy threw up her hands at Max. "I didn't know you had a basement phobia, but at least now you know where I get my obsession with bathroom etiquette."

Max cut through the kitchen, smiling at the ladies along the way.

"Make sure you lock the door," Nancy hollered.

"You're funny." Max blushed at the inside joke.

Nancy watched him disappear and turned back to the commotion in the kitchen. "Auntie, you get so crazy at times."

"Crazy is me helping you with a party I have nothing to do with," Claudette chided.

"Okay, Auntie. Let me just page Jimmy." Nancy reached for the phone unaware that Jimmy had just pulled in up the street.

"I'm here, I'm here." Jimmy huffed as his pager went off. Before he even looked at the screen, he knew it was Nancy. "Why did you have to be so damn beautiful?" he lamented aloud.

"Not now, Fiona is here," Ti Zoot joked.

Jimmy looked up surprised to see Ti Zoot and Fiona standing before him.

"First time you've shown humor," Fiona observed. "Is Jimmy the only person you show this side to?"

"I wouldn't call that humor." Jimmy wiped his brow, embarrassed to have been caught in a conversation with himself. "Ti Zoot, give me a hand. This cake is heavy. Help me get it out of the trunk."

"I thought you were bartending?" Ti Zoot asked.

"I was—I am. I just had a crazy run across town to get this cake. Long story."

"Is there a wedding cake in this big box?" Ti Zoot struggled to lift the other end.

"Big party," Jimmy explained.

"I can tell by the music." Fiona shimmied to the kompa playing in the background.

After lifting his end, Ti Zoot placed the box in Jimmy's care and slammed the trunk.

***

Max snuck up behind Nancy on the crowded lawn and whispered in her ear. "I want you."

"Oh, I thought you were someone else." She smiled and took her sweet time facing him.

"Fun-ny," Max rolled his eyes. "Did you reach your boyfriend Jimmy?"

"No, I didn't. And he's not my boyfriend."

"Who is?" Max got in her face.

"I don't know."

He shook his head at the reply. "Can we dance?"

She didn't answer. Instead, she took a step back and wiggled her hips, inviting him with her eyes. He joined her and did his best to keep up. Marie was dancing nearby with Ernie, a family friend. She pulled Ernie in Nancy's direction so the girls could talk.

"He can't take his eyes off of you," she whispered.

Nancy smiled and avoided looking Max's way.

"Everywhere you go, his eyes are on you," Marie repeated.

"Serious?"

"As a heart-attack." Marie resumed her dance with Ernie.

Nancy followed suit and wrapped Max's arms around her waist. "Parnell and Fredo can use some dance lessons." She craned her neck to watch the two fooling around with a couple of her co-workers on the dance floor. "You can use some too."

"Teach me," he said.

"Not enough time." She grazed her thigh on his zipper. "On the other hand, Steve is smooth, I should be dancing with him."

"Stop playing." He held her closer. "You're mine, and you know it."

She let the comment slide, but her thoughts remained on Marie's words. She liked the notion that he was very much into her. She certainly didn't want to chase him.

"I'm letting Emily stay with my aunt tonight," she whispered to Max. "She'll fall asleep soon. I don't want to wake her up."

"Can I come over?"

"No," she smiled. "Maybe."

"You're driving me crazy. I have to see you later."

"I said 'maybe.' But either way, we're not going to do anything."

"Come on, Nancy. You're purposely trying to give me a set of blue balls."

She'd just started to laugh it off when Marie cut in. "Let's switch," she insisted. "If Ernie has his way, I'll be dancing with him all night."

"Oh, Ernie knows how to dance," Nancy cooed. "My pleasure."

"Hope you don't mind, Max." Marie grabbed Max's his hand.

"Not at all. Happy Birthday." He kissed Marie's cheek. "Actually, I wanted to talk to you."

"Are you sure? Because your eyes are still set on Nancy."

"I'm sure," he grinned.

"Okay. Having a good time? Enjoying my fabulous party?"

"I am." He focused on Marie. "I see you're having a great time too, but I was told you didn't want a party."

"I didn't. I was going through a moment, but I'm loving my party. Plus," she raised her voice to gather his attention, "I get to dance with a good-looking guy who is really into my cousin."

"I wasn't looking over there this time, I swear." He laughed at the pleasantry.

"It's okay, I get it. Nancy is the bomb."

"You're not exactly her homely cousin. You two are what's happening here."

"Aww, thanks."

Max took a moment to regain his footing. Marie was just as difficult to keep up with as Nancy. The kompa required more than his normal two-step routine.

"I wanted to tell you something I saw earlier tonight," he said.

"Something you saw?"

"Yes. When you first arrived, I saw a guy standing at the gate. He stayed for a few minutes, but as he left, I realized it was your ex-boyfriend. The guy I met when we were in Times Square."

"Rudy…here?" She looked around.

"Yeah. He was here earlier, but he left."

"Wow, he showed up."

"You were expecting him?"

"No." She mulled over her earlier phone conversation with Rudy. "I don't expect anything anymore."

"Well, he came and stood by the gate, but he never moved beyond that. Then he just left."

"I invited him," she explained. "Yet, I still find it incredible he actually showed up." The realization sparked a fondness for what could have been. "Promise me you'll be good to Nancy."

"I will. I don't think I have choice."

"Because you know I'll come after you?"

"Don't worry. I'm crazy for her."

Marie's smile was wide. She placed her head on his shoulder mercifully slowing things down for him. She had already guessed he had feelings for Nancy, but it satisfying hearing him admit it.

She glanced over and saw Nancy break away from Ernie to meet Jimmy, who had arrived with the cake, Ti Zoot, and Fiona.

"Do me a favor, Marie?"

"What's that?"

"Please don't tell Nancy what I just told you."

***

"Thank you. Thank you." Nancy directed Jimmy to a long picnic table in front of the deck. "Ti Zoot, Fiona, where were you all this time?" She greeted the pair with French style double kisses.

"He takes forever," Fiona explained. "Worse than a woman."

"The place is packed." Ti Zoot looked around. "Did you invite all of Brooklyn?"

"And then some," she said. "Come in. People have been asking for you." Nancy went over to the table and cleared a space so Jimmy could unbox the cake.

"What would I do without you, Jimmy?"

"I can't imagine," he answered. "Okay. I guess I'm back to the bar. I hope there are drinks left."

"Thanks again." She embraced him with a kiss. "You're the best. Relieve Barbara, please. After that, you owe me a dance."

"You mean you owe me a dance," he corrected.

"You damn right." She blew him a kiss and took off in the other direction.

***

"You're still the man." Bigga patted Ti Zoot on the back. "You've been low-key. I don't see this guy anymore." He turned to Fiona. "Are you taking all his time?"

"Not me. Maybe some other woman," Fiona smirked.

"No way. You're too fine for him to dip."

"Merçi," she smiled.

"When is Claudette serving this food? I'm hungry." Ti Zoot waved a hand at the empty serving tables.

"I've been asking that since I came," Bigga agreed.

"All that loving this afternoon also made me hungry," Fiona added. "Let's at least find the hors d'oeuvres."

Bigga did a double-take and pulled Ti Zoot aside. "Damn bro, you're really putting that work in."

"Tiup. All for show," he said.

"She just said you've been slaying all day." Bigga clapped his hands. "All day!"

"Find the food, Bigga. Stop the bull."

Ti Zoot grabbed Fiona and made a turn for the kitchen.

"Oh, there's Ti Zoot and his porcelain doll," Claudette cried.

"Bonsoir." Fiona briefly bowed her head to acknowledge the elders in the room.

"Claudette, cheri, I'm hungry. Where's my plate?"

167

"Ti Zoot, get out of here. The food is coming soon. In fact, grab this tray and place on the table outside."

"I'm wearing a suit," he argued.

"Well, take it off or don't eat."

"Ket." He chose the tray with the cooked rice and dried mushroom broth mixture known as djon-djon and carried it into the yard.

***

Nancy was on the deck, dancing alongside friends. She had an elevated view of everything and remarked how tightly packed the big yard was. It was surprising Claudette hadn't pulled her aside and complained she had invited too many people. That was a sign her aunt was enjoying herself.

"Hey, couz." Marie stepped onto the deck. "Love you. Love everything tonight."

They embraced then took a few photos when a guy with a camera asked them to pose. A group of girls and Bigga swooped in and joined the photo session.

"You guys are going to break my deck," Claudette yelled from the kitchen window. "Get off!"

"Okay. That's my cue," Marie laughed. "Let me go to the lady's room."

The others quickly scattered for fear of Claudette's wrath, and Nancy found herself alone on the deck. She was a little weary, so she leaned against the rail just as she'd done hundreds of times as a young girl. She looked for Emily and spotted her with a friend and wondered how long before she would fall asleep.

Suddenly, it felt like someone was staring at her. She turned to the right, and sure enough, Jimmy was gazing. She smiled back, and he quickly turned to his duties at the bar. On the far end of the same counter, Max was also staring at her. He raised a glass, but she turned back to Jimmy and winked.

The dual flirtations gave her an idea, and she waved Barbara over.

"Hey, girl. What's up?" Barbara said, short of breath from dancing.

"One more favor. Can you give Jimmy a break for a few? I'm dying to dance with him."

"Wait, what about Max?" Barbara posed the question but quickly understood. "Ah, say no more." She danced her way to the bar and relieved Jimmy.

Nancy took the opportunity and made sure everyone saw her wave to Jimmy for a dance. Rather than walk down the steps, she slid over the rail and stepped on the grass surrounding the deck. She fixed her one-piece, then cradled Jimmy's neck with both arms.

Max, still watching, kept the smile on his face. Nancy had played this game all evening, and he wasn't about to lose his cool over her latest performance.

***

"Set the platter on this rack." Claudette pointed Ti Zoot to a serving table.

"I need a plate now," he demanded.

"Get out of here. Go dance with your doll," she shoved him toward the makeshift dance floor. "We're serving the food very soon. I know how Haitians act when they're hungry."

Fiona took the cue and led Ti Zoot to the floor. Despite the steely face and no non-sense demeanor, the guy could still rock a dance floor. It was what put him over at the Latin Lounge. They squeezed through the crowd and found a tight space big enough to dance. A couple came over and patted Ti Zoot on the back while greeting Fiona.

Nancy looked for Emily as she chatted with Jimmy. "Okay. She's out."

He followed Nancy's focus and saw Emily asleep on Margot's lap.

"That was fast." Jimmy raised an eyebrow. "She was running around only minutes ago!"

"That's Emily, like clockwork," she explained.

"Let me help you bring her inside," he offered.

"Not yet, we're dancing."

Marie pushed her way over to them. "Hey, Jimmy. Thank you for everything. I know how much you helped Nancy with putting this together."

"My pleasure." Jimmy reached over and gave her a hug.

"We have to celebrate you next, Jimmy," Nancy suggested.

"No. I don't need any big parties. I just like to attend them."

"It'll be a surprise then," Marie said and turned to Nancy. "I taught you well." She nodded in Max's direction.

Nancy reacted with a broad smile and watched her cousin nudge her way to the center of the floor where Bigga pulled her into spin.

"Jimmy, are you dancing with me or not?"

"Yeah, what do you call this?"

"Well, then hold me like we're dancing," she advised.

"You want to cause trouble for me? I can already see a lot of guys giving me the look."

"Well, I don't care about them. I'm dancing with you." She pulled him until there was no space between them.

"Lord, help me with the hawks at this party tonight," he half-joked.

Ti Zoot and Fiona tuned everything out. Not quite dancing to the DJ, but rather to their own ballad. Fiona thought about their week. She finally found a tiny opening into his mind. Their future was always a question, but the last few days had brought possibilities.

Max couldn't control his emotions even though he was fully aware what Nancy was up to. His mouth had gone dry with jealousy, but he was too transfixed to get another drink. He simply shook the cup, hoping the ice would eventually melt enough to drink. Meanwhile, his temperature rose until he saw opportunity in an attractive lady walking his way. He made a play and asked her to dance. That would get Nancy to behave.

"I'm sorry, but I'm here with someone…my boyfriend," she smiled. "Thank you anyway."

With that, there was only one option left. Step to Nancy and interrupt her flow.

He struggled through the busy crowd. Nancy glanced up and caught his approach, but shut her eyes as if she hadn't noticed.

"Sorry, partner." Max tapped Jimmy's shoulder, never taking his eyes off Nancy. "If you don't mind, I believe the lady promised me a dance."

Nancy smiled and signaled Jimmy to step aside.

"Thanks, homie." Max placed an arm around Nancy.

Jimmy inched back to the bar so he could resume his post. The interruption deflated him. He loved being around her even platonically.

Halfway to his destination, something struck a familiar chord. He suddenly recognized the broad-shouldered guy who now had his lips comfortably close to Nancy's ear. It was one of the guys that confronted Ti Zoot during that car wash incident. In fact, he was the one calling the shots that day. What's he doing here and dancing with Nancy? Was he one of Marie's friends? It didn't matter. Things were bound to get sideways once he and Ti Zoot saw one another.

Jimmy made eye contact with Barbara and held up five fingers signaling he needed a few more minutes. She consented with a wave.

He then looked for Ti Zoot and wondered how he could avoid another confrontation. Just then, his eyes landed on two more guys from the car wash. The hothead who pulled the gun that day the was having words with a young lady. This party was too dense with people and could turn ugly. There wasn't a clear way to get Ti Zoot out of the party unnoticed, but he had to try or at least warn him without drawing attention.

Ti Zoot danced in the center of the crowd with Fiona, and they were right behind Nancy and the guy. Jimmy's heart fluttered with panic, and he did his best to maneuver through the crowd. He estimated he had only a few seconds to pull Ti Zoot aside if he was able to create a suitable distraction. And if was really lucky, he'd be convincing enough to get him to leave the yard. It was a slim chance, but even a hardhead like Ti Zoot would have to realize the three to two odds weren't in his favor.

***

"You play too much." Max nibbled on Nancy's ear.

"I'm sorry. Maybe I was being a brat." She rested her head on his chest.

"Your outfit is killing me." He shook the ice in his cup. "That color looks great on you."

"Thanks." She briefly raised her head from his chest to offer a cheerful but weary response.

"Jimmy, what's good man?" Bigga asked as he twirled Marie.

"Nothing." Jimmy's eyes stayed on Ti Zoot a few meters away. "Sorry, I'm trying to get through, excuse me."

He had just made it around Bigga's massive frame, when he had an idea. "Bigga! Come on, man. Let's go over to Ti Zoot."

Bigga's six-foot, three-hundred pound presence might by an asset just the imposing Notorious B.I.G. from whom he cribbed his nickname. Maybe Nancy's guy would think twice about an altercation once he saw Bigga.

"Go over? I saw him already," Bigga explained. "And I'm dancing with my girl over here."

"You wish," Marie laughed. "Please, go talk to your homeboy." She patted his shoulder and exited as best as she could manage.

"Damn." Sweat poured from Bigga's his forehead. "Where's Ti Zoot anyway?"

Jimmy grabbed his elbow and veered toward Ti Zoot, but before they could reach him, he disappeared from sight.

"Christ!" Ti Zoot felt the rush of cold water on his leg and bent down to investigate. A cup of melted ice had fallen to the ground and drenched his pant leg. An accidental bump on the packed floor probably caused the spill. No harm really, but he had barely broken in this particular suit. He stood back up and turned around to examine his backside for more damage.

Jimmy continued to wade through the crowd and eventually regained sight of his friend, but they were still separated by three bodies.

As Ti Zoot turned to figure out the who, what, where, and why of the minor accident, a familiar figure appeared in the corner of his eye.

Max.

Stunned, Max narrowed his eyes and quickly pulled the Old G's image from his mental rolodex.

Ti Zoot reacted first, shoving Max in the sternum. He couldn't give the move his full force as the packed crowd made it hard for even air to pass through. Behind Max was Nancy, who was mystified by Ti Zoot's reaction.

"You're that motherfucker who was making threats." Ti Zoot straightened shielding Fiona in the process.

Bigga, still with Jimmy, took the lead and plowed through the crowd with the force of a locomotive.

Fredo and Pik came to life after seeing the Old G and Max face-to-face and took to shoving aside anyone in their way to the fray.

"Fight!" Came a cry from the crowd. And with that, the two titans locked horns.

Bigga and Jimmy beat Fredo and Pik to the scuffle by a step, but that was all they needed as Bigga was able to squeeze an arm between Ti Zoot and Max.

"Fuck outta my way." Fredo hollered as he launched a wild swing in Jimmy's direction.

The blow missed Jimmy and connected with Bigga's neck. He absorbed the blow and wasted no time decking Fredo and Pik in retaliation. Ti Zoot and Max were now buried under a crowd of bodies.

From a distance, it was difficult to determine who sought to bring order versus those who fueled the fire. More bodies piled onto the ground, and the scene turned into a full riot with some fleeing for the street as things grew more explosive. A bit across the yard, Steve realizing Max was involved in the scuffle literally jumped over several people, hopping into the middle of the fray, helping his partner take on Ti Zoot.

Hearing the commotion from the kitchen, Claudette slammed a food tray down on the counter and ran to the deck to witness the melee. She scanned the yard for Emily, who Margot had thankfully shuttled away in the nick of time. Her neighbor rushed up the deck's steps carrying the child who'd somehow remained asleep during the chaos.

"Quick, take her up to my room." Claudette raced down the deck into the vicious throng. "Lord what's going on? Stop it! Stop!" She charged at the mob and tried to pull people away from the ruckus. A few of the older guests attempted the same, but things seemed to get crazier by the second.

On the outskirts, Marie crouched frantically behind a young man who shielded her from harm. She scanned the area for Nancy, but she could hardly make out anyone in the fracas. Her gaze landed on Fredo, who was recovering from getting stomped. He eventually made it to his feet and reached into the pocket of his oversized shorts.

"Oh, my God. He's got a gun," Marie screamed.

Fredo used his weapon to plant several blows to the back of Bigga's head. Most of the crowd ran to the side or out of the yard completely as Marie's words echoed through the air. Even Max and Steve who got their hands around Ti Zoot froze and released him.

Fredo's wiry frame stood over Bigga as if he'd just conquered a giant.

One half of the broken cellphone dangled in his hand, the edge caked with Bigga's blood.

"It's not a gun," someone shouted. "It's one of those cellular phones."

Nancy was distraught. But despite being in the middle of it all, she was unscathed save for a broken strap on her sandal. She hadn't even realized it, but someone pulled her away from the mess. "Where's Emily?" she screamed.

"She's inside. Margot is with her." Claudette rushed over and wrapped an arm around her niece.

"What just happened here?" Marie demanded. "What the hell happened?"

Nancy went straight to Ti Zoot. "I can't believe this. Why did you do this?"

"Me? You saw this thug attack me. You were there!"

Nancy stared at Max with a mixture of venom and confusion.

"I didn't come to a party to get attacked," Max said. "He's been harassing me and my friends for months now."

"Bullshit!" Ti Zoot lunged for Max, but Claudette, Fiona, and a couple of older gentlemen were in the way, blocking the attempt.

"Ti Zoot, what are you doing?" Marie was now in tears. "Why would you do this here?"

"You blame me?"

"Fuck, yeah," Fredo taunted. Steve held his shoulder refraining further violence . "You been harassing me. You pulled a gun on me and my boy Pik. Fuck outta here, man!"

"Calm down," Nancy cried. "I don't know what the hell is going on, but nothing is going down in my aunt's house."

"Hold him," Claudette commanded the men still on Ti Zoot. She then stepped into the center of the much smaller crowd. "Everyone, please go home. Sorry, the party is over. Please go home."

"You guys have pushed my limit." Ti Zoot grabbed his ruined jacket from the ground and started for the exit.

"Ti Zoot, no! You stay." Claudette turned to Max and his friends. "You guys, please go peacefully. Enough. Don't make things worse. My neighbors have probably called the 67th Precinct by now. Please."

"Yes ma'am," Max said. Once his breathing steadied, he nodded his crew.

Fredo remained fixed until Max grabbed his shoulder and forced his exit.

"I swear Old G, it's on," Fredo said at the gate line. "That's my word!"

Nancy followed Max to the front lawn. "Look, please don't call until I can get some answers. I don't know what's going on or what you're involved in."

"Are you serious?" His heart sank another notch.

"I'm serious." She wanted to say more but remained stern.

Max shook his head in disbelief, repulsed by what he had just participated in. He followed his crew out with a limp, which he hadn't noticed until that point. As he drew closer to the car, he could hear Fredo's loud talk. A small group of twenty-somethings who had just left the party listened to his act from the sidewalk.

"That's why I should've had my burner tonight," hollered while Steve cringed.

"He's right." Pik dabbed at the blood trickling from his nose. "We can't be out here strapless with an animal like that Old G thinking he's running shit."

"Stop drawing attention," Steve said. "Let's roll before five-o gets here."

"Fuck that!" Fredo pounded on Steve, unleashing his anger.

Max limped in between the two and slapped Fredo on his jaw. "Get in the fucking car!"

With the added embarrassment, Fredo followed Pik into the back seat. Max sat on the front passenger side and glanced in the rearview mirror. He caught a glimpse of Nancy standing behind the front gate. He thought she'd returned to the house, but her position meant she'd just witnessed more erratic behavior on their part.

He was sick to the pit of his stomach as he watched her reflection lock the front gate and vanish.

CHAPTER 10

May 25, 1996

"Ti Zoot, can you explain what happened tonight?" Margot made her way down to the yard. She had gently tucked Emily in Claudette's bed, not wanting the wake the child in the middle of an all-out fight.

"I don't know what these thugs were doing here, Margot."

"But what the hell happened?" she pressed. "Thugs or not, why did it have to get ugly?"

"You saw everything," he exclaimed. "I was dancing in the area where you were sitting. You tell me!"

"I think I saw a drink fall on you. And the next thing, you're fighting, and other people jumped in. Everything happened so fast, it wasn't making sense."

"Ti Zoot, this was uncalled for," Marie said.

"Are you saying this was my fault?"

"Then who's fault was it?" Nancy interjected. She had stood silently against the deck after making sure Max and his friends drove off. "His drink fell on you. That's not a reason to attack someone."

"It's not about a drink, Nancy," he replied. "They pulled a gun on me and Jimmy a couple of weeks ago."

"They said you pulled a gun on them," she countered.

"Nancy," Jimmy interrupted still catching his breath,"what Ti Zoot is saying is true."

Nancy looked at him like he had just betrayed her. Sensing her doubt, Bigga presented the broken Motorola. "These are a bunch of thugs, just like he said. They cracked this drug dealing phone on my head."

"Look," Marie walked toward the house, "it doesn't matter who started what, but it has to end."

"Ti Zoot, please." Claudette placed her hands on his shoulders. "Don't let anything else happen. Do me that favor."

He shrugged at her request and grabbed a bottle of rhum from the bar. He needed some distance between himself and everyone else. The peaceful promises going back and forth tonight didn't carry weight. He was already thinking several steps ahead and anticipating possible counter moves.

Fiona went over to him."Let's go home." She extended her hand to him, but Claudette grabbed it instead.

"No, no. Stay here tonight," she stressed. "I don't want him out there."

"Relax, Claudette," he said. "I'll be in my bed tonight."

"I said, 'no.'" She turned to Fiona. "I have a room for you both upstairs. You'll find everything you need in the hallway closet."

"Merci." She didn't want to spurn Claudette's concerned gesture.

"Shit," Bigga cried, prying a piece of plastic from the back of his neck. Claudette went over and examined his head for more plastic shrapnel. She and Margot got some gauze and covered the wound. Bigga then limped over to Ti Zoot, Fiona, and Jimmy who had joined them the deck. Bigga and Jimmy did most of the talking, still amazed at what just transpired.

"Unbelievable," Claudette surveyed the yard. "Other than the couple of chairs that were knocked down, you would never believe something took place tonight."

"Good," Margot said. "No broken bones, no broken home."

"Excuse me?" Bigga pointed to the gauze on his head.

Margot went over to Nancy who sat in a corner and stared at the broken strap on her sandal.

"Are you okay, sweetheart? You're so quiet."

"I'm okay." She kissed Margot's arm. "I was just a little shaken. I guess we all were tonight."

"Thank God Emily slept through it," Claudette added.

"That's Emily." Nancy forced a smile. "She can sleep through an earthquake."

"Why don't you go upstairs and sleep?"

"No, Auntie. I need my bed tonight, and they should stay here tonight." She gestured to Ti Zoot, Fiona, Jimmy, and Bigga. "You don't need me taking space."

"Are you sure? Come over by me," Margot offered.

"It's okay. I want to sleep late tomorrow and put this night far from my mind."

"Okay, but Emily is sleeping here tonight," Claudette replied. "No need to wake the child."

"Thank you. I can't take her if I expect to get any sleep. All she does is come into my bed and kick me all night," Nancy explained.

"Just call me when you get home," Claudette said.

"I will." She rose from her seat. "I'll check on Emily and Marie before I leave. Excuse me." She stepped over the gang sitting on the steps and went inside the house.

"That was weird." Bigga shook his head. "It's like she didn't know us."

"She's been strange for a while now." Ti Zoot broke his silence. "Those friends she had here tonight are proof of that."

"She put a beautiful evening together. She's upset," Fiona advocated. "You have to understand."

Upstairs, Nancy made a turn for Claudette's room. She smiled, seeing Emily sound asleep. Nancy placed a couple of pillows alongside the child to prevent her from rolling out of bed. She kissed Emily's cheek and quietly wished her a good night.

Across the hall, she noticed the nightlight on in Marie's old room. She cracked the door open and expected to find Marie awake, but she was sleeping just as hard as Emily. Seeing Marie there summoned the memories that encapsulated their teen years.

The room's window overlooked East 38th and contained the ledge she and Marie used to chat with the friends on the sidewalk below. There were many conversations from with boys from that perch—at least until Claudette chased them off. Nancy loved the ledge because it gave her a great view whenever Ernse stopped by. From the sill, she could study his leisurely gait as he turned the corner during visits.

How could Marie fall asleep so fast after a night like this? She reasoned it was probably a way to bury everything that transpired. Maybe that would do her some good too.

"Sorry," she spoke softly. "Maybe we'll cut that cake another day."

***

"I want you guys to stay off these streets." Ti Zoot instructed Jimmy and Bigga. "I don't want any trouble. Just stay off these streets."

"Will you do the same?"

"Just stay home, Jimmy," he repeated.

Jimmy looked inside the kitchen and noticed Nancy was back downstairs. She took her keys off the rack then stepped onto the deck. "Okay, good night."

"You're leaving?" Jimmy rose from his seat.

"Yes. Guess I'll see you when I pick Emily up."

"I'll walk you to your car."

"Okay." She extended her arm, which he grabbed. "Good night,

Auntie and Ms. Margot. See you in the morning."

When they got to her car, Jimmy opened the driver's door.

"Thank you, Jimmy. You did so much to get me to this day." She fought back tears.

"Hey, come on, it was nothing. Don't be so down. Things could be w—"

"Could be what, Jimmy?"

"Well…" He couldn't think of a combination of right words to console her.

"Good night." She hugged him. "I'll beep you once I'm home."

***

"Remember when we were young, like them?" Margot swung a cup of wine in the direction Nancy and Jimmy had disappeared.

"Don't bother me," Claudette said. "What am I going to do with all this food?"

"A few people took plates home," Margot replied. "I sent the DJ and Barbara home with a couple of plates."

"That's not enough." She stared at Ti Zoot, Fiona, and Bigga on the other end of the yard. "We didn't even get to serve the food." Claudette's words focused on the food, but her mind raced with concern about her troublesome guests.

"But really Claudette," Margot asked, "do you remember when we were Marie and Nancy's age?"

"Dieu, if I could only go back to those days. We had it better then. It was the 1970s!"

"Amen," Margot smiled. "Times have changed, but I can't help but think Marie and Nancy are going through a lot of the same challenges we experienced."

"So much is different," Claudette countered. "Things were simpler and a lot more fun back then."

"Did we realize it at the time?"

"I didn't. It felt complicated because we didn't know how everything would turn out."

"So, things aren't different. Our perception of a time paints a landscape." Margot sipped her drink. "For us, the colors are quite vivid. Why? Because we lived through the 1970s."

Claudette let her words sink in before transitioning to the state of her yard, specifically a patch of green alongside the house she'd dedicated as a garden. Should she plant bell peppers or something she could easily share with friends like squash or greens?

"Claudette, I'm ready for my bed." Ti Zoot rose from the steps.

"Me too," Bigga agreed. "This knot on my head is giving me a headache."

"What a sweet potato," Claudette teased Bigga. "Ti Zoot, you know where everything is. Go on up with your doll. You won't see me in the morning. I'm going to church, I'll leave coffee on the table."

"What about me?" Bigga spread his massive arms. "I sent my ride home. I have to spend the night with you, mamie."

"You?" She looked at Bigga cross. "I hope you don't mean my bed. You're too damn big. I don't have anything to fit you."

The comment and her delivery got laughs out of Fiona, Margot, and Jimmy, who had just returned from escorting Nancy to her car.

"There's a convertible couch in the basement. Go down and open it," she instructed Bigga. "I'll be down in a moment with sheets."

"I'll get him the sheets." Ti Zoot brushed past her with the bottle of rhum. "Bigga can fix his own bed." Fiona and Jimmy followed his lead with Bigga bringing up the rear grumbling that his head was too sore to make his bed.

The yard was empty save for the two women sipping their drinks. The sound of an occasional car driving by was the only noise that could be heard on the now peaceful block.

Margot went to the bar poured another drink. "I'm not going to church in the morning, no need to remain sober." She offered Claudette the bottle. "If you had to do it all over again, what would you change?"

Claudette thought about it but couldn't come up with an answer.

"I know what I would change," Margot smiled. "Do you remember Walter Gerard?"

"Lelio's best friend? Yes."

"We had a thing."

"What?" Claudette stared like she was crazy. "What thing and when?"

"When? Right after I found out Lelio was cheating. I always found Walter attractive, but it never crossed my mind until things fell apart with Lelio. I was really upset about it all, and I called him up for advice, I guess. We met at the Woolworth downtown for lunch and discussed my failing marriage. It turns out he didn't know about Lelio's fling either. I couldn't believe it. I thought men always confided those things. Walter was almost as hurt as I was that Lelio never told him. In hindsight, I was using my dilemma as a way to get close to Walter."

"Why didn't you tell me?" Claudette sounded hurt. "I can't believe you kept this from me all these years."

"I couldn't tell anyone. What would you think of me?"

"The same way I've always thought of you, awona."

"Quiet." Margot giggled, almost spilling her wine. "Anyway, I made a pass at him."

"At the Woolworth's lunch counter?"

"No, at his apartment. The one on Park Place."

"I never knew the man's address." Claudette up her hands in innocence. "I don't need it now, and I can only imagine how you ended up in the man's apartment."

"Long story," Margot laughed. "Anyway, let me finish. So, we made love that afternoon. I went back every day for weeks. It was incredibly addictive sex. I don't know if the revenge part enhanced for me. It was unbelievable how quick Walter wanted to discard his great friendship with Lelio just for me. He was willing to come out with the secret, fully aware Lelio would never be his friend after that."

"So, what happened? Why didn't you end up together?"

"It was shortly after that my father got ill then my mother. The last thing I needed in my life was to explain why I was now with the best man at my wedding—my husband's best friend. Like you mentioned earlier, in the moment, I thought it was too complicated. I couldn't handle it."

"No, that one really was complicated, bitch."

"I regret that. I hurt Walter, but it was too crazy at the time, so I let it go. In the end, he kept his friendship with Lelio." She gulped more wine. "Lelio won twice."

"It's not about winning and losing, Margot."

"It feels that way." Her words were solemn. "I ran into Walter two years ago in Manhattan. He looked exactly the same, as if fourteen years hadn't passed since I saw him last."

"What happened?"

"He was on his way to pick up his wife from work."

"Goodness." Claudette mulled over the story. "I think Walter lied to you. I think he knew Lelio was having an affair, but he either protected his friend or he used that opportunity to gain your trust and have a relationship with you. Haitian men can be devious."

"You think so?"

"Ask him when you see him in another fourteen years."

Forgive me," Margot continued. "I kept this secret from you for so long, but I couldn't bear judgment."

"Give me break," Claudette smiled. "I would've given some to Walter Gerard if I was in the same position."

The two laughed and tapped their cups. A light from one of the bedrooms came on. Fiona appeared in the window and drew the curtains.

"One big regret," Claudette admitted. "I wish my sister was around for those two girls. She would've been their best friends. She was so young at heart."

"I can definitely see her with Marie and Nancy." Margot swirled her wine and savored its aroma. "She'd party with them."

"She would've related to those girls better than I ever could."

"You were raising two girls, you couldn't be their friends," Margot explained.

"Either way, they would've benefitted greatly with Veronique still around."

Margot nodded and polished off her wine.

Claudette rose. "I'm going to bed. Go home, Margot."

"I am. You don't have to kick me out."

"I think I know what I'll do with all this food tomorrow. You can help me. I'll buy some take-out containers and those who attended the party last night can come by to pick up their food. It's the least I can do."

"Good night, Claudette. And that's the last thing you will volunteer me to help you with."

"Walter Gerard." Claudette shook her head in disbelief and entered the house.

Margot remained seated in the yard listening to the ambient sounds.

***

May 26, 1996, early morning

"Why are you at my door?" Nancy was still upset. It was just past 2:00 a.m., and Max stood on the other side of her front door.

"I was just driving around with Steve. I can't sleep."

"And? Again, I don't see why you're at my door at this time of night."

"Can I please talk to you?" He wanted to blame the whole affair on Fredo and Pik. If only they hadn't been invited.

"No." She opened the door a crack so he could see the seriousness in her eyes. "I'm tired. I'm angry. I need to sleep, and I need to think."

"Is Emily here?"

She rolled her eyes, unwilling to answer.

"Nancy, I'm sorry. Can I please come inside and talk?"

"Can you lower your voice? I don't want my neighbors in my business."

"Please." He looked down at his foot. "It's a bad sprain. I can't walk back home. Please."

"Whatever," she said after takinga deep breath then let the door slam in his face.

She sat on the couch with her arms crossed and her legs tucked under her to add modesty to the sinfully short black T-shirt she wore as a nightie. Minutes passed and finally he turned the knob, slowly opening the door.

"Did you mean to leave it open?" he wondered after locating her on the couch.

She didn't reply, choosing to roll her eyes and blowing air through her mouth a couple of times, full of anger and frustration.

"Nancy, I'm sorry. But I really don't know what happened tonight." He stopped under the arch dividing the hallway and the living room.

"Look," she said, unmoving, "I don't think this is going to work out. I don't know much about you. You are shady and tonight exhibited that."

"How? Your friend, or whoever he is, attacked me." He grimaced after accidently shifting his weight on his bad ankle.

"I don't know what you and your thug friends are involved in."

"Nancy, you invited them. Do you remember that? I was against it from the start. The only person I hang with is Steve."

She was quiet. For a second, she thought of going to the fridge and throwing some ice into a Ziplock to ease his injury and pain, but she decided against that. "Look, I'm going to bed. Just pull the door shut when you leave in the morning."

He watched her leave and took a minute before limping over to the couch, took his shirt off, sat in his wife-beater then dozed off within minutes. When he woke, it was still dark, but he limped into the bathroom and showered. The water didn't relieve the ankle as he hoped. Afterwards, he couldn't find a towel, so he dried himself using the wife-beater.

He was about to limp back to the couch but decided she couldn't possibly kick him out of her room with his bad ankle. In the bedroom, Nancy was on the right side of the bed in the fetal position. He wasn't sure if she was asleep, so he gently lay on the left side.

"Tiup." She rose from the bed, grabbed her pillow, and left him for the living room couch.

Max shook his head and stared at the ceiling, eventually succumbing to a deep sleep. It was after 5:00 a.m. when sunlight struck the room. He thought he was dreaming when he found Nancy in the bed again. Between them was the black T-shirt she wore earlier in the evening, lined up as if it was an official marker line he couldn't cross. She was nude but very much asleep. He had no clue when she returned to the room, much less when she removed her top.

Torture, he thought. There's no way she could expect him to just lay there like this was normal. He tried looking straight ahead, but the mirror on her dresser only gave him a better view. He thought the situation through. At worst, she would push him off for trying anything or maybe even force him to leave. He'd be willing to comply if his advances were unwanted.

Eventually, he took a chance and slowly kissed her neck. Her eyes opened slowly, and she reciprocated the gesture with a kiss of her own.

"I'm hating myself in this moment Max, but I'm in desperate need of a hug right now."

Once again, she was the Nancy he had gotten to know the last few months. It was as if the last few hours had taken place at another time and place.

CHAPTER 11

May 27, 1996

Traffic was a monster. Watts Street was a parking lot of cars that stretched to the Holland Tunnel. Max sat in the passenger seat wondering how this Route 1/9 traffic could make the I95 in south Florida look like the autobahn. As usual, Steve drove while Fredo and Pik split the back seat.

From the time they left Brooklyn, no one had said much except for Steve, who cursed at the traffic before them. Even though it was Memorial Day, it was far too early in the day for this much congestion.

Regardless, there wasn't a lot say. In the wee hours Sunday morning, after they left a mess at Marie's party, a host of expletives were tossed around, resulting in Max attacking Fredo. From that point, everyone kept to themselves, not wanting to reignite the powder keg.

Fredo was doubly embarrassed that night. In reality, his shame originated from his very first altercation with Ti Zoot. So far, whether it was on the street, at the car wash or Saturday night at the party, Ti Zoot got the best of him in each encounter. The worst part, this issue was unfortunately under Max's purview.

After the party, Fredo exited the car at a stoplight after Max ordered they refrain from any retaliation against Ti Zoot. Too many witnesses, Max cautioned. He insisted Fredo and Pik swallow their pride for the moment. Fredo couldn't stomach the idea and exited the car in disgust.

Max had Steve pull over, and they all got out of the car to confront Fredo who couldn't calm down. Max lunged at him but aggravated his ankle in the process. From that point, all he could do was punk Fredo with a barrage of words.

"This shit is gonna change soon," Fredo promised Pik after Steve dropped them off. "Very soon."

Max glanced at the clock in the dashboard and checked it against his watch. The plan was to reach Newark twenty minutes early and to ensure there weren't a large number of cops trafficking the area. The news stories about Newark rattled his nerves. He wasn't about to take a foolish chance. Prior to leaving Brooklyn, he told everyone if they had as much as a toothpick in their pocket, toss it out.

Finally, they exited Route 1/9 and made their way through some backroads until they found Brick City. Steve pulled a note from the center console and followed its directions until they arrived.

Everything was just as Stilt described. The green and white house was in the middle of the block. Max studied the place. It needed a paint job and extensive renovation just like other homes on the block. Steve pulled in the driveway per Stilt's instructions. They stopped just before a canary yellow E36 sitting on a jack in the long driveway. They stepped out of the car and stood in the yard. No one spoke as they waited for Stilt.

Eventually, a side door on the garage opened and three guys exited accompanied by a trail of smoke.

"What's good?" The shortest of the three guy greeted them. He was a bit older, early forties with salt and pepper facial hair.

Max nodded. The one who greeted them had to be Stilt, but with his short stature where did he get a name like Stilt? The hood was funny like that. Guys named Tiny were always massive like Suge Knight.

"Stilt?" Max extended his hand.

"The one and only, homie." Stilt clamped his hand around Max's. "These are my couzoids Carey and The Short-Fuse."

"Just Short-Fuse, homies," the tallest one stressed.

"Glad to finally meet you all," Max said. "I roll with these cats right here. Steve, Pik, Fredo."

"One," Stilt tapped fist on his heart. "I'm glad you guys come through Pap."

"Most definitely," Steve agreed. "Pap is a good dude."

"Yeah, sorry about his bid," Carey lamented. "These streets show very little love."

"We out here trying a peaceful hustle but too much hate in Brick City," Stilt explained. "They only understand force. Know-what-I-mean?"

"It's like that on these streets. It's like that in government or wherever you go," Max said.

"Man, we on some deep political shit now," Stilt laughed. "Fuse, get the Henny. We gotta have a drink and smoke with our New York homies."

Short-Fuse returned with a couple of bottles. Carey whipped out the Dutch while they all sat in the yard and talked everything from neighborhood struggles to the upcoming November elections. It was exactly the trust Max was hoping to build before they could agree to an arrangement. Thankfully, Stilt came across as sincere and alleviated some of his concerns about Newark.

"That's a nice ass whip," Fredo said of the car in the driveway. His eyes were fixated on the E36 from the moment they arrived.

"I was trying to change the rims and stripped one of the lug nuts," Carey said.

"I see." Fredo spotted four OZ's leaning against a wall. "A set of those rims would look nice on a gold GS."

"What you pushin' now?" Carey asked.

"Shit. Just a hooptie." Fredo savored his cognac. "That's why I'm grinding out here. I need a GS bad."

"Shit, that's easy out here," Short-Fuse winked. "What color you want?"

"Serious?" Fredo's eyes widened. "What's it gonna take?"

Their conversation got Max's attention. He was always leery about talking in front of outsiders.

"Well, we can make it part of an ongoing transaction," Carey explained.

Max paused his chat with Stilt and Steve. "Fredo, chill." His tone was stern.

"My man." Stilt smiled and shook Max's hand. "Ya'll see this." He looked over to Carey and Short-Fuse. "This man is business all the time. From the moment he walked in here, he kept the social stuff to a minimum and talked business. Now if you two were soldiers like this, I wouldn't need to be arming myself all crazy." He laughed and pulled Max and Steve into the garage to tie a bow on their conversation.

"Looks like ya man just shut this down, homie." Carey crossed his arms.

"No problem dunny-dunn." Fredo played it cool then motioned Pik for his phone."I know the place. I'll be back here. Take down this cell number."

"Oh shit." Short-Fuse ogled the phone after Pik handed it to Fredo. "The whole time I thought you were packing a pistol in that pocket. Real Brooklyn ballers!" The four laughed it off.

"I had one too," Fredo entered Short-Fuse's number, "but I had to bust it over some fool's head Saturday night."

"It's crazy out in Brooklyn, huh?" Short-Fuse queried.

Minutes later Steve, Max and Stilt made their way out of the garage. Stilt, satisfied with the deal, offered everyone another round before declaring a toast. "To business and street hustlers all over the world!"

"Sounds good," Carey said."I hope I can walk these bricks in peace again."

"We're good," Stilt reassured his cousins. "Pap left us in good hands."

"Great," Short-Fuse raised his cup. "I just love the burst from a Tec-9."

The others laughed and raised their cups in agreement.

The detente lasted another round, along with small talk concerning details, after which Max informed his hosts they were leaving.

"Hey we got a little Memorial Day barbeque at some homies later," Stilt announced. "Why don't y'all just stay and enjoy the cook-out?"

"We're good." Max smiled and shook Stilt's hand.

"See," Stilt again turned to his cousins, "business!"

"It sure is a bitch getting here," Max commented on the way out.

"Don't tell me you took the Holland Tunnel?" Carey said.

"Yeah," Max admitted. "That's the most direct route."

"Nah," Stilt laughed. "Never take Holland. That shit takes forever, homie. You're coming from Brooklyn? You should back-door through the Verrazano. Trust me."

Steve took the note from the center console and flipped it over to write the alternate route to Brick City.

***

"Just checking up on you." Jimmy spoke into the receiver. "You can call me back."

Even though it was a holiday, he had tried Nancy at her job first since she told him she would be there for a half-day to complete some assignments. He then called her at home a couple times, but she never answered.

A minute later, his phone rang. It was Nancy.

"Hey, I tried calling you at work few times," he explained.

"I was going in midday then decided to stay in bed. I needed a day like that."

"Oh, sorry to interrupt then."

"Don't be silly," she countered. "I don't mind your calls."

"I was hoping to catch you yesterday morning when you picked up Emily from your aunt's place, but I guess you came much later," he explained.

"Yeah, I didn't pick her up until after three. By that time, everyone had left—even Marie."

"Okay." He didn't want to question her motives but decided she probably didn't want to face anyone and had planned it that way.

"It was strange, Nancy, but I felt I was reliving some of the post-party stories you shared about your aunt's from back in the day."

"Really?" her enthusiasm grew. "We're you guys up until early morning?"

"Pretty much."

"And did my aunt wake you all a half hour later for coffee and bread?"

"Exactly," he laughed. "But she didn't have Haitian bread on hand, so we made the best we could with sliced bread."

"The morning ritual was my favorite party of partying. I don't know if that makes sense."

"It does now," he said. "At your aunt's house, it makes all the sense in the world."

"I'm glad you got a taste of it."

"Me too."

***

"This way is faster." Steve flew down Route 440.

"Yeah, we'll definitely use this instead," Max agreed. "Fuck it. We'll just pay the higher toll."

"We can take this to go down south too," Pik added.

"Yeah, I guess we can," Max said. "Pik, lend me your cellular."

Pik had been gazing at the window and was caught off-guard by the request. "My cellular?"

"Yeah, your cellular phone," Max reiterated. "I can't ask Fredo for his anymore."

Pik struggled to pull the blocky device from his carpenter jeans. He looked at Fredo before handing it over, but his roomie quickly turned away, preferring to look out of his window.

Max keyed into the device and went through the menu while he addressed Fredo. "I'm the only source of communication when it comes to business." He deleted Short-Fuse's contact info. "We can't have side business going on. That's how shit breaks down." He flung the phone into Fredo's lap. He handed the device back to Pik and returned to his window.

When Pik looked up, he noticed Steve glaring at him in the rearview mirror. With the phone safely tucked away, Pik turned his gaze to the window as well.

Words were scarce the rest of the way.

"Be ready for Thursday." Max gave Fredo and Pik a stern warning as they stepped out of the car in front of their building.

"Yup," Fredo answered dryly.

"What are you thinking?" Steve pulled away from the curb.

"About Stilt?"

"Well, yeah. But also with those two knuckleheads."

"All good with Stilt. I see money out there. Maybe even an opening into Camden like Stilt mentioned in the garage," Max smiled. "And yeah, knucklehead is definitely a perfect description for those two."

"I know Pap ran with Fredo's brother back in the day, but he really made a bad call on that one."

Max nodded in agreement. A trio of lines formed on his forehead. Dealing with Fredo on a daily was more frustrating than he let on. "I don't know man. They're not the street soldiers they claim to be. You see the way they handle themselves? Everything about them is suspect."

"You think so?"

"Hell yeah," Max responded. "If they knew what they were doing, that Old G problem wouldn't have landed on my lap. Saturday night would have never happened."

Steve had to agree. "I still don't understand how both Fredo and Pik let that Old G beat the crap out of them."

"Were they packing that day?"

Steve laughed at the question but quickly realized Max was serious. "I don't know, but at this point, I wouldn't be surprised to find out they were packing and somehow got their asses handed to them."

"This whole setup is crazy." Max massaged his forehead. He didn't notice Steve had already reached his drop-off.

"Where you able to square things with Nancy?"

Max smiled, "Yeah I took care of that. We're good."

But the smile disappeared as soon as he turned away. He always kept a cool front even with Steve, so he left out the details of how things ended Sunday after the early morning tryst with Nancy.

They both slept until midday. He lost count how many catnaps he had, only opening his eyes occasionally making sure Nancy was still in his arms.

Once up, she made her way to the shower. Max got his bearings and used the time to brew some coffee and enjoy a cup. Once she finished, she grabbed some lotion and walked into the living room.

"Oh hi , Max." Her voice was breezy and she immediately returned to the bedroom.

He limped along on the still swollen ankle and stuck his head inside the room. "Coffee?" he asked holding up a mug.

"No thanks. Getting dressed. Please give me a moment."

He had just finished his second cup when she returned dressed in a bright pink romper. He moved over so she could join him on the couch, but she ignored him and chose the love seat instead.

"I'm really sorry about what happened," he spoke as gently as possible, "but I'm glad we're putting that past us."

"Past us? What makes you think it's past us?"

His eyes narrowed. "I mean last night, what was last night?"

She folded her hands and stared back at him.

"Wait, are you saying...you used me?"

Again, she was quiet.

"I can't believe this."

"Look, I think we should put this friendship or whatever on pause. I don't know you well enough."

"Friendship or whatever?" He rubbed his forehead. "I'm getting your message loud and clear."

He placed his mug in the sink, grabbed his shirt, and walked to the front door. "Are you coming to lock this door?"

"That's fine. Just shut it. I'll lock it."

"You're like night and day." His heart sank. "I swear."

"I'll call you if I need you, Max."

He shut the door with a little more force than necessary. Her words cut deep.

There was no way he could relay that version of the story to Steve.

CHAPTER 12

May 28, 1996

"Tell Fredo what you told me earlier," Pik said.

Pik had just walked on the block with Tyrique. He found Fredo in front of the bodega, just down the block from their apartment, jawing with a group of young men. Pik walked up and introduced them to Tyrique, just fourteen and all limbs. Fredo and his audience mostly ignored Pik and Tyrique, until Pik forced them to listen to the boy's message.

"Go ahead, tell Fredo what you told me earlier."

Tyrique refrained from looking at anyone in the eye, finding comfort staring at the sidewalk beneath him.

"Go ahead, little man," Fredo prompted him. "Spit it out."

"I told Pik…I know where Ti Zoot lives," Tyrique mumbled.

"And who the fuck is that?" Fredo shrugged his shoulders.

Tyrique looked at Pik every bit as confused as Fredo was.

"Wait, I know that guy," said Daze, a lanky furrow-browed fellow. "He used to be some kind of a name back in the day."

"Yeah, that's the Old G! Tyrique knows that Old G." Pik connected all for Fredo.

"Oh." Fredo's tiny eyes grew. "That's valuable info right there, little man." He patted the boy's shoulder. "So, where he stay at?"

Again, Tyrique looked at Pik as if he needed permission to speak. "Four hundred east seventeenth, down the block from my building."

Pik wrapped his arm around Tyrique's shoulder, nudging for more, "And tell us what he do every morning?"

"He walks to the bodega on Cortelyou and 17th and buys coffee and sometimes lottery every morning around eight thirty," the boy said.

Pik grinned as if he'd made the discovery himself.

"Little homie, you all right." Fredo shook his hand. "No need mention this to anyone. Homeboy is just an old friend we're trying to connect with."

"Okay." Tyrique nodded even though anybody who worked the streets knew enough to doubt Fredo's motive.

"All right, little homie, you good with me." Fredo turned and addressed anyone in the neighborhood within an earshot. "Any problem you got on the block, holla at me. This is almost too easy."

Tyrique was slow to walk off. He looked back, hoping to get Pik's who was in the middle of a word with Fredo.

"Pik," Tyrique cleared his throat. "Pik, can I talk to you?"

"What up 'Rique?"

"Well, you had promised...promised me something."

"Oh, shit, yo," Pik said,."Fredo, I promised little man here some sneaks."

"So," Fredo shrugged, "pay up or take homie shopping."

Pik shot Fredo a funny look and dug into his pocket, pulling out two twenty-dollar bills. He looked at Tyrique and the kid's beat up kicks. "Hold up."

Pik walked over to Fredo. "I promised little man a pair of Jordans. I only got forty. Give me sixty, and we can hook little man up."

"We?" Fredo stepped back. "Homie is your little man. Your connect, not mine. Besides, for a skinny little dude, he got some big ass feet. I can't pay for that shit," Fredo said to the amusement of his associates.

"Man pay up!" Pik barked at him. "Don't clown him. He came through."

Fredo was still laughing, but relented, feeling empathy for the kid. "Come here, my dude."

Tyrique drew closer as Fredo went into his pocket and pulled out a wad, loosening another forty dollars. "My dude, here's forty. Ask your mother for twenty and get yourself a fresh pair of Jordans, aight?"

"T-thanks." Tyrique nervously placed the money in his pocket and disappeared from the block.

Fredo moved the group away from the bodega closer to the corner. He was happy with the newfound information. But there was one thing blocking him—Max.

He hated the way Max dictated things and treated him like some minion. In fact, he was feeling the same animosity for Max as he felt for the Old G, to him they were one and the same.

***

"Nancy, do you think you can get those documents from LexisNexis now? I mean, I sent you a request this morning. It's almost two o'clock."

"Sorry, Andrew. I had a lot of work to catch up on. We had the day off yesterday, remember?"

"And?" He looked at his watch. "Your work productivity shouldn't be my problem."

"Fine. I'll get it to you soon." She rolled her eyes and logged onto the service to find precedent for one of his cases.

The desk phone rang. It was Marie.

"Hey, love. Having a shitty day? Can you come spend the night by me?"

Marie smiled at the rapid-fire request. "Well, hello, couz."

"Hi. We never spoke after Saturday. I need you. Girl's night?"

"Sounds good," Marie said. "In fact, that should be mandatory on

Tuesdays, the day with the least personality."

"Great," Nancy chuckled at her observation. "I'll grab some food."

"Something spicy," Marie insisted.

"Okay. Let me finish up the mess at this lousy job. See you later!"

***

Fredo, Pik, and their crew had moved into the apartment when Eddie knocked at the door.

"Where you been? I paged you a hundred times," Fredo screamed from the living room.

"I was sleeping, I barely got any sleep last night." Eddie moved lethargically through the hallway.

"E-Flow, you're fucking up. We need to handle major things. Are you in this shit or not?"

Eddie would've gladly backed-off. He wasn't ready for the vengeance Fredo insisted upon reaping. But in front of the crew, he had to maintain composure and keep his cred intact. He was well aware Fredo played against his insecurities.

"I'm in." Eddie flopped into a chair.

"Aight. Here's what he has to do." Fredo grabbed a bottle of malt liquor.

"This is big. We're taking this for ourselves. I got heat out there, and no one is doing anything about it. There's money out there I can't— we can't get our hands on," he hesitated. "So, I need everyone on the same page. Can I count on that?"

"Fredo, we can't be on the same page if you don't tell us the 4-1-1," Hustla D said from the window ledge.

"You're talking in riddles," Pik added. "Let everyone know. What's in this room stays here whether we all agree or not."

"Okay." Fredo made eye contact with everyone in the room. "We are getting rid of Old G ASAP."

"That's it?" Daze asked. "Old G's future being short and bleak was always a given."

"We're also taking Max down," Fredo added. Everyone tensed, surprised except for Pik who gauged everyone's temperature in the room.

"Out the crew?" Eddie asked for clarity.

"I said down! Just like Old G," Fredo restated.

"Wow." Daze's eyes widened. "That's a big order right there. Why Max though?"

"You really gonna ask that? You really think we're eating right? Max can't be the only one caking off!"

"Okay, I can get with what you're saying," Hustla D conceded. "But I don't know. This is disrupting a lot. And Pap—"

"Man, Pap is in prison! I can spin this shit," Fredo screamed. "But I need you gunners. Are you in?"

"All right we in," the collective agreed.

"What about Steve?" Eddie asked.

"Fuck Steve," Fredo said. "Him and Max are the same as far as I'm concerned."

"Nah, I'm cool with Steve," Eddie said. "Knew him forever. Nah."

"Listen, Steve won't do anything once the situation is resolved," Pik reasoned. "If he's down, he's down. If he ain't, I got no beef with him."

"Nah, Steve don't want none of this," Daze said. "He won't come at us like that."

"I don't know," Fredo said. "But we can definitely scope his reaction and then...whatever man."

***

"I'm pretty sure they'll hire you." Jimmy exited the subway with Ti Zoot. "I'm cool with Linette from Human Resources."

"We'll see," Ti Zoot said. He didn't take stock in things until they happened. Though he wouldn't admit it, he was confident about the interviews Jimmy had arranged for him. He went through three rounds. First the director, an assistant manager, and finally Linette from HR. In each, they all but embraced him. Jimmy had gone all out for him and encouraged him to apply at the records department in the same company which he worked in payroll.

"I'm still not understanding this 401K thing HR talked about."

"Don't worry," Jimmy laughed. "They hold a portion of your salary for retirement."

"If I live that long," he replied.

They were at an intersection crossing when Jimmy looked up and saw Max and Steve in their car waiting for a red light to change. Almost simultaneously, Ti Zoot looked in the same direction, locking eyes with driver and passenger. Max raised his right-hand gesturing for Jimmy and Ti Zoot to cross. The two continued and crossed the intersection, but Ti Zoot's eyes never left Max and Steve's.

Neither side blinked.

For Jimmy, the eight seconds felt like hours. Every step was like a slow sequence from a dream. Saturday night was fresh in his mind. Having a gun flashed in his face in front of a car wash on a leisure Saturday was equally indelible. Compelled to look back, he kept his nerves intact long enough for the car to clear the intersection. Ti Zoot didn't utter a word. They were half-way down the block when Jimmy spoke.

"That was crazy. I can't believe we ran into those guys."

"Believe it," Ti Zoot said nonchalantly. "Believe it."

Down the block, Steve pulled over to Lulu's Barbershop when he spoke. "What do you think?"

"Think about what?"

"The Old G we just ran into."

"I don't think much," Max said. "Nah, you know what, I think Old

G is lucky to be walking around breathing."

"It's not like I was there, but I get the feeling this beef was one-sided and caused by Fredo and Pik."

"I'm not doubting that for a second, especially with Fredo." Max smacked his hands together. "In fact, from the little I've seen, that Old G carries himself with a certain decorum. He might even be respectable, but I can't deal with this motherfucker Fredo."

***

"Emilyyy…Auntie Marie brought us Cinnabon!"

Emily ran into the foyer after the announcement. "Is that the surprise?" She planted a pair of kisses on Marie's cheeks.

"Well, the surprise was just your godmother coming to spend the night, but I had no idea she was bringing Cinnabon!"

"What do you mean 'just'?" Marie pinched Nancy's side. "What's a girl's night without Cinnabon?"

"Easy for you to say," Nancy said and placed the pastry box on the kitchen counter. "You can afford to eat this stuff. You work out."

"Please, Nance." Marie kicked off her shoes and went straight for the Chardonnay in the fridge. "You weigh the same as you did in high school."

"Well, it's catching up to me," she admitted.

"You should spend the night with us more, Auntie Marie," Emily pined.

"Aww, but I have my own apartment. Who will watch my place?"

"Maybe we can come over and watch it with you."

"You're too adorable, but no! When your mommy and I get together, we have too much wine, and we both have to go to work in the morning."

"What's in the oven?" Marie wondered. "I thought you were ordering something."

"That's just some jerk chicken I picked up and keeping warm in the oven."

"Well, I can't say they complement one another—Chardonnay, jerk chicken, and Cinnabon—but what the heck, it's our night!"

The phone rang. Nancy looked over and read Claudette's name on the caller ID. "It's Claudette! Pick it up for me," she asked.

Marie hesitated, but picked it up. Any other day, she would've told Nancy 'hell no.' But something had changed since Sunday morning.

"Hello."

"Marie?" Claudette asked. "I just dialed the wrong number. I was calling Nancy."

"No, it's not the wrong number. I'm at Nancy's apartment."

"Okay. How are you today?"

"I'm fine. We're just here talking." Marie sat down.

"Where's Nancy?"

"She's busy at the moment."

"I'm not busy," Nancy whispered, giving Marie a funny look. She hadn't seen or heard tension free conversation between the two since Marie was a teenager. This little phone exchange was actually friendly.

"I'm just spending the night," Marie continued.

"Tell Nancy her jury duty requests keep coming here. She has another one."

"Okay. I'll tell her. Bye, Mom."

Nancy raced over to Marie. "Bye, Mom? What was that all about?"

"I said bye. What's the big deal?" Marie sipped her drink.

"I can't remember the last time you referred to her as Mom."

"Mamie, mom…what's the difference?"

"There's a difference," Nancy countered.

"Mommy, what movie are we watching tonight?" Emily wondered.

"Anything you choose, Em. But why don't you go put your PJs on? We'll eat and then have some Cinnabon. I'll bribe your Auntie Marie to comb your hair."

"Not happening tonight," Marie said frankly. "I'll be too drunk."

"Okay, mommy," Emily said. "Can I stay up past my bedtime?"

"Only a half-hour, you still have school tomorrow."

***

"Kasav?" Ti Zoot offered Fiona. "Mamba?"

She had tried the snack once and found Haitian peanut-better too spicy for her tastes. But seeing him in his underwear at the kitchen table reeled her in.

As soon as he got home, he removed his suit and immediately went for the comfort food he loved since childhood. The big jar was almost done. It was one of the few items he brought back from Haiti during one of his last two trips. He couldn't recall if he brought it the first trip, which would have been the week Ernse was killed, or his second three weeks later for his mother's burial. Details from that time period became increasingly hard for him to put into context.

He scraped the bottom of the jar with a knife—and came up with enough to coat the kasav he offered her. She had just come home herself, having had another interesting day at Patricia Field.

"I'll need water for this spicy peanut-butter." She filled a glass with tap water.

"Did you have a good day?"

She looked at him and placed the back of her hand on his forehead checking for signs of fever. "You feel normal, but your behavior is far from normal."

"Why?" he asked, half laughing.

"You have never asked how my day was." She sat and bit into the kasav.

"Maybe I wasn't ready to listen before this point."

She reached over and touched his hand. "Who are you? Vous êtes un imposteur."

"An imposter wouldn't offer you kasav and mamba."

She took another bite and watched him scrape the jar for more spread. "How did the interview go?"

"Good, I think. But I'm tired of interviews and filling out forms."

"Patience."

"Jimmy is confident they'll hire me."

"Good." She bit the kasav. The more she ate, the more palatable the combination seemed with the peanut-butter.

"But I'm still worried," she continued.

"About Saturday night?"

"Yes." Her face revealed some uncertainty.

"No need to worry," he rose and tossed the empty jar in the garbage. "I just ran into that guy from the party—Nancy's friend."

"Today?" She looked at him surprised.

"After my interview, we locked eyes on my way here."

"What happened?"

"Nothing," he replied. "And nothing will happen."

"I wish I could believe you, but as stubborn as you are…I can't."

"Trust me," he said. "Nothing is going to happen. When we looked at each other, I knew it. I don't like him, but I'm not seeing him instigating anything either. He's caught in the middle of something."

"Okay, so what does this all mean?"

"It means, I'm removing myself from street politics." He leaned back on the chair. "I've been thinking about something for the last six months."

He took her arm and pulled her to his side of the table.

"What are you thinking?" She eased herself onto his lap. "And why am I afraid of what you'll say?"

He laughed and gently rubbed her forearm. "Remember my aunt and cousin living up in Haverstraw?"

"Yes, Cathline and her son Reginald, I think."

"Yes. They've been telling me to move up there for years now. I've never seriously considered it, not for a second. But lately, it's been on my mind, and it feels like a good move. I mean, I'm almost forty."

"You would leave Brooklyn? I didn't think that was possible."

"Me too. But maybe I need change—maybe we need change," he said.

"Dieu. The last few days you've had more surprises than the entire time we've been together."

"I mean it. I'm serious."

"It's scary when you're this open, but I love it," she admitted. "But what about this job? You just interviewed for it."

"I can take the Metro-North. We both can."

She placed a kiss on his forehead, and the two sat happy to share space.

***

"She's asleep," Nancy said, having tucked Emily in. "Too much excitement for her on a Tuesday night."

Marie was lying on the throw rug ignoring the TV just above her. "Is there any Cinnabon left?"

"Yeah, it's on the counter." Nancy planted herself on the bed.

"Okay. Last round. More wine and Cinnabon?" Marie offered as she started for the kitchen.

"Just a wine refill, please."

Marie poured the remaining bottle and grabbed the pastry. "Okay real talk." She returned to the living room. "What is going on? Saturday night was crazy."

"Wish I knew." Nancy sat lotus-style on the bed. "I wish I could explain. Everything took me by surprise, and I'm sorry that drama ruined your night."

"It didn't ruin anything." She placed her roll back in the box.

"Maybe it's because I'm older now and see how fragile things are, but I was genuinely scared someone would get shot or worse killed."

"Me too," Nancy admitted. "It scared me on another level. I realized how little I knew about Max. I don't who he really is, yet I've shared myself with him." She tucked her head into her hands.

"It's okay." Marie leaned in and stroked her cousin's hair. "It happens. Don't be so hard on yourself."

"I feel so naïve. The very things that attracted me to him made Saturday inevitable."

"Look, I won't let you blame yourself. You don't deserve it, but if I may pry, I'd like to know what's going to happen next."

"Nothing," Nancy quipped. "I'm done with Max."

"What about this thing with Ti Zoot?"

Nancy paused and thought about the question along with everything else. "I asked him, and it's all that street bullshit that had me sick years ago when Ernse put me through it. I'm not going down that path again, so I ended things with him."

"Just like that? He really likes you Nance."

"Why are you so sure?"

"Come on, Nancy. Be serious. He's crazy for you."

"I don't know the guy," she argued "I know it's only been a few months, but he's too mysterious. Saturday is just a sign I'll pay attention to, for once."

"I can't fault your logic, not if you don't know what he's involved in, but he's so damn fine," Marie lamented.

Nancy felt the same but kept it to herself. She didn't want to convey her anxiety. She was trying to find the will to put things behind her, but the short time they spent together proved difficult to wipe from her mind. That was also true the moment they met earlier in the year at a cocktail bar and lounge thanks to her friend Barbara pestering for a social hang out. "I'm glad you came," Barbara welcomed her upon arrival. "Even if it's only for an hour."

"This is very nice." Nancy said impressed by the swanky lounge's Mediterranean theme. It was across the street from Bryant Park, and she liked the way it was hidden from street view. You had to go down a flight of steps to enter the quaint hideaway. "But don't try to keep me here. You know my aunt."

"Claudette can wait. It's been forever since you hung out."

Barbara tried at least once a month to get Nancy out for a night. When that continually failed, she bumped up the calls and requests to a weekly basis. This time she proposed a cool lounge on 40th between Fifth and Sixth, and Nancy finally agreed to meet Barbara after work. A quick call to Claudette about a work emergency got her a babysitter for a few hours.

"Honestly, I feel like a fish out of water." Nancy sat down at the table. "I haven't been out in so long, and anytime I went out before, I always had my partner by my side."

"Well, you need to change that," Barbara advised. "I want you out of your shell and living like the young woman you are."

The words warmed Nancy. It was good to know someone was in her corner and willing to invite her out. It was still early, but the lounge had a decent crowd inside.

"What are you drinking?" Barbara scanned the menu.

"Wait, let me run to the ladies' room. I didn't bother using it at work because I didn't want to get roped into a conversation."

"That way," Barbara pointed and returned to the drink menu.

The bathroom was located on the far end of the lounge. Nancy turned a corner and saw what looked like two closets with bathroom signs but neither indicated sex. She turned the knob on the closest door, but it was locked.

"Busy," said a voice on the other side.

She moved on to the next one, which was unlocked, so she opened it wide. "Oh, God," she screamed. A man was inside using the toilet, his member fully exposed as he moved to place it back in his pants. Their eyes locked briefly and Nancy slammed the door shut.

"Occupied," the man yelled.

"Well, you should've locked the damn thing." Nancy kicked the door and raced back to Barbara.

"Barbie, some pervert was in the bathroom and exposed himself."

"What?" Barbara rose from her seat. "Let me get the manager."

"No, no. I don't mean on purpose." Nancy took a breath. "He didn't lock the door. Maybe he forgot. I don't know. I think I'll just wait until I get home."

"Girl, please. I'll escort you," Barbra added.

"No, you don't have to. Let's just sit. I'll go in five minutes. I don't want to run into that guy again."

"Or his ugly thing," Barbara quipped.

"Well, I didn't say it was ugly," Nancy corrected.

The two laughed it off.

"Guess I'll have to go stand at the bar for drinks," Barbara said. She had tried getting a waiter's attention a couple of times, but he never looked in her direction. Luckily, another waiter, who had been working tables closer to the bar, came to their table with a pair cocktails.

"We didn't order these." Barbara stared at the glasses confused.

"They're from that guy sitting over there." The waiter pointed to a man sitting at the end of the bar with a drink in hand.

"Oh, how nice, really nice." Barbara smiled at the man who returned the gesture with a friendly wave.

"Barbie! Don't drink that." Nancy slapped Barbara's hand before she could reach the cocktail.

"What? Why not?"

"That's the guyfrom the bathroom!"

"Him?"

"Yes, him!"

"But he's fine," Barbara smiled.

"Barbara!"

"I'm serious," she said."It's not like he's Flava Flav. Far from that."

The man stood up, with drink in hand, and made his way to the women.

"Oh, my God. This is so embarrassing."

"Embarrassing?" Lost on the man's looks, Barbara had forgot the bathroom story Nancy had just relayed.

"His penis was inches away from me only minutes ago." Nancy slid down her seat as if the man wouldn't see her.

"Hello." The man leaned on the corner of their booth.

"Hi...and thank you." Barbara held up her drink.

"I'm Max," He smiled and looked at Nancy, who avoided eye contact.

"Hi, Max. I'm Barbara. This is my dear friend Nancy."

"Nice to meet you, Barbara. I, uh, accidentally met your friend in the bathroom."

"I wasn't in the bathroom." Nancy corrected him.

"Well, you pulled the door open on me."

She looked up, "You didn't lock it."

"Well, the normal way is to knock first and check if someone is inside."

"Look, why don't you have a seat Mr. Max?" Barbara offered.

Nancy rolled her eyes.

"Are you sure?"

"Yes, of course. Are you here with friends?"

"No. Alone. Someone cancelled last minute, so I decided to have one drink but ended up on my fourth." He slid into the booth.

"Well," Barbara clinked her glass with his, "very kind gesture on your part but next time lock the door as Nancy suggested."

"Okay. That's fair." He glanced at Nancy. "Aren't you going to drink?"

Nancy stared at the libation like it was something dirty."I don't know…did you even wash your hands afterward?"

"Nancy," Barbara cried, "he's apologizing."

"No, I didn't wash my hands." Max inched closer to Nancy. "But go ahead and have that drink, I didn't mix it myself."

"I think I'm enjoying this," Barbara mused. "Come on, Nancy. Cheers."

She reluctantly took a sip of the cocktail, sneaking glances at Max.

"Are you okay?" Marie asked.

"I'm fine. Something came to mind." Nancy shook her head to clear the memories. "I know he has feelings for me, but I can't open myself up to heartbreak. It's over."

***

It was just before 10:00 p.m. Fredo, Pik, Hustla D , and Daze had just returned from scouting Ti Zoot's building. They had done so to check out the proximity of the lobby to the sidewalk and to uncover which corner of the block was closest to the building. Daze had a good understanding of the logistics and guided the other three through the hazards. Fredo ultimately liked what he saw, and his confidence in the plan grew.

Per Fredo's request, the crew remained in the living room, so he could illustrate their next set of moves based on what they'd observed. He reveled in the way they sat around him and how his words now meant something. He felt like a general directing his lieutenants and couldn't help but equate himself to Nino Brown from *New Jack City*.

"Okay. This is how it's going down. We have a transaction in Newark in two days, but before that, we're going to take care of Max and Old G simultaneously. Hustla D and Daze, you two head over to Old G's place early morning. Daze will wait in front of the lobby's entrance, and Hustla D will double-park in front of the building. Leave the car running, butHustla , make sure you stay outside of the car. Don't sit in the car waiting! I don't want Old G seeing any movement from either of you until it's too late."

"Got that." Hustla D nodded.

"Daze, understand?"

"Easy."

"Good. As soon as Old G walks out that lobby, Daze give him space, wait a couple of feet, but follow him out of the courtyard. Make sure you're both ready to pop him. He'll be trapped. Once you're done, take off normal. No need to speed off that might draw attention. It's morning and not too many people out anyway. Drive to the Belt and meet us at the end of the 86th Street exit."

"Bay Ridge?" Hustla D was unclear.

"Yeah, but more on that later." Fredo held up his hand to signal patience.

Pik sat on the far end of the room impressed. Fredo never struck him as the strategic type until this moment. On top of that, he had received the info from Tyrique just a couple of hours ago. Maybe transitioning from Max would be easier than he imagined.

"I have a plan to corner Max. I'm going to get him to leave around the same time Hustla D and Daze are handling Old G."

"This is some Michael Corleone type shit," Daze remarked.

"This is my shit." Fredo snapped, unfamiliar with the reference.

"Wait, what makes you think Max will take this bait, whatever it is?" Eddie asked.

"Okay," Fredo smiled. "I'm going to tell Max we were robbed of our Newark inventory. Once he hears that, ain't no way he'll wait around for anything. He's gonna come over here and confront me with a thousand questions."

"That may work," Pik said.

"That will work," Fredo corrected. "So Pik and I will bring Max to the car where E-Flow will be waiting around the corner."

"Why around the corner?" Hustla D was confused.

"I don't want Max suspecting anything once he's on the block. E-Flow, I'll beep you when it's time to come around. Hustla D and Daze, we'll be meeting you at the 86th Street exit. Take the Verrazano across. At that point, we'll escort Max to some backroads off the I-278 leading to Newark. When we drove there the other day, I saw plenty of places we can drop a body."

"I gotta give it to you." Daze gave Fredo a pound. "But what do we do after that. aren't we meeting those Newark dudes at like 3:00 p.m.?"

"We celebrate," Fredo laughed. "We find a diner or hopefully a strip joint open during the day so we can kill time."

"Brilliant," Pik said. "But one problem: How are we going to explain to Stilt that Max is no longer involved?"

"Forget that. You think Stilt is gonna give a shit when I got two fenders stacked with tecs? What's he going to say, 'Nah. I'm only dealing with Max. Take those back.'"

"True," Hustla D nodded.

"Besides, we already have Stilt and his homies in pocket." Fredo beamed with confidence.

"Liquor store run," Pik announced. The others started shuffling a deck of cards on the table.

"I'll make that trip too," Hustla D offered.

"Hold on, hold." Fredo placed his cards down. "I just thought of another brilliant part in this plan."

Eddie, mostly quiet throughout due to his reservations, spoke up. "What else could there be?"

Fredo looked around making sure he had everyone's attention. "Pik, I'm going to need you to put me in contact with that Nancy chick. I think she's going to need some consolation."

"Kill that," Pik said. "She's not going for that."

"I'm serious," Fredo laughed. "And after I console her. I'll just casually mention a street rumor that it was Old G who clipped Max's wings."

***

"I've been in the same environment too long, letting my fears dictate my life," Ti Zoot explained.

They were in bed and Fiona sat next to him thumbing through *WWD Magazine.*

"Does that mean you won't have nightmares anymore?"

He thought long and hard before responding. "I don't know. Possibly. There are things I'll have to confront. If I don't, I'll go crazy."

"Were you ever sane?" She smiled and tossed the magazine on the floor. "I like what I'm hearing. I don't care how corrupt we are, I think we can always overcome and redeem ourselves."

He reached over and hugged her. "This is like the last time I went to confession."

She found comfort in the statement, placed an ear against his chest and listened to his heartbeat.

CHAPTER 13

May 30, 1996, 7:55 a.m.

Fredo made three early calls all at different times. During each, he simply spoke the word 'now' into the receiver to which Daze, Hustla D , and Eddie set the plans outlined into play. The crew had spent most of the prior day going over the plans, poking at possible loose steps. Each time, Fredo, Pik and occasionally Daze provided an answer.

He looked over in the living room and saw Pik loading a clip. He checked the clock and made a final call. "Max, we got robbed!"

"What? Robbed what?" Max was still groggy and very much in his bed. "What the hell are you talking about?"

"The tecs. I went downstairs, checked the car and both fenders were damaged. The wheel wells were hanging off the front tires," Fredo frantically explained.

"How the fuck is that possible?" Max sat on the edge of the bed. "I don't see how. We installed them inside a garage. No one could've known that."

"Max, I don't know, but what are we gonna do, man?"

"Stay right there. I'm coming over right now," he stated.

"Great." Fredo hung up and smiled. "Come on over, Max." He

turned to Pik, who sat patiently with the gun on his lap. "You can go now," he instructed. "You know what to do."

***

May 30, 1996, 7:56 a.m.

Back in his apartment, Max hurried to the bathroom and got dressed. He grabbed his semi-auto, placed it in the inside pocket of his all-white tracksuit, and stuffed his phone in one of the outer pockets. He unbolted the door and opened it but then shut it. He walked down the hallway and went straight to the back of the closet where he stored a vest. He unhooked it, removed his top, and strapped on the Kevlar so that it would fit snuggly under his tracksuit.

This time, before exiting, he pulled the phone out and dialed. "Steve, pick up," he demanded.

No answer.

He jerked the door open and raced down a flight of stairs. Inside the car, he kept redialing Steve's number to no avail.

Something felt wrong, and he needed Steve—not to help deal with Fredo and Pik— he could easily do that by himself. He really wanted Steve's take on what Fredo related concerning the Newark merchandise. How could the tecs get ripped from the car's fenders? If the whole car was stolen, that would've made sense. Only their tight circle was aware of their transportation methods. Was Fredo running his mouth and got robbed as a result? Or was this a set-up?

He could never fully trust Fredo. His tolerance was in part to keep his word and to keep Pap calm. He tossed the phone on the passenger seat and dialed three, four, three on his pager, hoping Steve still used his and would respond. He had to know if Fredo was lying. From that point, he would know how to react.

***

May 30, 1996, 8:39 a.m.

"Morning." Fiona applied her makeup in front of the medicine cabinet.

"Morning," T-Zoot grumbled. He flipped the toilet seat and urinated for what felt like minutes. "Coffee run?"

"I'm late, but if you hurry, we can go."

He squeezed next to her and brushed his teeth but decided against getting fully dressed, choosing to visit the bodega in his pajamas. He did that sometimes for their morning stroll. He got the idea when he saw a front-page article on the *New York Post* about a mob boss walking the streets in his bathrobe, and it supported the image most people had that he was a little loose in the head.

Just outside of Ti Zoot's place, Daze stood in front of the lobby door like Fredo had instructed. He had a clear view of Hustla D, who sat in the idling car, double-parked in front of the building entrance. Half-dozen people had exited the structure. Each time, Daze was careful to look out the lobby window. If he tilted Yankees cap down, Hustla D knew to remain in the car for the moment.

Daze looked at his watch, 8:46 a.m. Well past 8:30. Where the hell was this Old G? He looked out and saw Hustla D checking the clock on the dash likely with the same question. Was that Tyrique kid wrong or just hustling them for some sneakers?

Hustla D kept the radio low most of the morning but turned it off at 8:20, anticipating the Old G's approach. Things had to go smoothly without distractions. Fredo never provided a contingency in case the Old G was late, or hell, what if he never came out? How long were they supposed to wait? They had been waiting since 7:41 a.m. Sixteen minutes after Fredo's call.

"Shit, Crown Vic." He noticed a police car in his rearview mirror. He looked over to the left but couldn't make eye contact with Daze, who was fixated with something inside the lobby. He rotated his eyes to the rearview mirror again. Two cops. The one riding shotgun stepped out of the Crown Vic.

A ticket. He's just writing a ticket on a parked car, Hustla D realized to mild relief. The police unit was a good five car lengths away, but the knot in his stomach made it feel like the cops were breathing down his neck.

***

May 30, 1996, 8:17 a.m.

Max reached Fredo's block but drove right past it. He drove an extra block, deciding it was a better idea to park close but not directly in front of the apartment. If something went down, he'd be better on foot. He would run the opposite direction and take the long route back to his car.

Since things didn't sit right, even if Fredo was telling the truth, he calculated it was better to get rid of him in the long-term. Did he cut a side deal with that crew in Jersey? Is that the side conversation they were having the other day? He parked the car, checked his pistol and walked over to Fredo's block.

Things were quiet—a huge contrast to the hotbed of activity normally happening on the block during warm weather. Save for a middle-aged woman having a coffee and cigarette from her window ledge, no one was in sight.

He checked his pocket, but he didn't feel the bulky phone and it was clear he'd left the device in his car. He scanned the block and saw no signs of Fredo's car. That was another indication something was possibly wrong. Instead of going back to the car and getting the cell, he thought it better to call Fredo from the corner phone. A pay phone would catch him off-guard. The element of surprise, made it easier to detect anxiety in his voice.

He found a quarter, checked the receiver for a dial tone and then removed a paper from his wallet. He had everyone's number on that paper.

"Hello. Hello?" Fredo looked at the phone confused. "Hello."

"It's me Max."

"Max? Where are you calling from?"

"I ran out of my place so fast, I forgot to grab my phone," he explained.

"Oh, so where you at? I thought you were coming here?"

"I'm here…on the block. Meet me by the pay phone at the corner," Max instructed.

"On the corner? But why—"

He hung up. He didn't want Fredo to suggest coming to the apartment.

"Fuck!" Fredo pounded his fist on the table. But he quickly thought the situation through and realized he could easily forge ahead with his trap. All he had to do was meet Max at the corner. From there, he could tell him they should go and check the car fenders. Max would be too focused on salvaging the tecs to refuse.

Max drove his fist into his palm. He was still at the pay phone. Everything he needed to know surfaced in Fredo's voice. It was tricky but obvious trap. Fredo had to be only a minute away, so he had to find where the car was located then react. If it meant clapping Fredo right after he found out, even better. The guy had it coming. Who else was involved? Pik, of course. But what about the others? And where was Steve? Could he possibly be aligned with these guys?

Max pocketed those thoughts as soon as he saw Fredo walk out and pause on the sidewalk. Fredo looked down the block before facing the pay phone on the corner. They locked eyes, and Max studied Fredo for a flinch or anything out of the norm.

Fredo started his approach, the trot from the corner was a twenty-second jaunt, but it felt like a long walk at high noon. Two cowboys facing off with an empty plastic bag taking the place of tumbleweed in the background.

Fredo had gotten his first taste of this game at fourteen. Pap was like a big brother he followed everywhere. Pap loved his spirit but wouldn't let him in his circle for fear Fredo was too young and rash. But occasionally, he would let Fredo hang out at his apartment as long as the boy ran his errands and provided a report about what happened on the block when he wasn't around. In between chores and errands, Pap started explaining the mechanics of his business, maturing Fredo in the process.

Max knew he wasn't in the clear as soon as he saw Fredo alone. Pik had to be close by. But even so, it would be hard for them to ambush him on the main corner, which is why he made Fredo come his way rather than meet on a lesser used side-street.

"Crazy shit, right?" Fredo extended his hand.

Max ignored the gesture. "Where's Pik?"

"Pik?"

"Yeah, where's Pik?"

"Oh, he's at the car," Fredo said.

"How come the car ain't on the block?"

"Max, I couldn't leave a car with the fender torn open on the block. Even a dumb ass cop would figure that one out."

"Well, why aren't you taking me to the car?"

"Oh, oh yeah," Fredo nodded. "Let's go."

Max waited a half step, walking slightly behind Fredo so they were never side-by-side. At the same time, he checked the empty block and casually looked at the roof lines. No sign of anything or anyone, except for that middle-aged woman still at her window now drowning the cigarette butt inside her coffee mug.

***

May 30, 1996, 8:48 a.m.

Daze was concerned. Every time he tried to make eye contact, Hustla D looked elsewhere, namely his rearview mirror. His attention should be the courtyard.

As outlined, Daze would sit in the back seat with Old G while Hustla D drove them to the location Fredo chose. Daze was going to stick his .32 in the Old G's side in case he got any ideas. A couple of rags were positioned under the passenger seat in case he had to wipe the Old G's liver off the back seat.

The cop placed the ticket under the vehicle's wiper arm. Finally, the police were on their way and the Old G hadn't stepped out yet. Hustla D sighed with relief. But instead of pulling out, the police cruiser creeped up behind his double-parked car. He figured they were probably going to tell him to move, so he placed both hands on the wheel prepared to drive off.

Daze spotted the Old G stepping out of the elevator. He held the door open for a stylishly dressed woman, but the man himself wore a bright blue pajama set. A detail Tyrique should've mentioned, and the omission made Daze uneasy.

Daze decided all he had to do was let the woman walk through the door then step in front of the Old G and pull up his T-shirt to make sure the Old G saw the .38. He would then inform the Old G they should have a word in the car.

Daze looked up and noticed the Old G approaching the exit, but he also noticed the Old G held hands with the woman. Maybe she was a jump-off he was just walking out the building? If that's the case, no big deal. He'd follow Old G back into the lobby and enact the scenario he'd just laid out in his head. He turned his attention to signal Hustla D , but he was still consumed by something else in his rearview mirror.

"What the fuck!" Hustla D's heart skipped a beat. From his peripheral, he saw Daze coming his way. He didn't divert his full attention as he was worried about the police car just behind him. They didn't blow their horn or pop their siren urging him to move. But he also couldn't drive off on his own as that would draw suspicion. He turned his head slightly and realized the Old G was actually in front of Daze in some aqua-colored pajamas and slippers. On top of that, he was flanked by a woman.

Again, Daze struggled to make contact. What the hell was going on with Hustla D? Then he saw the unmistakable blue fender of an NYPD patrol car pull up behind Hustla D . In hindsight, it would've been better if Hustla D had been circling the block. There was no way they could carry this out. All he could do now was watch and figure out why the police parked behindHustla D.

"No more spaghetti," Fiona complained. "You need to cook something else."

Ti Zoot didn't respond. Instead, his attention was focused on a man who stood in the courtyard, right next to the building's entrance. He didn't recognize him, but that's how it usually worked. They send someone you've never seen before to pop you.

Ti Zoot kept hold of Fiona's hand but slowed down. A cop car idled a few feet from the front of the building, casing an occupied vehicle that was double parked. Something told him the guy in the courtyard and the one the cops monitored were connected. Guys like these two rarely circulated streets this early.

"What's wrong?" Fiona asked when their pace slowed. "Remember, I'm running late. I have to catch the next train."

He didn't answer but squeezed her hand. She understood the message and paid attention to the cop who stepped out of the cruiser.

"Can I see your license and registration?" the officer asked. His partner stepped out from the driver's side of the patrol vehicle and proceeded to inspect Hustla D's backseat through the open window.

"I was just about to move the car," Hustla D said.

"License and registration." The officer restated and glanced over at his partner who had made his way to the passenger side of the car. Hustla D slowly pulled the documents from his wallet.

Ti Zoot watched the transaction. He then turned back to Daze, still in the same spot in the courtyard, but Daze quickly looked away and placed his attention on Hustla D and the cops.

"This vehicle is listed as stolen," the officer said. "I need you to slowly exit this vehicle now."

"Stolen?" Hustla D was shocked. "I got all my papers."

"Please exit the vehicle." The officer's hand hovered above his holster.

"Nothing to see here folks. Just keep it moving." The other officer called to Ti Zoot, Fiona, and another passerby.

Ti Zoot kept the slow pace but did as he was told, crossing the street with Fiona—although he kept an eye on the scene and caught the cops putting Hustla D in handcuffs while the guy in the courtyard slipped away before he could be implicated.

"What is this about?" Fiona asked as they reached the corner.

"For once, I don't know," he admitted. "I need my coffee. See you later." He planted a kiss on her cheek then entered the bodega.

***

May 30, 1996, 8:24 a.m.

"So, where'd you park the car?" Max paused.

"I had to put it in my cousin's yard. It's not far—just the other side of Beverly."

"When did you find the car and notice the fender?"

"Early this morning. I was up and came out, and I was, like, 'Oh, shit!' That's when I called you."

Max looked down the street and recognized a car in front of Fredo's building. It wasn't the car Fredo referred to, but a car he often saw

Fredo's associates riding around in. Maybe it was Daze or Hustla D's car—he couldn't remember which—but this was a teal-colored car, and he could see someone in the driver's seat. In fact, the person's arm was hanging outside the driver's window, but they tucked it in as he and Fredo approached.

"I'm stopping right here." Max stood three buildings before Fredo's.

"What?" Fredo turned to face Max. "Fuck you mean?"

"I mean bring me that car back with all my tecs motherfucker!"

"Yo." Fredo pivoted to make sure Pik could see their interaction from the car. "I don't know what the fuck is wrong with you, Max." He pulled out his semi-auto and fired.

Max anticipated the move, jumped from the sidewalk, and slid in between two parked cars. By the time he landed, his .38 was out, and he was already returning fire.

Fredo waved for Pik to join him on the sidewalk. The two moved cautiously, but they knew Max was trapped. A shot came low, Pik swore as it ricocheted past his foot. He dashed across the street and took shelter behind a minivan.

Max rose quickly and started firing left and right. Fredo returned shots, which hit a parked car. Max backpedaled but continued to fire. He didn't have a clear shot of either of them but needed an extra second to keep them at bay so he could jet to the nearest corner and disappear.

Ambushing him on their block was stupid. But then again, they were idiots. He fired in Pik's direction first since he was farthest away then fired a couple of rounds at Fredo, who commando rolled behind a brick gate in front of the building closest to him. Max raced for the corner, but he was a step slower from his recent ankle sprain. Fredo responded by leaping from his spot and clearing his clip.

When Max got in the game, he was taught to count bullets under fire. He was sixteen when that ability helped him during his first altercation. It was easy when everyone used six shooters. But in a world of rapid fire automatics, it was an impossible guess as he raced for his life.

"Got that motherfucker!" Fredo shouted as Max went down hard just before he could clear the corner.

"Let's get outta here," Pik advised. "Let's go!"

Fredo didn't budge, mesmerized by what he had just done.

Pik took his friend's semi-auto, placed it in his own pocket, and yanked Fredo's arm in the direction of the teal vehicle.

"You got him?" Pik asked once they sped off.

"Of course! You saw it. He went down." Adrenaline coursed through Fredo's veins. "I popped him at least three times. Bye Max!"

CHAPTER 14

May 30, 1996, evening

"It's me, Lulu!"

"Lou who?" Nancy squinted through the peephole.

"Lulu! The call me Antoine. You know my barbershop. Your husband used to come and get his cuts from me."

Nancy shook her head. Other than seeing him in the neighborhood occasionally, she never interacted with this man, save for courteous greetings.

She cracked opened the door, her eyes were immediately drawn to his jet-black hair, and she wondered if it was an afro-wig.

"Yes?"

"Ms. Nancy, you don't recognize me? I knew your husband well."

"Yes, but why are you here?"

"Ms. Nancy," he lowered his voice and looked down the hall in both directions, "I have some news for you. Can we talk privately?"

"Privately? This is private," she snapped. She was tired and had just come from work after picking Emily up from her afterschool program. All she could think of was jumping in the shower. "Whatever you need to say, you can say it from there."

Lulu couldn't hide his annoyance. He had come all the way to this woman's door twice. The first trip, a little before 10:00 a.m. He had summoned an ambulance after a bloodied Max crawled past his barbershop, only to pass out a few feet away in front of the laundromat next door.

His forearm looked like it was torn from his elbow and blood engulfed his tracksuit. When Lulu ran out of the shop, he noticed the blood trailed well past the crosswalk and extended to the previous block.

"Shit, they got young blood in a bad way," Lulu grimaced. "Chiro, call 911 we need an ambulance now!" He told the owner of the laundromat.

He looked at Max's face and imagined the young man's pain. He was sweating buckets, mostly from his forehead. Lulu tried to give some first aid to Max's elbow, but the wound was too gruesome.

A passing car slowed to rubberneck at the scene and Lulu took advantage. "Hey man, give us a ride to the hospital."

But the man sped off.

Chiro returned and handed Lulu a towel. "I called 911. Wrap his arm to stop the blood."

Surprisingly, the ambulance arrived within minutes, and Lulu decided to ride the ambulance alongside Max, who had passed out cold.

"Aww, shit, young blood." Lulu peered out the window. "You really got bad luck today, they're taking us to Caledonian!"

At the hospital, Lulu explained Max patronized at his barbershop, but he really didn't know much about him. When a nurse from the triage noted the patient had on a bullet proof vest, Lulu left the hospital in short order. He figured the cops would be on the scene to investigate this as a gang related matter, and he wanted no part.

The first thing on his mind was to inform Nancy even though he had to go out of his way to get to her place. Upon arriving, he rang the doorbell a few times but decided she was likely at work.

Now on his second trip, Nancy didn't have enough etiquette to let him inside or even offer some lousy tap water. "Well, Ms. Nancy, I'm guessing you haven't heard?"

"Heard what?" Her tone conveyed more annoyance than curiosity.

"Ms. Nancy, that Max guy you've been involved with was shot this morn—"

"Oh, my God!" She stepped back from the door in shock.

"He took one in the arm, but he should be okay. I escorted him to Caledonian myself."

"My God. I can't believe this. Who shot—"

"Hmm. I don't have info on that, Ms. Nancy. I found him a bloody mess crawling to my barbershop. That's when old Lulu did a good deed and made sure I got him to the hos—"

Nancy slammed the door shut and dialed Claudette.

"Auntie, I have an emergency. Would you please watch Emily for a little while?" She tried her best to mask the worry in her voice.

"Emergency?"

"One of my girlfriends is feeling sick. I just want to go over and see if everything is okay, but I don't want to take Emily there and expose her to anything."

"Bring her," Claudette replied.

***

"Shot?" Marie gasped. "Goodness!" She was already short of breath, having just entered her apartment from a day at work. She'd raced to answer the ringing phone only to be confronted with Nancy's disturbing news. "Were you with him?"

"No, I was at work. It happened this morning. I just found out. I'm heading over there now. I'm not telling Claudette." Nancy hung up.

Marie did the sign of the cross and said a quick prayer. She then changed out of her work attire and left the apartment to meet Nancy. As she got into her car, the events of the party came flooding back to her. Ti Zoot looked and behaved like crazed man that night. Could he possibly have something to do with this, or did one of his associates retaliate on his behalf? She really didn't know Ti Zoot's business or want to get involved, but she compelled to confront him and erase all doubt.

"Hi, Fiona." Marie stood awkwardly in the doorway. "Can I talk to him?"

"Alo, Marie. I just got home. Let me see if he's in the room."

"Marie?" Ti Zoot looked up from his paper.

"Meet me in front of your building in ten minutes," she told him.

"Okay." He didn't bother to ask why, but he knew it had to be serious. Marie could be a lot like him, curt and succinct.

He dressed quickly and decided to use the extra time to buy his numbers before meeting Marie.

"You're leaving?" Fiona asked.

But the door slammed shut before he could hear the question.

***

Nancy's feet were a lot heavier the closer she got to the third curtain. That was where the nurse at the desk told her she would find Max, unless they had moved him to recovery. Unsure what to expect, she couldn't shake the panic ever since that Lulu character detailed how he found Max. She also regretted the way she ended things days ago, but there wasn't room for questionable things in her life.

She parted the curtain and found Max asleep. His chest was bare, save for the gauze and tape use to keep the electrodes for the heart monitor in place. Another set of wraps, just around his elbow and under his arm pit, dressed his damaged limb. Thankfully, this was post-op, and the image was more subdued than she imagined, alleviating some anxiety.

"He was up twice." Nancy jumped at the sound of the nurse's voice. She'd entered the curtain while Nancy stood absorbed in thought about Max's present state. The nurse went to one of the many monitors and made a series of checks on her clipboard. "Related, or is he your boyfriend?"

"Just friends—just a friend," Nancy stressed.

"He's very handsome, but his type looks like trouble," she whispered as she exited.

Nancy moved closer to the bed and touched his good arm. He felt warm. She kept her hand on long enough to feel his pulse. She traced a finger over the scar on his forehead. and he opened an eye. He recognized her but wasn't lucid or strong enough to utter words. She shut the eye and kissed him. She went back to holding his good hand and wished the past week could have been erased, especially this day.

"Ma'am, is this your boyfriend?"

She looked up and found a cop standing just inside the curtain. She'd seen him near the emergency room triage section when she'd arrived. He'd been leaning against a wall drinking coffee, but she didn't think twice about him.

"I'm sorry. My name is Officer Numa. I was hoping to have a word with Maxwell. Are the two of you related?"

"No." She noticed the officer's gaze shift to the hand she'd placed in Max's open palm. "He's a friend. Who are you?"

"Officer Numa," he repeated. "The nurse told me it might be a while before he's able to have a clear conversation. Maybe you can help in the meantime?"

"What's the problem?"

"Well, I'd like to know if you or anyone you know can identify who shot him. I'd also be interested in finding out why he was wearing a bulletproof vest. Can you answer either of those questions?"

The inquiries made her antsy. "Look, I don't know what you're talking about, but can we do this another time? He's in pain and unconscious."

"Okay Ms.—Mrs.?"

She bowed her head and stared at Max, hoping the officer would think she hadn't heard him. She was clueless as to what to do next, but the officer's presence had her mind racing.

"Witnesses say your friend was involved in a gunfight. We collected shells…can't locate any firearms though." He turned to exit. "I'm only trying to help. There's no way he'll be so lucky next time. I'll be back."

***

"Fuck you mean Hustla D got pulled over by cops?" Fredo moved the phone from his ear and stared at the receiver as if Daze had mixed his words up. "Talk straight man. We waited for you guys the whole time. You never called or paged me."

"I'm telling you, that's exactly what happened," Daze yelled through the receiver. "The cop said the car was stolen. Next thing I know, they're hauling him off."

"Fuck! Why didn't you get that Old G yourself then?"

"What the hell are you saying? That Old G came out the same time the cops pulled up onHustla D."

"Why the hell am I hearing from you now?" Fredo screamed.

"I left my pager in Hustla D's car. I have everyone's phone number in that thing. I just found my old phone book, which is why I'm just now calling. Plus, I started to think maybe those cops arresting Hustla Dwasn't so random. I was laying low. Maybe this was a setup."

"Daze, what the fuck are you trying to say here?" Fredo braced a hand on his hip.

"Maybe I'm buggin' right now," Daze admitted. "Let's get together and clean this mess up. I'll check with Hustla D's sister to see if she heard anything and what the deal is."

"Well, we have to get those tecs to Stilt and his crew tomorrow. I had to explain things to him earlier, and he was pissed. Bring one of those semi-autos with you tomorrow. We'll throw that in as a peace offering."

"Okay, but we still have the same problems we had yesterday. Old G and Max are still out there."

"Fuck are you talking about? I bodied Max this morning!"

"You haven't heard?" Daze's eyes narrowed.

"Heard what?"

"Lulu is going around telling people he took Max to the hospital this morning, and he's going to make a full recovery thanks to him."

"Lulu is a fucking liar! I bodied him."

"I told you!" Pik sprang up from the couch. "You have to walk up to a body up close, and 'BLAM,' especially when he's down."

Angered, Fredo threw the phone, which struck the wall just above Pik's head.

***

Ti Zoot was on his way back from playing his numbers when he found Marie sitting in her car in front of his building. She must have been expecting him to approach from the lobby because she jumped when he knocked on her window.

"What the hell is going on?"

"You know I'm tired of you never greeting me." He slipped into the passenger seat.

"Not here for laughs. What the hell happened today?"

"What are you talking about? Nothing."

"Max was shot."

"Who?"

"Max, the guy you threatened Saturday night. Nancy's friend."

"Shot? I saw him the other day."

"Are you sure you didn't see him this morning?"

"Marie, please."

She immediately regretted the inference. Clearly, the news was upsetting, even for him. She hadn't thought about it much, but her relationship with Ti Zoot had changed since Ernse's passing. Had she subconsciously blamed him? In the back of her mind, she felt Ti Zoot knew more about Ernse's death than he let on. Either way, there was no denying he was riddled with the pain of losing his best friend and carried the event on his shoulders. Maybe it was time to let him off the hook.

"I'm going to the hospital to meet, Nancy," Marie said. "Are you sure there's nothing about this we need to discuss before I see her?"

"Not a thing." Ti Zoot's voice dripped with sincerity. "Let's go."

***

"Looks like you're waking up."

Nancy opened her eyes. The voice came from a man in scrubs. Fatigue and the stress of waiting had forced her into a catnap. She spotted the tag on his top and realized he was another R.N., but he wasn't talking to her. He was having a one-way conversation with Max.

"That was a nasty wound," he continued. "The trauma unit did a great job though. You'll be out of here before you know it." He turned to Nancy. "He's heavy on painkillers now, so there will be some discomfort as they wear off."

"Thank you," she responded. She rose from her seat and held Max's good hand.

"Okay, the doctor will be in to check on him in a moment. He should be moved to a room after that." The nurses stepped out and shut the curtain.

"Hi." Max's first word came out dry and slightly mangled.

"You have a bad cut on your lips." She took some lip balm from her bag and rubbed it over his mouth.

"Must've fallen," Max said.

"Yeah, fallen," she repeated, peeved at his ill-timed humor.

"What happened?"

"That's what I'd like to know."

Nancy spun around. The last comment came from Officer Numa. She rolled her eyes and turned back to Max.

"Look, I'm here to help." Numa pulled out a pen and small notebook. "If there's someone after you, we'd like to put a stop to that, but I'll need some questions answered."

Max ignored the officer, preferring to face the wall. Nancy say awkwardly between the two, unsure if she should say something or wait until Max spoke.

"We'd like you to identify who shot you," Numa said.

Max remained quiet, so the officer moved on to a series of questions dealing with his gang affiliations and whereabouts over the course of the day— none of which Max acknowledged.

Suddenly, she felt light-headed and wobbly, but she remained upright by bracing herself against the bedrail. Neither Officer Numa nor Max noticed her discomfort, but the officer's questions were becoming unbearable. She eventually excused herself and stepped out into the hall.

Max managed to raise his head enough to see Nancy exit the curtain. The officer continued on with his interrogation, but Max made it clear he wouldn't talk without a lawyer present.

On the east end of the floor, Steve turned a corner and walked up a ramp pointing to the ICU when he saw Nancy coming down a long hallway in his direction. She never looked up, but as she got closer, it was clear her eyes were red and she was in tears.

"Nancy?"

She sidestepped him.

"Nancy," Steve repeated.

"Steve?" She turned, finally hearing him. Maybe he could answer the questions Max wouldn't. He'd always played it straight when she was around. "What happened today?"

"I don't know. I got a couple of pages from him earlier today, but I was asleep. I didn't know anything until one of the guys at the barbershop paged me. When I got there, everyone filled me on how Lulu found him this morning."

"So you mean to tell me, you two are joined at the hip, and you didn't even know why he got shot this morning?"

"Nancy, if I knew, I would've rushed right over here. I was supposed to meet him midday. I thought it was strange he didn't respond to my pages. If I hadn't check the barbershop, I'd probably still be in the dark."

"Okay, but you know Maxwell better than anyone, who could have done this?"

He was compelled to point out the Old G from Marie's party Saturday night, but he refrained knowing Nancy the two were friends. "I'm not sure."

"You're not sure? There's that many people?"

He shook his head. "I'm just not sure."

"Well, there's a cop questioning Max right now. Maybe you can go in there and tell him how unsure you are about everything."

Steve looked down the hallway in the direction she pointed. He could rattle off a half-dozen names, but what good would that do? If anything, the cop would start looking into his background, and there's no gain in that scenario whatsoever.

"Aren't you going to see your friend?" she wondered.

He was at a loss for words. He noticed an exit to St. Paul's Place and stepped in that direction. "I'll catch you later, Nancy."

She bit her lip and shook her head. Running off was the best he could do. She resumed her stride and noticed a set of familiar faces barreling down the hall, Ti Zoot and Marie. She opened her arms wide as the drew closer and fell forward into their arms.

"Look at you. You're crying." Marie wiped her tears. "You shouldn't be here alone."

"I know, I know." She squeezed them tight. "I need a moment."

"Come, sit here." Marie led them to a bench in the hallway.

"Thank you." Nancy stared at Ti Zoot. "I can't believe I ever doubted you."

CHAPTER 15

May 30, 1996, evening

Esther had another long day at the clinic, but the overtime was coming in handy. It was great her job was walking distance, but one of the challenges of working late was coming home to a filthy kitchen and living room. Amar sat in the living room barking orders at the twins, but of course, nothing was ever done. He only raised a finger to play his video games.

He sat in front of the TV fully animated, displaying energy she wished would make its way elsewhere. His routine was wake-up midday, watch Jerry Springer or Maury, and play video games through the night. In between that, he had a voracious appetite ready to eat the dinners she cooked or the takeout she was forced to bring home on the nights her job got in the way.

By then, Esther only had enough energy for a cursory glance at the kid's homework. Sometimes she would fall asleep trying to decipher a math problem. It was all taking its toll, but she was riding it out until Amar figured out how to join the work force.

And then there was her little brother Tyrique. He was the fourth and final child and quite the surprise to Esther who was nearly fifteen when he was born. As the only child home at the time, she was instrumental during his early years. So when their mother died from breast cancer a year ago, Esther took Tyrique into her home. Her older siblings showed no signs they were willing to make the same gesture.

The boy could be intelligent, but he seemed to have lost focus since their mother passed away. He was more reserved, and she was unsure if puberty and teenage years was cause for the change.

The other day, he came home with some expensive sneakers, but he couldn't tell her where the money came from. She didn't know where she'd find time, but she was going to have to dedicate more of it to the boy before things got out of hand. All those thoughts raced in her head when she walked into her building. She was about to climb the staircase when she heard voices, one of which was Tyrique's. The other two voices she didn't recognize, so she remained at the bottom staircase, hoping to get the gist of their conversation and the identity of her brother's friends.

"Those Jordans look great on your feet, little man." Fredo remarked, unable to take his eyes off Tyrique's shiny new sneakers.

"Thanks." Tyrique responded politely even as he was confused why they followed him inside the building just for compliments. He had just run an errand for Amar, who ran out of sugar in the middle of making lemonade. Just as he was walking up the stairs, Fredo and Pik came running after him.

"'Rique, I think those Jordans would look great with a nice tracksuit." Pik wrapped an arm around the boy's shoulder.

Tyrique remained still, unsure what was happening.

"You don't think so?" Fredo prodded. "You'll be looking fresh out there."

"Y-yeah…I guess."

"So that's where he got the sneakers," Esther whispered to herself. Her anger rose, but she remained at the bottom of the steps. Why the hell are they making these offers? Was it drug related?

"Little man…scratch that I'm, going to have to start calling you big man from now," Fredo said. "We need you to come through one more time."

"I don't understand. I thought everything was okay with Ti Zoot."

"Oh, it's okay," Pik explained. "We need one final favor then we're good." Fredo placed a hand on Tyrique's shoulder to stress the importance. "We need his apartment number. We're just running a prank, but you can't tell anyone about this. No matter what."

"Why didn't you ask him? Didn't you see him going to the corner store like I said?"

"We saw him 'Rique. Trust us, he'll get a kick out of this too," Pik reassured.

Fredo pulled a hundred dollar bill out his pocket and placed it in Tyrique's hand. "I want you to have that tracksuit. Those Jordans need it."

Tyrique inspected the bill with renewed interest. "It's 5D."

Esther's heart sank. Their voices said it all. This was shady.

"Okay. That's great," Fredo smiled. "So, you've been there?"

"A few times."

"Tell me the layout of the apartment."

Tyrique studied the money. The shiny new bill felt good in his hands, crisp like it had just come off the press. It felt like he could do anything with it.

"It's a regular apartment. You enter through the living room and the kitchen is down a hallway on the right. I think the bedroom is further down the hallway, but I've never been inside that room."

"And what about when you get off the elevator, left or right?" Pik asked.

"Right…you make a right. It's the apartment straight ahead and down the hallway, 5D."

Fredo faced Pik with a big smile. "I love this little man."

"'Rique, good work." Pik gripped the young man's shoulders. "Get the hottest tracksuit at Albee Square, baby. And remember, no one better find out about this, no matter what happens."

"We'll be getting in touch with you soon, so stay quiet," Fredo winked.

And with that, the pair marched downstairs.

Esther's mind raced. What the hell was Tyrique involved in? But there was no time to think and wonder any further. She couldn't take the chance of running into the two men, so she dashed into the tiny space under the staircase. The rumble of Fredo and Pik's feet vibrated over the steps above her head. For a second, she worried they'd seen her hiding and that she'd be trapped, but they trotted out the exit and never looked back.

Even so, she couldn't move. What would their mother say if she'd lived to see Tyrique involved in such a nefarious scheme? She slid down into the corner and held onto her legs, trapped with the uncertainty of what to do.

She lowered her head. Maybe it was nervous energy, but she still had that empty feeling inside even though several moments had passed since Fredo and Pik had their cryptic conversation with Tyrique. She took a deep breath, wiped the tears, and walked up to the apartment.

"Hey babe," Amar held up a glass. "Lemonade?"

She continued past him until she came upon Tyrique, who was in the living room with the twins.

"Where were you?" She grabbed him and shoved him inside the kid's bedroom.

He tripped from the momentum, and she used the moment to get right in his face. No one had ever invaded his space like that. He was his mother's baby and got away with things Esther and her siblings could only dream of. But then again, their mother was much older when it was time to rear him.

"What were you doing with those two guys?" she screamed.

"What guys?" Tyrique shrugged off her question.

"The two hoods you got those sneakers from!"

He looked at the sneakers. How had she figured it out?

"Negotiating with thugs? Our mother would be heartbroken if she was still alive."

Tyrique teared at the thought, and it wasn't long before he detailed the entire series of events involving Fredo, Pik, and their supposed plans for Ti Zoot.

"I'm beyond disappointed," she cried. "They're going to kill that man!"

***

Ti Zoot looked up. It was eight o'clock. Nancy and Marie had finally exited the hospital and were heading his way. A sudden chill struck him as they drew closer—specifically from Nancy, who had gone back inside to say goodnight to Max.

"Are you okay?" He tucked Nancy's arm under his as they walked to the parking lot.

"I will be," she said with a sigh.

"Come by me tonight," Marie offered.

"No, I have to stop by Claudette's to pick Emily up and take her home. There's school and work tomorrow. I wasn't prepared for any of this."

Her pager buzzed through her shoulder bag, and she checked the number. "It's Jimmy. I have to let him know what's going on."

"No need. I left a message on his answering machine," Ti Zoot explained. "He probably just heard it and is reaching out to you. I'll update him when I get home."

"Where'd you park?" Marie asked. "We'll walk you to your car."

"Love you two." Nancy gave them both a squeeze.

"I'll pick Emily up this weekend so you have time to check on Max," Marie offered.

"Thanks, that will help—although I'm not sure if I'll be visiting that often."

"Either way," Marie said. "I'll pick her up."

Ti Zoot watched Nancy climb into her car and felt the same chill again. He reached out and placed a hand on her door before she could close it. "We should talk. Things have gotten out of hand, not just Saturday night, but for a while now.—But it's a conversation for when you're in a better place, and you have time."

"Sure," she conceded and drove off.

CHAPTER 16

May 31, 1996

Ti Zoot sat on his windowsill. His apartment was on the rear side of the building, so all he had to look at was a back alley. It was midday, cloudy, and he hadn't stepped out, not even for his morning coffee, but for a change he was okay with that. Some music played on the stereo. Occasionally, he grabbed the remote and skipped to the next song of a bachata compilation.

His pager went off. It was Fiona again. She had already paged him a half-dozen times. Each time he returned the call, he told her not to call him and that he'd be in contact at some point. He was tired of all the talking. They were on the phone well past 2:00 a.m. the night before. She had tons of questions, but he refused to answer any, prolonging the conversation.

Still he'd found time to call both Jimmy and Bigga. He first called them the night before, right after he'd dropped Fiona at Claudette's. He'd warned both guys to stay off the streets for the next few days, especially this weekend. They didn't bother to press him why because the incident from last Saturday night was still etched in each of their minds. Both guys knew if Ti Zoot told you to lay low, he probably heard something was going down. After he'd got those calls out of the way, he paged both of them occasionally making sure everything was okay. He was planning on doing that most of the weekend.

"Hello?" Ti Zoot picked up the ringing telephone.

"Mr. Phillipe?"

"Yes?"

"This is Ms. Sumlar at Pitney. Congratulations, we'd like to make you an offer."

"Thanks," he was surprised. He was told to expect a call between Friday and Monday, but events from the prior day dominated his thoughts.

"We're overnighting you a package. would you be able to come in Monday at 10:00 a.m., execute and submit the documents?"

"Yes, no problem."

"Great. We'd like you to start the following Monday once everything has been processed."

"Thank you, Ms.—"

"Sumlar," she replied. "Have a great weekend."

Another hour passed. Still on the windowsill, he leaned his head against the jamb and shut his eyes until the lobby's buzzer reanimated him.

He muted the stereo and made his way to the intercom. "Who is it?"

"UPS, delivery," a voice announced.

He hit the 'door' button allowing the delivery man to enter the lobby.

***

Down in the lobby, Pik held the door open as Fredo tied his sneaker. Once he finished, they looked around, specifically at the stairways on each wing of the building. The layout was important in case they had to deviate from their plans. In the elevator, both performed a quick check, inspecting their clips before the doors opened on Old G's floor.

"Come in. The door is open." Ti Zoot had turned the stereo back on, but managed to hear the knock on the other side of the door.

Fredo looked at Pik. The plan had been to knock on the door under the guise of delivering a package, duck down so as not to be detected through the peephole, and ambush Old G when he opened the door to retrieve his item. "Too easy," Fredo whispered.

"This fool thinks he's getting a package, but he's about to get a real special delivery," Pik smiled.

Fredo pushed the door open with his foot and entered with his pistol raised.

"Freeze." Ti Zoot stood with a P89 Ruger pointed firmly at Fredo's temple. "Drop it slowly," he ordered. "Come on in," he barked at Pik, who tried to quietly step back out. "Lay yours on the floor too," he instructed.

Pik followed just as Fredo did since Ti Zoot now had the drop on them both.

"Move in there." He pointed them over to the living room with his free hand.

"Come on man," Fredo objected. Ti Zoot simply locked the door and kept the P89 at pointed at them the entire time.

"Take a seat. Don't sit on my couch." He pointed the weapon toward the heavy-duty grade garbage bags laying neatly on the floor. "Right there."

"Hey man, can we just squash this?" Pik pleaded. "Everything got out of control."

"Sit your asses down." Ti Zoot watched them flop down like a pair of schoolboys. He squinted across the living room and observed 1:37 p.m. on the VCR. It was earlier than he expected, but he was okay with that.

He sat in a chair opposite his two guests and rested the P89 on the chair's arm, never releasing his grip on the metal.

"What are we sitting here for?" Fredo's voice was laced with worry.

"Did you think it would be so easy to track me down, and come at me like this?"

Neither had a response.

"You come at me hard on the street. You do the same again at a car wash. Saturday night, you show your audacity in front of everyone."

"It's just a misunderstanding," Pik said. "We can squash this right now."

"Now you sound so reasonable." Ti Zoot admired the P89's barrel.

***

Claudette walked up the basement steps, struggling with the laundry basket. This was her final load. She'd spent all morning washing everything from the curtains to the rugs. She placed the basket in the living room where planned to fold the dry laundry.

"Are you sure you don't want my help folding this?"

Claudette turned and stared Fiona's way. Every time she managed to forget the young lady was around, she appeared and reminded her all over again. But then again, what else did Claudette expect? They were the only two people in the house.

"Well…" Claudette counted the six baskets on the living room floor. "Are you sure you can fold? You don't look like you've ever folded anything in your life. You might damage those fancy nails."

"I fold every day." Fiona smiled despite the knock. "I'm in retail."

"Yes, you did say that." She handed Fiona one end of a curtain.

"I'd love to help."

"You're such a happy person, how did you end up with someone like Ti Zoot?"

"Dieu," she laughed. "I fall in love with any man who can dance."

"Why aren't you working today?"

"Friday is my day off." Fiona placed the folded curtain on the couch.

"Right." Claudette looked at the folded curtain. Not bad. Fiona's meticulousness wasn't lost on her. Maybe her tidiness applied to more than just appearance. "Why did Ti Zoot rush you over here in the middle of the night? I don't understand any of this."

Unable to answer the question, Fiona continued to fold. "All he said is that it's an emergency and I'll be safe."

"What emergency? When he called last night, he said he had to prepare and train for a new job he got. Is there really a new job? That man is so erratic."

"He did get a new job," Fiona replied. "Jimmy helped him get it."

"Well that sounds better," she said. "I was a little worried it has something to do with Nancy's friend."

"He and Nancy's friend saw one another of the street the other day. Ti Zoot was with Jimmy, and he just looked at each other, but nothing happened."

"I'm not surprised," Claudette said. "A lot of men will posture in public, but when no one is around, it's another matter altogether."

"I hope so."

"Are you sure he doesn't have another woman in that apartment right now?"

"No." Fiona was quick to dismiss the question. "He wouldn't do that."

"I don't understand all this mystery. My husband—my estranged husband was always like that. Plenty of questionable moves and a lot of half-truths."

"Well, I'm giving him until Sunday like he said then I'm just going back home."

"Hmm, you're going to wait that long?" Claudette asked and took the last curtain.

***

"Man, I don't want to insult you, but the truth is we weren't coming here to do anything crazy," Fredo said. "We just wanted to talk this out."

Ti Zoot chuckled. "Talk it out? With guns in hand? I believe you because that's exactly what I'm doing right now, talking this out with a gun in my hand."

For Pik, this Old G came across peculiar from his demeanor to the weird manner in which he covered half the floor with trash bags. They'd only been there about ten minutes, but it was starting to feel like hours. He looked over to Fredo, hoping his partner had a plan to get them out of this predicament, but Fredo hadn't moved an inch after Ti Zoot had shot down his last comment.

Ti Zoot looked at the gun's barrel and released his grip, leaving it on the chair's arm. The move eased tension just slightly. "I have an idea, you guys want to make a quick payday?"

The duo looked at each other, unsure if they'd heard right.

"Yeah," Fredo said, "let's make that money."

"I'm with that," Pik agreed, fearing the alternative.

Ti Zoot leaned forward. "My real problem is with your boss, Max."

"Max?" Pik repeated.

"So, what do you want us to do? Fredo nodded his head like a bobble toy.

"There's a grand for you each if he goes away. I don't care how you do it."

Fredo leaned back. If he had a cigar, he'd light and smoke it on the spot. Not only were they about to walk away from this but with a grand apiece to top it off.

"Consider it done," Pik said.

"In fact, the job is halfway finished," Fredo added.

Ti Zoot's eyes squinted."I don't understand."

"I'm saying," Fredo sat forward. "We already clipped Max, finishing him off won't be a problem."

"I see." Ti Zoot rocked back in his chair. "This will be another cross for me to bear."

"What's that supposed to mean?" Fredo wondered.

Ti Zoot casually placed his hand over the P89. "It means a number of times in my life, I've had to do things that held my conscious in prison. These are things I've done to protect those around me. At times, they've allowed me to see a sunny day."

Pik turned to Fredo before posing his question to TiZoot. "What does this have to do with Max?"

"Nothing. But it has everything to do with us here and now."

***

"You really think someone is over there?"

Glued to her television, Claudette hadn't budged since taking a seat on the couch. Folding laundry had tired her even with Fiona's help.

"Claudette?"

"What is it?"

"Do you really think Ti Zoot would disrespect me with another woman in that apartment?"

"Who knows?" Claudette replied. "No, he wouldn't. Not this time. But I still don't understand why he would rush you here in the middle of the night. This is the first day of my two-week vacation. I'm not playing host and servant to anyone during my time off."

Fiona couldn't shake her anxiety. The abrupt way he'd escorted her out of the apartment kept replaying in his mind. She hoped a clue would stand out and might explain what was going on in Ti Zoot's world.

She recalled him storming into the apartment calm. It was obvious his mind was occupied with something heavy because he kept walking around and examining everything from furniture to the windows. He paced up and down the hallway several times before grabbing the phone. He spoke creole, but she knew he was on the phone with Claudette. And though he tried to hide it, she was certain he said 'Fiona' at least once.

"There's not much time." He'd set the phone aside and entered the kitchen. "I have an emergency. I won't be able to explain until everything is over."

"Emergency?" The word made her panic. "What emergency?"

"Fiona, you will have to take my word," he said. "We have to get out of here. Pack some things, we're going over to Claudette's for a few days."

She knew he wouldn't answer questions from that point, so she decided to comply.

Oddly, he was pleasant—almost relaxed in the car. He'd talked about how well his job interview had gone and the potential benefits package outlined by HR. She'd kissed his cheek and congratulated him. Suddenly, the future had direction.

"I am cooking a special dinner for Jimmy next week," she announced. "He did an amazing thing when he got you that interview."

"My charm helped," he winked.

When they arrived at Claudette's, his somber tone returned. "You stay here. I'll be in touch, don't come back to the apartment until I pick you up."

"You're being irrational," she contested.

"Please." He took her hand and held it firmly. "I really need you to trust me on this."

She had an urge to open the door, leave the car, and flee. Instead, she waited for him to get her bags from the trunk and followed him inside.

Inside, the smell of mint tea pierced their noses. Claudette offered them each a cup, but both declined. Ti Zoot kissed each lady goodnight and quickly parted. Fiona stood in the kitchen and watched Claudette stir honey into a mug. Between the clangs of the spoon against the side of the mug, she heard Ti Zoot start the car and back out of the driveway.

The future had no direction.

The memory left Fiona cold. "Can I call him?"

Still weary from the laundry, Claudette looked up from her television program. "You know where the phone is."

Fiona walked to the kitchen. The times she'd called earlier, he was slow to pick up and cut their conversation after a minute. Ending each exchange with 'Please don't call. I'll call you.'

She dialed and let the phone ring for what seemed like a dozen times.

"Hello?"

"Why haven't you called me back?"

"Sorry, I was a little busy."

"Busy doing what?"

"Just cleaning up."

"There wasn't much to clean," she replied. "I'm coming home."

"No," he said. "Tomorrow. I'll call you later."

"Pourquoi est-ce que tu ne me parles pas? Talk to me!"

"I'll will. Give it time."

"I love you."

"I love you too," he said and hung up.

Bizarre, she thought. He had no problem saying he loved me.

"Did you find your man?" Claudette strolled to the kitchen sink to wash her mug.

"We spoke." Fiona twirled the phone by its cord. "He's such a sweet man."

Claudette shut off the faucet in surprise.

"He's okay and will pick me up tomorrow."

"You are strange. Both of you." She turned the water back on.

Fiona was feeling good. There was no way someone else was in that apartment. He was uncharacteristically cavalier with his last four words.

***

After running piping hot water over the mop in the tub, Ti Zoot emptied the floor cleaner into a bucket. The solvent bubbled, letting off a strong pine odor in the tiny bathroom. He drenched the excess water from the mop, swirled it in the bucket, and dragged both items into the living room. He'd made progress with the mess, but the two pistols he'd forced Fredo and Pik to place on the floor where still in his foyer. He debated what to do with the metal. He thought it was ironic that the older he got, the wiser he felt, but his self-doubt had also increased. His younger self never doubted or debated.

He walked over to the kitchen and grabbed some rubber gloves from under the sink so that he could handle the guns. One of them would've surely brought his demise. He carefully placed each piece into their respective heavy-duty bags. It wasn't difficult to recall—Fredo's had a shiny finish while Pik's was dark and blocky.

Fiona's call was well-timed. He was about to touch base with her anyway. One of the many plans he calculated during his time mopping. He was waiting for night to come, so he could dispose of the bags. The last twenty-four hours were surreal, but it all went as well as he could've possibly hoped. That was largely in part to Esther and Tyrique, who cared enough to share what they'd overheard. He asked them not to mention any of that information to anyone when Esther pled for him to involve the authorities. Under tears and sniffles, she promised Ti Zoot her and Tyrique wouldn't discuss any of it from that day forward.

With the mopping job completed, Ti Zoot performed a final inspection of the couch and floor. He was about to take the cleaning equipment back, when he noticed a crimson droplet just under the couch. It was of course blood, but he had a hard time figuring how it managed to splatter under the couch. He got on his knees, wiped the underside of the couch with a rag, removing the droplet.

CHAPTER 17

June 1, 1996

"I got the job."

"I knew you would." Nancy high-fived Ti Zoot. "Jimmy was very confident you'd get it."

"Well, Jimmy did everything," he admitted. "He was pushing for me to apply at that company for a while. I just wouldn't do it."

"Not a surprise. You're a stubborn mule, but I'm sure you charmed whoever interviewed you."

He walked to the living room window, parted the curtain. and looked out. A tree branch partially blocked his view of the street below. "I wanted you to be the first to know I'm leaving," he said.

"Leaving what?" She drew closer.

"Brooklyn. Remember my Aunt Cathline in Haverstraw?"

"Yes, I remember you took us up there for a party once," she said. "You're going up there to live with her?"

"Yeah," he turned. "She's been telling me to move up there for years."

"I don't understand. You just got that job."

"Yeah. We'll be commuting down."

"We?"

"Fiona is coming too."

"Yes, of course," she said. "I didn't see this coming."

"Yeah, I think it's time for a change," he explained. "I'm that boy raised on the streets of Port-Au-Prince. Brooklyn saw the man in me, but it's time I changed the scenery. I'm ready for the farm."

"Haverstraw isn't farm life," she said.

"Compared to Brooklyn?"

"Okay. When does this take place?"

"End of June. Or maybe I'll wait until September." He circled the room. "I don't know, but definitely by fall. I'll go up there and stay with my aunt and her son for a couple of months until we get our own place."

"Good for you." She gave him a hug.

"How's your friend?"

"I went to see him earlier. He's okay, I guess."

"I don't want to get in your way anymore," he said. "I just want you to be careful. Especially—"

"Especially since you're leaving?" She raised an eyebrow just as the phone rang.

"Hello. Hi Auntie."

He waved his arms in front of his face to signal he wasn't available.

"Why did Ti Zoot leave that girlfriend of his at my house?" Claudette asked loud enough for Ti Zoot to hear.

"He did what?"

"She's been here since yesterday."

"I'm not sure why," Nancy said. "Let me page him for you, Auntie."

"Why did you exile Fiona at Claudette's?" She hung up phone. "Can I make some coffee or tea for you? You look tired."

"Coffee, please."

"Come." She grabbed his arm and sat him down in the kitchen.

"So why did you leave Fiona over there?"

"I had to make a long drive." He watched her set the percolator on the stove. "I just didn't want to leave her home alone."

"How sweet." She poured the ground. "Except I don't believe you."

"Long drive." He leaned his head against the wall.

She looked back and realized his eyes were closed and he was napping.

After the coffee brewed, she placed a mug in front of him and took a seat at the other end. "Wake up. The coffee is ready."

"Thank you." He took a spoon of sugar and stirred it in the cup. "You look like you could use a cup too."

"I am tired," she admitted. "But no coffee. I'm okay. I want a lot of sleep later."

"This coffee is good." He inhaled the steam. "Is there anything you do bad?"

"You'd be surprised." She pulled out a brown paper bag. "You forgot this, but I don't have any peanut butter."

"Kasav. Thanks." He bit into it. "Uh, hard. I might lose some teeth eating this."

"You'll eat every crumb I'm sure." She took her seat again. "I'm going to miss you."

"I'll be here all the time," he smiled. "I'm moving, but I'm not leaving Brooklyn."

"It won't be the same," she sighed.

He dug into his back pocket, pulled out his wallet, and took out piece of paper which Nancy thought was folded a dozen times into a perfect little square.

"Someone was handing these out on the train one day for a contribution. Each was a different message. When I read mine, I felt like it was meant just for me." He read he note aloud.

Yesterday I was clever, so I wanted to change the world. Today I am wise, so I am changing myself.

"That's beautiful," Nancy smiled. "I never thought you'd carry something like that in your wallet."

"You won't find anything else like it in my possession. Best dollar I spent."

She rose and kissed his cheek. "I think I understand, Ti Zoot. God bless."

She sat down and closed her eyes while Ti Zoot finished his cup. He stared at her profile against the wall. In many ways, she was still that delicate twelve-year-old kid he met only weeks after arriving in Brooklyn. Of course, she had filled out into a beautiful young woman, mother, and friend, but there was a fragile side he was always able to identify in her.

"There's something else I wanted to speak to you about." He swallowed his last drop of coffee.

"I know you didn't just want to speak to me about a new job or your move." Her eyes were still shut and she'd leaned her head against the wall with her arms folded across her torso.

"I'd like to talk about Ernse. I'd like to talk about the night I found him."

"Okay," she nodded.

"I lost my spare keys, or specifically, Ernse lost my spare keys. We never found them. After I found his body, I pieced things together as much as I could. I thought he was killed by a neighborhood gang—"

"A gang related to that woman he was seeing?"

"Yes," he nodded. "That's what I thought. I also thought Ernse must've lost my keys during a fight he had with someone from that gang and somehow the gang got the keys and left him in my trunk. I thought that was their statement. It was the easiest way to make sense of the events that transpired. Everything happened so fast."

He wiped a hand across his mouth and took a moment.

"I thought putting him in my trunk was a message specifically sent to me, but it wasn't. We had the same car, same color. It wasn't a message to me. They were just confused. Ernse's body was supposed to go in his car's trunk, but my car was parked there that week. His car was around the block. That's all it was."

He reflected on the night he returned from Haiti and picked up the car keys from her place. As she listened to the words, her eyelids sunk deeper as if permanently shut.

"I got to the car, and just before I opened the trunk to put my suitcase, I heard something. Since it was raining, the sound was faint. I couldn't tell where it was coming from. I opened the trunk, and there he was…in a bag. I didn't open the bag to confirm, but I knew it was him. I felt it in my bones."

He shuddered. "I heard the sound again, but now it was clear. It was the buzz his pager created against the metal in the trunk. I removed it from his pocket and kept it. At the time, I didn't think anything of it." He scratched his head. "I had no idea what to do, but I knew enough to create a diversion. I placed his body where I knew fingers couldn't be pointed. I'd be begging for trouble if I tried explaining things to the police. Besides, something didn't sit right with me. I couldn't figure it out. I didn't want to."

"I started having these dreams and nightmares. One kept recurring. I saw Ernse walking down a long, dark corridor. I'm following from a distance. The longer he walks, the stronger the light becomes at the end of the corridor. It eventually leads to a tunnel and now the light is overpowering at the end. Once he got to the end and the reached light, he turned back, opened his hand, and dropped a key on the floor. He took another step and disappeared into the light. I followed, hoping to grab the key off the floor, but I could never reach. The key got further from me, no matter how hard I tried.

One day, I woke up, interrupting that sequence and it dawned on me, when I found Ernse, he had no keys in his pockets. No house keys, no car keys. Only his wallet and his pager. There were no keys on him."

He went into the inner pocket of his sport coat and placed Ernse's pager on the table. He looked over, a tear dangled on her chin then fell on her arm.

"When I got around to looking through it," he continued, "I realized prior to the day I left for Haiti, there were no messages on his pager from you. I kept hearing your words, 'he hasn't been home in days.' Yet, no pages from you. Not a single page."

She placed herself back to that day in early February 1994. "The irony is for the first time, he did listen to you, Ti Zoot. After you left for Haiti, he spent the next few days in the apartment, never leaving until he got one page. I didn't hear who he called, but not even five minutes later, the buzzer from the lobby rang. Ernse went down despite my protests, but he wasn't gone more than ten minutes. He didn't say much upon his return. He just sat down in the living room and listened to music."

"What's wrong?" Nancy asked as she entered the living room. She thought he was uncharacteristically quiet, but he had the *Songs of Freedom* album rotating in the CD changer.

"Is Emily still sleeping?" Ernse asked.

"She's out like a light."

He hit forward on the stereo, skipping to the next track, "I'm Still Waiting."

"Come here." He motioned for her to join him on the couch where he sat.

"No," she smiled. "You know I love that song. You just want to have sex."

"Aww, come on," he pined. "Let's talk."

"It must be serious if you're doing that."

"Doing?"

"Anytime you interlock your fingers with mine it's serious," she explained.

"Never noticed," he said with his nervous laugh. "I've always felt if we met another point in time—any point in any time—we would always fall in love. Madly in love."

"You think so?" She reached for his other hand.

"I know so. My heart is forever yours."

An easy feeling washed over her. "My heart just dropped on the floor."

He rose from the couch and knelt before her. "I did something incredibly wrong."

"Just say it, Ernse."

"Remember a few months ago, you told me about an incident you had in a checkout line with Emily. Two women behind you were talking Spanish—"

"I do. I didn't understand, but I knew they were talking about me. They even said my name a couple of times during their conversation, especially the dark haired one. I don't speak Spanish, but I knew they didn't mean well. It was confusing and even scared me. I never met them in my life. I just knew I had to get out of there with Emily as soon as possible."

"She wouldn't dare touch you and Emily."

"What?" His comment made it all too clear. The event raced through her mind. She'd hurried home and relayed the story to Ernse . He thought she was mistaken and had overreacted. "The two women were probably gossiping about some other Nancy. Just a coincidence," he assured her.

"I did something wrong," he continued, his eyes full with tears. "I know one of the women on the checkout line that day."

Nancy pulled her hands from hi and turned.

"I got involved with her, and I knew it was wrong, but my head wasn't right."

"I think you're trying to say something else," she sniffed. "Say it and get it over with."

"Nance, I love you." He dropped his head in her lap. "I really, really love you."

"Excuse me." She pushed his head away. "I'd like to get up."

He gripped her thigh, pleading for a chance to finish the confession. "Nance, I got that woman pregnant."

"I never told you," Ti Zoot interrupted the story. "And I'm not sure if Ernse ever explained, but that's the reason I didn't want him on the streets. The woman he impregnated was this street dealer Quico's girl. The guy ran with a gang of thugs who bodied people all over Brooklyn and Queens. I hoped to settle things somehow as impossible as that sounds. I needed to figure it out."

"After he told me that, all I could do was run to the bathroom. My world had collapsed," she admitted. "The crazy thing is, I knew he loved me. We loved one another deeply. That much I knew."

"Anyone who knew the both of you could see that plain and clear," he added.

"I kept asking myself 'why?' I couldn't understand why he would do that. The same guy who had essentially been my knight from the time we met. The same guy who comforted the pain I endured for years after losing my parents. The guy who held me so close I swore we were one at times. How could that guy, that same person, do that to us? I kept seeing images of him with that woman in intimate ways, doing the things he and I did. I lost all thought and any real consciousness after that, I snapped."

Ti Zoot faced the kitchen window. He knew what was coming. It was torment and a constant reminder in his thoughts and dreams. Despite that, it wasn't a moment he was prepared to hear.

Nancy buried her head in her knees. Her back was against the tub. Tears poured for what seemed like hours, but she continued on with the story.

Ernse knocked on the bathroom door a handful of times, begging her to unlock it. He wanted to talk things out.

Finally, he went back to the music in the living room. Maybe she'd be able to talk in the morning. He shut the lights off and lay on the couch. Only the brightness from a streetlight kept the room from being completely dark. Bob's words would provide answers to this problem, he hoped.

There had to be an answer. He would never give her up. He laid out the upcoming week in his mind. Ti Zoot would be back soon. They would figure everything out from that point. The outcome was almost guaranteed to end up bloody, but Ti Zoot would be by his side.

But even more pressing, he had to patch things up with Nancy. He was going to sit her down and bare his soul. He also had to address the elephant in the room. Altagrácia was pregnant and there was nothing he could do about that. How was Nancy going to cope with that? How was he going to explain that to Emily when the day came?

He stood, reached for the rhum he poured earlier, and walked to the light from the window. There was nothing interesting outside of that window. The streetlight was the only object he was drawn to. As a kid, he threw countless rocks on these city lamps. Sometimes he struck one dead center and the light would fade, darkening that section of the street. There was no reason. He and his friends just did things like that, sometimes boredom…always boredom.

He shut the curtain. This was his thing, music in a completely dark living room. Sometimes Nancy joined and squeezed next to him on the couch.

He didn't realize how much time passed until "Real Situation" came on, which meant only a handful of songs remained on the CD. He turned to look at the number on the CD changer and saw Nancy's silhouette. She had quietly entered the room. He was happy. She was ready to talk. He took a deep breath and welcomed her with open arms.

"I don't know when and how, but something was in my hand and I just struck him with it. The room was dark. I don't even remember the sequence just a flash here and there. The lights came on. There was blood on the floor, Ernse's blood. I was holding a knife, Ti Zoot."

A cry bellowed from deep within the pit of her stomach, and she buried her head in her hands like a child who had just been disciplined. Ti Zoot went to the other side of the table and consoled her. He found himself absorbing the pain she just detailed. Her screams and cries were gut-wrenching. He buried his head against hers and let his tears flow.

This was everything his dreams had danced around, but never spelled out. More accurately, he rejected any sign that pointed her way.

"Why did I do that?" she wailed. "It was me, but I was on the outside looking at me doing it."

"It's going to be okay," he hugged her tight.

It took them a moment to overcome their regret and sorrow, but he was finally able to get up and put some water in the kettle for chamomile tea.

Nancytook a single sip. . Her eyes were red and puffy from the tears, so he suggested she wash her face and maybe lie down.

She shook her head. "No."

He left her in the kitchen and went into the bathroom. Dry tears had marked his face like the scar that ran down from the back of his ear to the side of his neck. A kid from the streets of Port-Au-Prince.

It wasn't how he imagined the confrontation. She hadn't denied or evaded anything. In fact, he got the sense she was relieved. The weight was off her shoulders. For two years, they both carried the same burden but for different reasons.

He ran the hot water and waited until it was intense, nearly searing. Fiona always complained of the damage that would cause his skin, but he was used to it. He washed his face thoroughly and thought about the restart he had planned: the move, the job, and committing to Fiona. None of that could move forward until he and Nancy had this moment in the open. He dried off and went to the kitchen. He thought about having a drink, but Nancy was doing something in front of the sink. He decided to give her space and quietly went to the living room.

He looked at his watch. It was almost time to pick Fiona up, but he first wanted to stop by the fruit and vegetable market where he saw some beautiful mangoes. If he bought those for Claudette, it would mute her bark when he got to her place. His pager had not buzzed, but he knew Fiona would bombard him with messages soon.

The thought was interrupted by the sound of a body dropping—a distinct thud of flesh and bones on ceramic. A noise without give.

"Nancy?" He raced to the kitchen.

"Ti Zoot...I killed my...husband..."

She was on her knees. The thud he heard was her knees smacking the tiles. A knife handle was sticking out of her mid-section. Blood poured as her eyes went blank.

"God, what have you done?" he gasped in horror.

"...I killed Ernse as...our daughter slept....in our bed..." She forced the words. "I killed him..."

"Nancy why did you do this?" He laid her gently on the cold floor as blood spread across the beige squares. He grabbed a rag and quickly tried his best to make a tourniquet to limit the flow. Again, tears poured. This time, they were his alone.

EPILOGUE

Nancy kept a polite smile as she struggled to pull two bags of cleaning items out of the elevator.

"Good luck." The young woman waved as she exited the lift. Nancy returned the blessing with a word of thanks.

She walked halfway down the hall before realizing she made a right when it was really a left. Pregnancy brain. She was close to term, and her new elderly neighbor joked she was hiding a ball under her dress because her belly was so perfectly round.

"It's a boy," the ancient woman announced in her pleasant accent. "I've never been wrong. I've always predicted correctly with pregnancies from the time I was a little girl in Barbados."

Things were scary at first, but she had finally started to feel good about her and Ernse's move. The friendly neighbors were making the transition easy. She kept wondering how things would turn out when it was just her and Ernse living together. And there was the baby, of course. Soon, they'd be welcoming a baby and both weren't even twenty.

A sharp pain forced her to stop midway down the hallway. She set the bags down to calm her belly. "Ease up in there. I just need to clean up then I'll rest up. Okay?" She summoned her strength, grabbed the bags, and entered the apartment. Would it ever truly feel like home, or was this just a quick stop in her life?

"I'm back," she yelled. Ernse and Ti Zoot didn't bother to answer from the living room if they had even heard. They were on a break, surrounded by the boxes and furniture they had just moved. Both men were seated with a plastic cup in hand. A bottle of rhum lay on the hardwood between them.

"Your mom sent you a case of this? Damn, this is hard!" Ernse said before sipping the rhum in his cup, only to gruntas the liquid lit a fire in his chest.

"I'll give you a couple of bottles. I have a feeling your cabinets will be empty for a while."

"Yeah man, I had to buy some stuff for this place; that set me back," Ernse poured more rhum.

"How much is the rent again?"

"Five-hundred and thirty-five."

"Tiup! Just make sure you pay on time every month. Claudette and I put our names on the line. Don't screw us over."

"I got this Zoot. I'm about to be a father. Crazy, but I'm stepping up big time."

"Stop talking a good game and just do it," Ti Zoot advised.

"I am. I am, but I'm going to need a nice ride. I can't have wifey and my baby on these streets like that."

"Tiup! Just handle this and stay focused. You can't afford any bullshit!"

"How's that bullshit? You got a phat new ride, why can't I?"

"Stop trying to be me," Ti Zoot warned.

"Well, I need a ride, gotta hustle to keep my new family on point."

Ti Zoot leaned back on the chair. "Nancy come and get your man, I'm about to smack him."

"Aren't you guys hungry yet?" She pulled out a few cleaning supplies.

"Very," Ernse shouted.

"If you run to the grocery, I can make some spaghetti," she offered.

"Nah, babe. You really should rest after you finish up. I'm going to order some Chinese food instead."

"Chicken and broccoli," she shot back.

Ernse walked across the room, plucked a menu from a box and dialed. "Let me get a small chicken and broccoli. A half-chicken and shrimp fried rice, no onions." He placed his hand over the mouthpiece and turned to Ti Zoot. "What are you having?"

"Same thing...half-chicken."

"Make that two orders of half-chicken and fried rice and no onions."

"I want onions in mine," Ti Zoot corrected.

"No onions in one of the half-chickens. Yeah no onion for the other one. Not sure this will be enough for me. Add two eggrolls and a chicken satay to that order. 717 Avenue C, Apartment 4C. Oh, and a ginger-ale and two cokes."

He placed the phone down and dug into his pockets. He pulled out his wallet, opened it, and grimaced when he realized there was no paper inside.

"Zoot man, you think you can spot me a few dollars to get this food?"

"And this big-shot wants a fancy car?"

"Come on, man."

Ti Zoot rose and went into the kitchen. "Nancy, you need help?"

"No, it's okay Ti Zoot. I've got most of the kitchen wiped down. I'm going to take a break after I sweep. Is he driving you crazy again?"

"I get a headache just talking to that guy," he sighed.

"You know that's your brother," she laughed.

"Only thing I know is he's a clown,." He opened the fridge to find a lone, empty egg tray. Luckily, the freezer had two trays full of ice. He took a couple of cubes and dropped them in his cup.

"You know it's up to you to keep Ernse in line," she said.

"He doesn't listen," Ti Zoot insisted. "I'm going to focus on you instead. You're smart enough to listen and make the right moves."

"He's matured, a little…emphasis on little."

"Well, I don't have any kids. I'm not about to raise a grown man."

"I heard that!" Ernse's voice echoed from the living room.

Nancy removed the latex gloves from her hands and hugged Ti Zoot as much as her belly allowed. "Thanks for everything, you really went to bat helping us get this place. I don't know what we'd do without you and my aunt."

"Don't worry, someone owed me a favor," his voice warmed. "Everything is going to work out."

"I know, I know. It better work. I love my aunt and cousin, but it will be embarrassing to have to return to their house with my tail between my legs with a baby."

"Don't worry." He pecked her cheek. "How's the job situation?"

"Tough. You know." She pointed to her belly. "Every time I walk in, they smile and say, 'we'll call you back,' but they never do. The agency gets me steady temp assignments though. I'll find something permanent after the baby is born."

"I'm here if you need me."

"Of course, as always," she beamed. "It's all exciting and scary at the same time."

"I can't believe little Nancy is about to be a mom."

"Neither can I."

"My beautiful wife." Ernse stood in the kitchen doorway nursing his cup.

"Hmm, we're not married yet…can't call me that."

"Well, we're going to take care of that soon," he promised. "After that, you're legally mine for the rest of your life."

"We'll see about that." She caressed her mid-section

He embraced her with short kisses from her earlobe to the nape of her neck. "You're all mine."

Ti Zoot left them alone, returning to the living room to add more rhum to his cup of ice. He heard their laughter. It wasn't just the rhum, but the moment itself warmed his insides. Everything was going to be all right. He'd make sure of that.

It wasn't long before the doorbell rang, and Ernse walked into the living room. Before he could say anything, Ti Zoot cut him off and planted a couple of bills in his hand. Ernse looked at the paper, it was much more than the delivery guy would need, but that was Ti Zoot.

"Babe, food is here," he announced.

"I'll eat in a bit," she said. "I hate stopping in the middle of cleaning."

"Too hungry, I can't wait." He passed a paper plate over to Ti Zoot.

"Don't worry about me." She rolled her eyes and sighed. "I'm just days away from giving birth."

Her dig was lost on Ernse who was too busy rummaging through the brown paper bag for a fork.

"Zoot, thanks for the money man."

"Don't thank me. That's a loan. Pay it back for a change."

It was late fall, and the sun went down early capturing the edge of night in the unfurnished room. Just as they had done countless times before, the two scraped everything from the Styrofoam containers, washing it all down with cola. At that point, Nancy had just finished cleaning and started sweeping.

"That hit the spot." Ernse mixed the last of his cola with a little rhum.

"To your new family." Ti Zoot raised his cup.

"Thanks, bro." Ernse leaned back to reflect. "You know when you told me where this apartment was located, I didn't want any part of it. I thought it was too far from the hood. I was like 'Kensington is way out there and too quiet.' But the first time I visited it, I knew it was perfect for Nancy and the baby. Hell, it might even be perfect for me. Maybe it's what I need."

"That's exactly why I pushed you here," Ti Zoot explained. "I don't want you on that side of town. It's a warzone."

Ernse thought about the comment. He loved the street, the comradery, and the drama. This situation pulled him out of that a bit. It would take time to get used to.

"Crazy...baby soon...new apartment. Everything happened at once. Is that how it works?"

Ti Zoot sipped slowly. "That's how it works in your world. Things happen how you make it happen."

"Well, this is going to be good, Ti Zoot. I really love that girl." He smiled as he watched Nancy sweep the adjoining room.

Ti Zoot turned and looked along with him. "Don't mess this one up. Some chances only come once in a lifetime."

"I won't, man. I promise. You know I have very little family. Building my own is special to me." He gave Ti Zoot a pound and emptied his cup. "Man, this drink is above everything else."

Ti Zoot picked up the bottle and turned it so Ernse could see the label and crest, which read fondè en 1898. "Do you know why this rhum is different from any other?"

"It goes down different?" Ernse guessed.

"Other rhums are made with molasses. This one is isn't. This one is refined with sugarcane...different from any other. In my world, there's no molasses in rhum."

"A plate of Chinese food, this rhum, my wife-to-be in my new home, I think life is perfect."

Once more, they raised their cups and sat there admiring Nancy's silhouette, her round belly in particular. A broom firmly in her hands as she swept away.

GLOSSARY

akasan – a beverage made from milk, corn flour, anise stars, vanilla and cinnamon; drunk warm or cold

akra – a fried appetizer made of pureed coco, garlic, scallions, pepper, and herbs

bouyon bef – a hearty Haitian beef stew soup

djon-djon – rice cooked with a dried mushroom broth, often referred to as 'black rice')

fritay – an array of fried food that usually includes meat, fish, plantains, cassava

kasav – flat bread made from yucca

kitè sa – leave it alone

pain-patate - sweet potato pudding

maren – godmother

sòs pwa – rich black bean puree

woy, pitit – an exasperated sound followed by 'child'

ACKNOWLEDGMENTS

Andrea, Alexis, Emir, Lexi and Lisa-- you are a super team! I have enjoyed every minute of this side of publishing thanks to your efforts.

ABOUT THE AUTHOR

When he's not writing late at night, J Duval is busy raising his kids.

RIZE publishes great stories and great writing across genres written by People of Color. Our team consists of:

Lisa Diane Kastner, Founder and Executive Editor
Andrea Johnson, Acquisitions Editor
Chris Major, Editor
Chih Wang, Editor
Laura Huie, Editor
Pulp Art Studios, Cover Design
Standout Books, Interior Design
Polgarus Studios, Interior Design
Alexis August, Product Manager Intern

Learn more about us and our stories at www.runningwildpress.com/rize

Loved this story and want more? Follow us at www.runningwildpress.com/rize, www.facebook/rize, on Twitter @rizerwp and Instagram @rizepress